W9-BMA-457

# Slim Chance

Also by Peter Helton

*Headcase*

# SLIM CHANCE

Peter Helton

CARROLL & GRAF PUBLISHERS
New York

Carroll & Graf Publishers
An imprint of Avalon Publishing Group, Inc.
245 W. 17th Street
11th Floor
New York, NY 10011-5300
www.carrollandgraf.com

AVALON
publishing group incorporated

First published in the UK by Constable,
an imprint of Constable & Robinson Ltd 2006

First Carroll & Graf edition 2006

ISBN-13: 978-0-78671-742-2
ISBN-10: 0-7867-1742-4

Printed and bound in the EU

*For Jess*

# Chapter One

'Give me a quid, man, or I'll puke all over you.'

Charming. Though I had to admit it was a refreshing departure from the usual refrain of 'Got any spare change?' On second thoughts, 'refreshing' was probably a misnomer. His blood-rimmed eyes, swaying stance and evil breath suggested he was quite capable of making good his threat to deposit his stomach contents on my favourite shirt and freshly laundered jeans. Not to mention my cinnamon toast and Earl Grey. How had he got into the Pump Room, anyway?

'Save your ammo, Chucky. You know it won't work on me,' I said casually, being far from certain that it wouldn't.

He refocused his bleary eyes and brought up an apologetic smile instead. 'Oh, it's you. You're all right. What's your name again?'

'It's Chris, but you can call me Mr Honeysett.'

He shrugged inside his sodden overcoat and spattered drops of water from his lanky hair. Behind him, a waitress in regulation black and white had finally spotted Chucky as an unlikely customer amidst all the Georgian splendour and made a speedy beeline towards my table.

'I wouldn't pull your stunt in here, they're likely to call the cops. Wait outside until I've finished my breakfast, I'd like to pick what's left of your brains. Might be a few quid in it for you.'

'You asked me some stuff a while ago. Didn't know

nothing then.' He looked past me through the french windows at the rain-driven shoppers hurrying through the Abbey Church Yard.

'I know, but you still got a couple of cans of Special Brew out of it, didn't you?'

'Yeah, I s'pose.'

'Is this man bothering you, sir?' The waitress addressed me without taking her eyes off Chucky.

'He's just leaving.'

He switched to the pathetic routine. 'It's fucking pissing it down out there,' he said sweetly. And rasped out a continuous burp for a full five seconds. Free sample. 'Can't I wait inside somewhere?'

The waitress offered him a deep-frozen look. The Pump Room Trio finished their inoffensive piece of Mozart to polite applause. I replenished my cup of Earl Grey from the pot.

'All right, but don't be fucking ages,' Chucky said, 'I've got things to do.' Like puke on tourists who mistake his threat of disgorgement for an empty boast.

The waitress escorted him away from a downwind position, not just out of the Pump Room but off the premises of the Roman Baths. Then she reappeared at my table with an interesting smile. So I ordered a Danish pastry and coffee.

Being a painter (the arty type) as well as a private detective has its upsides and downsides. Upsides: expense accounts, flexible hours and an excuse to get really mucky whenever I feel like it. Downsides: everything else. And those flexible hours can drag interminably on a grotty night parked outside some place or other, waiting for things to happen or people to show up.

Living in an unpredictable kind of world I hold breakfast sacred, especially one taken so close to the sacred spring of Aqua Sulis, which is the raison d'être of Bath after all. I even named the business after it: Aqua Investigations. This one, admittedly, was a second breakfast, purely to escape the rain. This morning I had been 'instructed' (not asked nicely or hired, mind) by Messrs Longbottom, Prangle and Fox (Solicitors), to ascertain the whereabouts of Billy, and had already been out for hours in his damp pursuit. Billy the tramp.

Not Billy the homeless person, or Billy the street person, as Mr Prangle of LP&F put it. Billy was a tramp of the old-fashioned type, and would have described himself as such if he did much describing. Chucky might know where Billy was hanging out, but if he got bored and left before I finished my breakfast I would soon find someone else to ask. There were harsher and much uglier towns to be homeless in which made Bath a popular place for beggars, *Big Issue* sellers and anyone pretending to play the penny whistle.

The pastry was fresh and moist and the coffee piping hot and drinkable, which was one of the reasons the Pump Room remained high on my shortlist of okay-places to have breakfast.

Chucky's face told me that I had tested his greed for money to its outer limits. It was still raining steadily so I joined him under the awnings of the antique jeweller's across the church yard where he'd been sheltering.

'Come on, man, whatcha wanna ask me? It's wet and I'm freezin' my arse off here,' he complained.

'Billy the tramp, you know him?'

'Not really. I know who you mean, but I've never had anything to do with him. Keeps himself to himself. Probably thinks he's better than the rest of us. Flies off the handle at nothing. No wonder he's got no mates,' Chucky concluded.

I myself had 'known' Billy for quite a while. And Chucky was right. Though Billy was a fixture, almost a feature of Bath, he never appeared to have company. When I had last seen him the steel wool of his beard was as white as the remaining wisps of his hair, and the missing chunk in his left earlobe gave him the air of an old and tired

9

family dog. He'd asked me for money for a bottle of wine. Billy was always scrupulously honest about the reasons for his begging, which is why I didn't mind subsidizing his habit from time to time. I hadn't seen him around for a few weeks but Bath is a compact city and I was confident of finding him without great effort.

'Seen him lately?' I asked.

Chucky screwed up his eyes and stared into the rain, thinking about it. 'Don't think I have, now you mention it. What d'you want him for, anyway?'

I ignored the question, mainly because I had no idea. I had been told nothing more than that it was 'to his advantage' to contact LP&F. 'Here.' I handed him my card. 'My numbers are on there. Fiver if you find him.'

'Make it a tenner. Fiver now, fiver later.'

'Get real, Chucky.'

'Bastard,' he burped and trotted off towards Stall Street in search of well-dressed tourists.

A cold and rainy April day was not the ideal time to go looking for a tramp since he'd be sheltering somewhere but I was going to give it a go for a while. I turned in the opposite direction, across Abbey Church Yard. The steady downpour, which soon found its way down my upturned collar, had washed the paved expanse clean of its usual encrustation of camcordering tourists, fire eaters, recorder players, pamphleteers and jugglers. I love the rain.

Past the east face of the Abbey and an empty taxi rank – taxi drivers also love the rain – through Orange Grove towards the river Avon. Billy seemed to like water. Not for drinking or washing, mind, or when it fell from the sky like it did now, but rivers, ponds and canals. More often than not you could find him occupying a bench by the weir or the sports centre, or lying on a patch of grass by the boating lake in Victoria Park, alone, with or without a bottle.

Despite the wet a fair few people were lining the Grand Parade, peering down at Pulteney Weir which, since last weekend's storm and the subsequent almost continuous rain, had taken on a more ferocious roar.

I joined them at the balustrade. Below, just above the white-water swirl of the river where it rushed over the horseshoe of the weir, a rigid inflatable boat of the fire and rescue service was holding station, tethered to a stout rope on the shore as well as using its engines to fight the current. Two firemen in waterproofs and life vests were in the bow, swinging poles with grappling hooks while a third manoeuvred the RIB. On the colonnaded walkway below us other figures – police and more firemen – were heaving on ropes thrown over a pile-up of debris under Pulteney Bridge. What looked like an entire tree had managed to get stuck under the left arch, where it had turned into a collection point for all the flotsam the storm-swelled waters were carrying downstream.

'Can you see a person in all that lot?' my immediate neighbour asked her companion. 'Someone said there's a person in the river.'

'Perhaps it's the missing woman,' said the lady sharing her minute umbrella. 'Gosh, I hope not.'

'Nah, it's a cow,' the man to my right enlightened us. 'Dead cow. It probably drowned during the storm. It's upside down in the water, you can just see its legs sticking up. They're trying to get a rope round it now.'

'I do hope they find this one alive,' the first woman said. 'Not like the last one that disappeared. Brr.' She gave a theatrical shudder inside her plastic raincoat. 'Have we seen enough?'

'Yes, let's go on.'

On the opposite bank a similar huddle of people watched the watery drama. I scanned the group and the area behind for any signs of Billy. A man with a sandwich board, waving a black book as he spoke to the backs of the crowd, got little attention. I couldn't hear what he was saying of course but I took the book to be a bible or prayer book. It was a fair guess, since the front of his board suggested we all REPENT.

The recovery of dead cows so soon after breakfast held limited appeal so I walked on. Parade Gardens looked near deserted. I gave the young woman at the ticket booth Billy's description.

She shook her head. 'We're not allowed to let in drunks, beggars or homeless people anyway,' she said. 'Not that many want to come in. It's the admission charge.'

'But it's free to Bath residents?'

'It is if you have some kind of proof. But of course you wouldn't have that if you were homeless.'

An excellent point. 'So how do you spot a beggar?'

'You can tell, can't you,' she asserted.

I didn't ask about drunks. She probably had a breath-alyser kit for those. Further along, the bill board of the *Bath Chronicle* outside the Bog Island newsagent confirmed the words of the umbrellaed women: NIKKI REID: NEW APPEAL FOR WITNESSES. With the second abduction in six months the police had to be desperate. And the first woman found dead just weeks before the second was snatched off the street. Happily as a private eye I didn't have to deal with gruesome cases like these. I wondered if these appeals for witnesses ever worked. OLD WINO DISAPPEARS, POLICE WIDEN SEARCH. An unlikely headline. Who cared about winos coming and going? And if you were truly homeless, I wondered, could you be said to have disappeared if you couldn't be found? Disappeared from where? Your usual doorway?

I stepped into a deep puddle and my shoe got swamped and my hair stuck damply to my head and neck. My leather jacket was springing a leak. Stupid. In the valley where I live just a few minutes' drive from the city I'd have been wearing decent boots, a rainproof jacket and a hat and wouldn't have minded the rain. The wind picked up as I crossed North Parade Bridge. I checked my watch: noon. I was still half an hour early for my next appointment but since I'd arranged to meet at the Bathtub Bistro that would hardly constitute hardship. At the south side of the bridge a spiral staircase led down to the towpath. The evil ammonia smell testified to its frequent use as a toilet and made me wonder about the olfactory capacities of those lingering long enough to daub graffiti on the walls. Among the mindless tags and swastikas I was being assured that Darren was a dickhead. (Yes, but was *he* stupid enough to hang around in a piss-stained stairwell?)

The cow rescuers were still struggling on the other side of the river. The crowd in Spring Gardens had thinned now that the wind was driving the rain harder, and even the sandwich board preacher was wrapping the good book into a Tesco carrier bag, calling it a day. A short tunnel and sharp turn right brought me into Grove Street and the Bathtub Bistro.

I wished I could shake myself dry like a dog. Instead I slumped my sodden jacket over a chair by the upstairs window table, grunted a greeting at Clive who grinned at me from behind the bar and made for the toilets where I stuck my head under the hand dryer. Relative comfort restored I squelched back to the table where Clive had thoughtfully deposited a bottle of Pilsner Urquell.

'How are you doing?' he asked, looking up from some paperwork. The place was quiet, only one table downstairs was taken so far.

'Fine, apart from wet feet.'

Clive bent down, rummaged behind the bar and emerged with a blow heater. He plugged it in and shoved it under my table. 'Anything for the Great Detective.'

I do love this place. I often meet clients here. It's central yet nicely tucked away and dead cosy. It had just got cosier, with under-table heating.

'Are you eating or meeting?'

I'd just had breakfast. But then it *was* lunchtime. 'What's good?'

'Bangers and mash. Venison sausages with a red onion sauce. You'll like it.'

'You talked me into it.'

I was finishing off the creamy mound of leeky mash when my client's representative arrived. A lanky scarecrow of a man in his fifties lost somewhere inside a pale blue M&S suit, he'd have been six foot four if he'd straightened up. Instead he crumpled himself even further to shake hands with me. 'Giles Haarbottle, Griffin's.' The insurers. I'd done work for them before but hadn't met this specimen. I knew what this was about, all but the details, that was. He waited until his double gin and tonic arrived before snapping open his imitation leather briefcase and extracting a lemon-yellow file, adorned with the Griffin logo. 'I'm informed that you have done similar work for us before, Mr Honeysett, so you'll be aware of the nature of these unfortunate transactions we are sometimes forced to make. Absolute discretion is imperative of course.' He gulped some of his gin before flipping open the file. 'It pains me to give money to criminals but . . .'

'. . . it saves you a lot of dosh.'

'We are working in our client's best interest, you understand. And, as you will see, the nation's,' he said sniffily.

Insurance companies, in case you hadn't noticed, aren't about insurance at all. They are gamblers and their only interest is winning. Insurance companies gamble on the chance of actually having to replace your TV/house/car/ oil tanker against the money they can extract from you, based on that promise. They're bad losers too. So if they can save themselves a bob or two, even though it means bending the rules a little, they will. And then they come to me. Or some other mug who is willing to do what the police can't and the insurer couldn't possibly ask of their employees. It's called 'recovery of stolen goods' and goes like this: a valuable item gets nicked. It's well insured. Instead of flogging it on the open market (where he gets a fraction of the value and can be traced back if someone

14

gets picked up) the crook offers it to the insurance company for less than they'd have to pay out if it stayed lost. The company shells out, the owner gets his valued baubles back, and crook and owner are happy. The insurance company isn't happy but (a) it saved some money, (b) it can always put its premiums up and (c) it will. The police have learned to turn a blind eye to the whole thing since the victims get their stuff back and because, frankly, there isn't a thing they can do about it.

Haarbottle handed over the open folder with long fingers. Three laser prints of images, each with a sheet of notes. 'Watercolours. Dimensions and descriptions are in the notes. Make absolutely sure before you hand over any money.'

It was my turn to get sniffy. I'm not a fan of art thieves. Handing over money to them was something I wouldn't enjoy one bit, so yes, I was going to make damn sure. I briefly examined the images. Two were ink and watercolour jobs of American natives dancing in a circle during an equinox celebration, the third of some sort of plant or rather a seed head. I recognized all this instantly because it said so in the margins. I turned to the notes. As usual nothing had been left to chance. The notes were very precise, down to the flocking of the paper and other superficial damage and where to find it.

'Okay. Who nicked them, where and when?' I enquired.

Haarbottle reached for his glass. 'That's none of your concern. Just do the meeting, check that it's all there and hand over the money.' He sucked up more gin as though the long speech had parched his throat.

'Wrong. If I do this kind of thing at all I want to know as much as possible about what kind of villain I'm going to meet in a dark alley while I'm carrying . . . how much?'

Haarbottle cleared his throat. '£120,000. We beat them down from two hundred.'

I couldn't help giving a whistle at the figure. 'For three watercolours? Try a bit more beating.'

'The works in question are by John White and are absolutely priceless.'

I looked at the photographs again. 'John White? The Scottish guy? Are you sure?'

'Wrong White. This John White was active in the late sixteenth century. Went to America with the colonists. Hence the Red Indians. Very few examples of his work remain. These were part of an exhibition at the American Museum up at Claverton.'

'They were nicked from the *museum*?' I hadn't heard of a break-in at the American Museum. I was sure I would have.

'No, no. They were stolen from the private residence of the owner who had loaned them, the very day they were returned.'

'Was much else stolen?' I wanted to know next.

'I don't see how that is relevant to our business here,' Haarbottle said, giving me an exasperated look.

Extracting blood from a stone suddenly appeared an attractive task by comparison. 'Okay, let me explain. If nothing else was taken then the thief targeted the items specifically. On the other hand, if it was a common-or-garden variety break-in then we're probably looking at some local talent who found out later what it was he had nicked.'

'It appears to have been a routine burglary. TV, stereo . . .'

'Which you wouldn't bother with if you knew you had your paws on some priceless artefact. How long ago was the break-in?'

'Just over three weeks.'

'That's very soon to get in touch with you. But it could mean it hasn't changed hands yet.' Stolen art often gets sold on from villain to villain or exchanged for favours for quite a while before it is offered back to the owners. You can't really do much else with high profile stuff. 'Good, I'd rather deal with a local blagger than a big outfit that took

16

it on in lieu of payment or the like. When's the handover arranged for?'

'We told him to get in touch again tomorrow.'

'Good. Get the dosh to me, then give him my mobile number.' I pushed my card across the table. 'I'll negotiate the where-and-when. Agreed?'

'Satisfactory.' Haarbottle unfolded himself, slotted my card into a pocket of his briefcase, snapped it shut and gangled off without paying for his drink. Perhaps I needed insurance insurance. Or to put my rates up. I settled with Clive, stuffed the file under my sweater and walked the hundred yards or so through the rain to my favourite supermarket. Only two weeks ago when it was warm and sunny I'd have zoomed in on squeaky salad leaves, cool cucumbers and cherry tomatoes. Now, dripping and squelching through the aisles, all I could think about was soup, give me stuff to make soup . . .


If anything it was raining even harder by the time I turned the DS down the waterlogged track towards Mill House. The wind had picked up again too, snatching at the beech trees and flattening the grass in the meadows. The mill-stream was in noisy spate and the pond would need clearing of leaves and fallen branches. The sagging out-buildings had held up surprisingly well; all that could fly away had flown away years ago. The yard was full of cars, so I knew the whole gang was in.

Even in this foul weather Tim's black Audi TT stood sparkling, clean and immaculate on the small remaining island of intact stone cobbling in the yard, surrounded by a sea of mud. Tim is the all-seeing eye of Aqua Investigations. An ex-burglar and safe-cracker made good (kind of), he's now an IT consultant for Bath University (I can't afford to employ him full time) and lends his entire reper-toire and considerable muscle where and when I need him. He tried to teach me how to pick locks and use a computer properly but I'm a hopeless case. Even a padlock takes me ten minutes to open with the set of picklocks he gave me and my computer skills are of neolithic standards. But what's the point of doing your own barking?

The green collection of scrapes and dents with a Land Rover badge at the front belonged to Annis. Annis treats life a bit like she does off-roading – always in four-wheel-drive, changing gear frequently, stopping for nothing. She managed to blag her way into my studio as an assistant when she was still an art student at Sion Hill. Before I knew it she had moved in, was working with me on Aqua business too and had started to outshine me in the studio we share. We share other things too, though not as often as I'd like.

I parked my Citroën next to a heap of metal that had started off life as a white Beetle in the seventies but had since acquired a blue off-side mudguard and a rust-red bonnet and was probably held together with hair bands. This relic belonged to Alison. Alison was a recent addition to the household. Another painter and ex-forger (or so she said) and old friend of Annis's, she'd been at Mill House since last summer when her dream cottage in Cornwall was deliberately set on fire with her and Annis inside. Chained to the bed. In the nude. It's a long story.

I found Tim at the kitchen table fighting his way out of an extended family-sized bag of mini doughnuts. His grin was dusted with sugar crystals. 'All gone,' he announced in a tragic voice.

I dumped my shopping on the table. 'I was going to ask you to stay for supper but since you've eaten . . .'

Desperation clouded his sugar-crazed eyes. 'No, no. Starving actually. Hence the, ehm . . . snack.'

There were two sides to Tim which I found hard to reconcile. He lived in a flat of near pathological neatness in Northampton Street; polished wood floor, a glass and chrome affair that bristled with banks of dust-free computers and gadgets, and a semi-automatic kitchen that kept laboratory standards of germlessness. Yet hand the man food, any kind of food (but not a jar of mayonnaise if you can help it) and within minutes the surrounding countryside needs mopping.

'All right. Don't let Alison see the doughnut bag, she's gone on another diet. Not that I think she really needs it.'

He nodded seriously. 'Exactly. I was just removing temptation by . . . destroying the doughnuts. Sacrificed myself, in fact. Hate doughnuts. Horrible sugary things.'

I stood by the back door and squinted at the barn at the top of the meadow which served as a draughty studio I now shared with both Annis and Alison. 'The girls are working, I take it?' They were frantically preparing for their imminent joint show at Simon Paris Fine Art.

'Yes, and they tried to bite my head off when I stuck it round the door earlier. I wish I had their work ethic.'

'I wish you had too. Did you do your invoices?'

'Ah. *Je regrette . . .*'

I'm terrible at paperwork but Tim is worse. There was only room for one chaos merchant at Aqua Investigations, I decided. 'Get upstairs and do them now, you can use my computer.'

Chris looked up at me through his woolly fringe like a five-year-old who has been told to tidy his room. 'I hate your computer, it's ancient.'

'It's two years old.'

'Exactly.'

'Well, it's that or help me cook supper for four,' I offered generously. 'You could start by washing these bags of . . .'

Tim's feet were hammering up the stairs to my office before I could finish the sentence.

# Chapter Two

'What are they anyway?' Alison asked in a voice that was aiming for indifference and missed.

'Fillets of sea bream on wilted spinach, baby new potatoes, dressed with olive oil and lemon juice,' I recited.

Annis, Tim and I sat in front of our steaming plates of food, waiting for Alison to show the smallest sign of weakness. I'd become worried about her ridiculous diet lately and had also cooked for her on purpose. It didn't work. She pushed her plate into the centre of the table.

'At least have some salad.' I shoved the bowl in front of her. 'It's ninety per cent water anyway.'

'It's swimming in olive oil. And it's got Parmesan on it. Nah, I'll stick with my shake, that way I'm allowed some wine later.' I had long (but quietly) suspected that Alison's obstinate weight owed much to this calorie trade-off.

So I gave up. I've never counted calories. I've no idea what they look like. Annis of course had one of those indestructible figures that no amount of food intake could touch, a fact that Alison bewailed loudly and frequently. Perhaps the bright and hungry flame that burned deep inside her incinerated calories as soon as they arrived. 'Good day in the studio?' I asked her. She nodded with a mouth full of food.

'Nightmare. How about you? What did Longbottom and Thingummy want, more boring process serving?'

'Nope. They want us to find Billy the tramp. Remember him?'

'The guy who looks a bit like Aqualung,' Tim said, which earned him a blank look from Alison. 'You know – Jethro Tull.'

'Jethro Tull's the bloke who invented the seed drill,' Annis explained helpfully to Alison. 'I learned that at school. Why you'd want to drill seeds they never said.'

'What do they want with him? And why not go to the police?' Tim asked.

'Not a criminal matter. He's sleeping rough somewhere but I've no idea where. Can't be that hard to find though, someone will know.'

'Good, if that's all you've got on the books then you won't need me,' Annis said. 'I'm still hellishly busy. At the rate I'm going half of it won't be dry in time to be framed.'

'I've also got a recovery to do, stolen watercolours, but the date hasn't been set yet.'

'Make it after sunset and I'll cover your arse during the handover but as long as it's light I want to be in the studio. Let's go, Ali.'

As they walked out of the kitchen door into the garden we heard Alison say, 'So this bloke invented a drill but he sleeps rough here in Bath? It didn't make any money then?'

Tim's eyes blinked rapidly at me. 'It's her diet. Brain starved of nutrients. No other possible explanation,' he concluded and started demolishing Alison's untouched plateful of food.


By next morning the wind had blown itself out, leaving behind an unmoving sky set in wet cement. I was inspecting the rubbish that had floated to the near end of the millpond above the house when I heard a car approaching along the track. I always loved the fact that Mill House had no passing traffic – the track ended in the yard which gave plenty of advance warning of any visitors. Not that many strangers found their way here.

I didn't give out my address lightly and I hardly ever received clients here.

I didn't recognize the car, a nondescript hatchback, so I jogged down to the yard. When I got there Haarbottle was already unfolding his length from the tiny car. From the passenger side a pale and podgy young man in a blue suit identical to Haarbottle's emerged, chained to an aluminium briefcase.

'With a sum like this I thought I'd deliver it personally. This is Daniel Bung – Mr Honeysett,' Haarbottle introduced us. Haarbottle and Bung. They looked like a cut-price comedy duo and promised to be just as much fun. 'Lovely place you've got here. Quite isolated though, we took a couple of wrong turnings before we found you.' I gave him the that's-how-I-like-it smile. He let his eyes travel over the precariously balanced outbuildings and the mossy roof of the house. 'Are you insured with us? Just out of interest.'

'Relax, I'm not. Is that for me?' I pointed to the shiny briefcase.

'Oh. Oh yes.' Bung fumbled for keys in his pocket and unchained himself, then tried to slap the handcuff on me as I reached for the briefcase.

I withdrew my hand sharpish. Chaining yourself to a wodge of money is one of the stupidest things I can think of. It's also the best way of advertising your mugging potential and if anyone's determined to have it off you they'll probably have your arm with it.

'Just set it down.'

'Oh. Sure. Okay. Ehm. The keys. Are here,' he staccatoed and handed them over.

Haarbottle produced three sheets of paper stapled together, printed in tiny writing, which he wanted me to read, sign and initial on each page. It was the usual devil's pact condemning me to harsh words and hard labour should I lose the ransom without recovering the goods, or breathe a word about the transaction to anyone. I didn't read it. That much small print gives me a headache. I just scrawled my yours-truly under it. Then it occurred to me that Mr Bung was there purely to witness the whole transaction. What was the big deal? A hundred and twenty grand was a lot of money for me but surely chicken feed for Griffin's.

'He rang me first thing this morning,' Haarbottle intoned. 'I passed on your number. You should be contacted very soon. They seem a bit nervous but keen to get the transaction over with.'

'All right, I'll let you know when it's done,' I said. I picked up the case and walked toward the house.

'Don't you want to count the money, Mr Honeysett?' Bung called. Bless him, he probably thought he was in a gangster movie. I stopped without turning round and gave him what he wanted.

'If there's as much as a quid missing you're a dead man, Bung,' I said over my shoulder. Which was kind of me, I thought. It gave him something to talk about down the pub tonight, which would probably be a first.

Then I went inside, cracked open the case and counted the money. Just to make sure *I* didn't wind up a dead man.

So there it sat, a hundred and twenty grand in tens and twenties. Unmarked. Non-consecutive. On my sofa. I walked around it a couple of times. Mmm . . .

That's when the strangest little idea slipped into my mind. Which henceforth we shall refer to as Stupid Idea Number One.


With the improved weather the buskers had reappeared. What am I saying? The whole freak show was back, cluttering up the streets around the Abbey like medieval mendicants hoping for alms. Juggling; what a useful skill for when your fruit bowl is full and there's no place to put the last three oranges. Standing very still and doing nothing unless someone offers you money? My plumber does that extremely well. Mime artists should be shot on sight (with a silencer, naturally) and anyone practising Dylan songs on an amplified guitar should only be given money on a promise never to try it again.

I scanned the crowds, an automatic habit by now, for any signs of Billy or anyone who might know him. A scrum of spectators around two uni-cyclists made progress slow. I negotiated an orderly queue of French school kids dressed in Technicolor, waiting noisily to be let into the Roman Baths, dodged a recorder player in Georgian costume but stopped to give money to an octogenarian violinist since he played beautifully and wore a meticulously patched suit. I had planned to walk down York Street to sniff out the galleries there while I was in the area but found it full of uniformed police, press photographers and a BBC West TV crew. Smiling PCs (always a scary sight) with clipboards chatted to passers-by. Police noticeboards at all corners read *Reconstruction – Nikki Reid. Were you in the area on 29th January?* with the phone number of nearby Manvers Street police station. A well-fed woman in her mid-thirties, dressed in the now familiar lime green business suit Mrs Reid had worn on the day she disappeared, was walking down the length of Cork Street towards Bog Island. Camera flashes followed her down the road. I could see Superintendent Needham, the bane of Aqua Investigations, talking to reporters in front of the teddy bear shop across the street. Appropriate for Needham, I thought, since he's quite bearish himself, although I wouldn't want to try cuddling him.

Needham's not overly fond of Aqua Investigations which he thinks sails dangerously close to the winds of legality that are blowing from his direction. He's more or less right about that, even though he has no idea of Tim's shady past (since he's never been caught), but he also knows I'm generally on the side of the angels. Except when it comes to my gun. He knows I have an illegal handgun, a World War Two Webley .38, which I inherited along with Mill House and of which I'm inordinately fond. Catching me carrying it has become a bit of an obsession with the dear Superintendent and he likes giving me a quick patting down whenever we bump into each other.

Trying to avoid such attention I smartly sidestepped the police street theatre into Abbey Green and nearly barrelled into sandwich board preacher man in the process. Today his board read HE WHO PRAYS AND GETS NO ANSWER MUST FAST. I dodged the mutely offered leaflet and was wandering aimlessly across the cobbled round of Abbey Green when I spotted a dog just below the large iron hinge of the old city gate, tethered to a dustbin by a piece of string. Where there's a dog on a string there's a beggar. This one was a chocolate brown specimen of uncertain parentage (the dog, not the beggar) but just young and cute enough to enhance the takings of his owner who emerged from Evans, the fish and chip shop by the gate, with a biscuit-coloured rucksack over his shoulder and a large bag of fries in one hand. I didn't budge from the side of his dog and he walked up and stood very close. 'You want something?' His voice was the kind of deep rasp I'd last heard from a man with one vocal cord missing.

The vinegary smell of his French fries nearly made me say, 'Yeah, one of those,' but he stared down anything flippant I might have wanted to say.

The man had been in a fire. His face certainly looked like it had. If this was the kind of miracle reconstructive surgery could work these days then I'd be more careful with matches in the future. From his eyebrows down, or rather where they should have been, his face was a permanent mess of puckered, purple scar tissue. While his right eye was deeply and crookedly lidded the left seemed to have no lid at all, which gave it a perfectly round, lizardy quality. It was this eye that scrutinized me aggressively while the other one gave the impression that he was half asleep. He popped a chip in his mouth. His hands, I noticed, were unscarred.

25

'You seen Chucky around?' Surprisingly Chucky hadn't got in touch, not even to sell me bogus information about Billy.

'Who wants to know?' Another one brought up on B-movies.

'I do.'

Wrong movie. 'Well, you can fuck off then.' He unslung the dog's tether and made to turn away.

'Okay, okay.' I produced a tenner from my pocket and made sure he saw it. Not a flicker of interest. 'I'm Chris Honeysett, I'm a private investigator and I'm trying to find Billy the tramp. I've got some good news for him. Chucky was looking out for him on my behalf. You wouldn't have seen either of them around?'

'Billy went up north. Scotland, I think. Never heard of the other one,' he said quietly and walked off towards the Marks and Spencer passage with his dog wagging its tail in French fries frustration.

In my considered opinion Billy had never been beyond the city limits. As far as he was concerned Scotland and Tasmania were probably equally remote. And everyone on the street knew Chucky. If only by smell.

I shoved the tenner back in my pocket. Now I'd seen it all. A street guy who told porkies but was too honest to take money for it.

I rejoined the ant trail of shoppers in Stall Street and walked into Southmead. All this astonishing ugliness would disappear soon: 1960s and '70s concrete jobs with a token half-inch sandstone cladding would be torn down and replaced with twenty-first-century concrete with a quarter-inch of sandstone cladding.

I turned left and right again. Here, a depressing concrete corner in the perpetual shadow cast by a multi-storey car park had attracted transients and beggars for years. If you find yourself homeless and arrive in Bath this is where you will go – two hundred yards from Bath Spa station and half that from the bus terminal, just around the corner from the public toilets and one minute from the night shelter. Reasonably dry. And of course there's Iceland. The busy ground-level exhausts of the frozen food shop pump out enough stale warmth to keep you alive through a winter's night if you didn't make it into the night shelter. Be prepared to use your fists in defence of your place in front of the ceaseless hum and clatter of the fans.

Two men in their late twenties were standing near the entrance of the supermarket, picking out what they considered likely candidates for their appeals for change. The larger one merely muttered his spare change mantra at all and sundry while the wiry red-haired one had a different philosophy. He was willing to engage with his public. Right now a large woman laden with bags emerged from the Iceland shop. He tried to head her off with an 'Excuse me . . .' She ignored him. 'Excuse me . . .' He drunkenly tried to keep up with her for a few paces but she kept her eyes rigidly to the front and kept going. 'Excuse me . . .' The beggar stopped. 'You don't even know what I want yet, you stupid fat cow!' he shouted after her.

I was about to turn towards the night shelter when I spotted a larger group of men sitting behind shopping trolleys in the corner of the dark recess created by the overpass of the car park. I circled casually through the gloom of the concrete cavern. There were six of them, sitting on bits of cardboard by a large pile of blankets, cardboard and sleeping bags. Two figures rose and came towards me, quickly blocking my progress. 'Got any spare change, mate?' said the younger and shorter of the two. The other one, a hard street face backed up by lean street muscle, simply stood, looking over my shoulder. I turned slightly while making a show of searching for change in my pockets. Both of the men on supermarket duty had moved across, now sentinels behind me. This was quite a ballet. I extracted a handful of change from my jacket pocket, making sure both saw I was carrying a supply of notes as well. During the transfer into the younger man's outstretched hand I let most of it fall to the ground. He ducked after it automatically, long enough to give me a better view of the group behind, which had drawn closer together. At their centre was a mound of man-shaped blankets.

'Toilets back here?' I asked.

'Round the corner, mate.' The taller one pointed exaggeratedly across my field of vision.

'Ta.' I sauntered back into the light and rounded the corner. There I went into the public toilet and spent some time washing my hands, while keeping an eye on the mirror. Nothing. I kept washing. Just as I was beginning to wonder what was wrong with my money today one of the two beggars who had been on lookout duty appeared large in the mirror. Rumours of money travel fast. I kept washing. He playfully pressed the button for the soap dispenser and stood close enough to make me wish he'd use some.

'Give me a twenny,' he said flatly.

'And then?'

'Then you can tell me what the fuck you want here.'

'Wrong. I give you a tenner and you tell me what happened to Chucky,' I suggested. I handed over two fivers with the cleanest of hands.

He folded them into an inside pocket of his faded army jacket. 'You saw, then. He doesn't wanna talk to you. Right now he looks like he last puked on a Thai kick boxer, man, and it's your fucking fault.'

'Will he be okay?'

'Caring type, are you? Forget about Chucky, the stinking bastard's been seen to.'

I unfolded a twenty and held it up to his angry face. 'Will he get this?'

He snatched it from my fingers. 'You really are an arsehole, whoever you really are.' He thumped the soap button hard and turned away.

'Where's Billy?' I said to his back in the mirror.

'Never heard of the fucking bastard, all right?!' He shouted loud enough for several people at the urinals to start hurrying procedures.

The Bell in Walcot Street at lunchtime is just big and noisy enough to discuss a Stupid Idea without being overheard. I was early. Alison's belly dancing class (another weight loss scheme) at the YMCA down the road hadn't finished yet. There was no Pilsner Urquell so I ordered a pint of Guinness, which anyway suited my mood much better, and made for an empty table at the back.

'Hey, gumshoe, come sit here.' Eva Keen (yes, really), freelance reporter for several West Country papers but still hopeful of better things, waved me over with a length of French stick, scattering bits of lettuce. 'Brighten my lunch break, Honeysett, tell me about the wicked world of Bath.'

'What are you doing in Bath? I thought you were a Bristol girl now?' I asked and sat down. I liked Eva. She had a deep font of local knowledge into which she had dipped several times in the past to supply me with information that would have taken me ages to ferret out by myself. And she was good to look at into the bargain. In fact, just the privilege of watching her eat and drink was enough to justify her acquaintance. Right now she was trying to inhale most of a baguette stuffed with salad and hummus by her well-known ram-it-all-in-my-mouth/pull-out-my-frizzy-hair-afterwards technique.

She washed half of a generous measure of Scotch down her throat, secure in the knowledge that she wouldn't put on a milligram of weight. 'Bristol girl? Only because I can't afford to live here. My heart, what remains of it, is still in Bath.'

'Didn't you do a piece on homelessness in Bath once?'

'Bath, Bristol, Gloucester, yeah. It's a big issue, pun intended,' she said and stuffed some of her blond strands behind her ear so they wouldn't catch fire while she lit her lumpy roll-up of vile Extra Zwaar. Eva's the only woman I know who can eat, smoke, drink and talk all at the same time in perfect coordination.

'Did you get to know any of them when you did your piece?'

'Quite a few. Talked to anyone who was willing. Most of it didn't make it into print, naturally. Attitudes to homelessness are the problem. The *Chronicle* gets more letters about beggars than anything else, I reckon. Most want them swept off the streets like so much rubbish and put somewhere where they don't see them. That's what they did in Bristol. Zero tolerance for begging. Where did they all go? They came to Bath. Ten minutes by train. Some suggested the police paid for their rail fares.' She glanced at her watch, inhaled smoke, hoovered up more whisky, exhaled and crammed down more baguette. One day she'll get the sequence wrong and set fire to herself.

'Did you come across a guy called Billy? Old-fashioned kind of tramp, not your Special Brew crowd. Wino, quite old, hard to tell of course, beard and long silver hair?'

'The name doesn't ring a bell but then when did you last see an old wino anyway? Seems to me there's a whole generation missing on the streets. There's some old geezers at the night shelter every day, but the streets are full of young people. Druggies, Special Brew crew and winos don't mix.' She checked her watch again. 'Hang on, I think I might have time for another sandwich,' she said and whooshed off to the bar.

As she reappeared with another foot-long baguette and a pint Alison arrived at the table, carrying a glass of red and her holdall. The two women took a couple of seconds to examine each other, the tall nervy blonde in a suit, with bits of hummus in her hair, and the short, could-lose-a-couple-of-stone dark-haired one in sweatshirt and jeans, decided they were from different planets and sat down, smiling expectantly at me.

'Eva, Alison and vice versa. Eva's a journo, Alison's a

painter. She lives at Mill House too, now.' Elegant or what?

Eva's eyebrows rose a fraction as they exchanged greetings. Eva's eyebrows stayed up.

'Another painter, not a different one,' I added for her benefit.

'Oh, right. How *is* Annis?'

'Busy,' Alison and I said in unison.

'Annis and Alison are preparing for a joint show at Simon Paris,' I explained. 'Opens here, then goes to his London branch. But you know Annis . . . She goes into hyperspace when she's got a show coming up.'

'She talks of nothing else, does nothing else, sees nothing else. God is in the detail and all that,' Alison elaborated. 'She'll probably be painting away in the back of the van when we drive our stuff down to the gallery.'

Eva's mobile bleeped. She looked at the display. 'Guys, I gotta shoot,' she said, draining her pint. 'Nice meeting you, Alison. Will I get an invite to the show?'

'Sure thing,' said Alison.

'But you've finished all the paintings for the show?' I asked when Eva had left in a shower of crumbs.

'If I started anything else now it would never dry in time anyway. But every one of Annis's paintings will have wet bits on it, she seems to be working on all of them at the same time. Poor John's going to have a fit.' 'Poor John' was Simon Paris's gallery assistant, in charge of framing and hanging shows.

'So, are you nervous?'

'About the private view?' Alison smiled into her glass. 'It's funny, I'm much more nervous about my own work than . . .' She had a quick glance about. 'Than I was about the forgeries. I knew I was good at those but then I could compare them to the originals, you see? Or at least the style of the artist, like with the Turner studies I did. Copying is easy if you have the knack.'

31

'And you certainly had the knack. You were very good at it. Ever miss it?'

It was too casual. After Alison's last spate of forgeries had landed her and Annis in a burning cottage, requiring urgent rescue from Tim, Alison had forsworn fakes and returned to honest, original painting. In fact, I had made it a condition when she moved into Mill House.

Alison fixed me with dark narrowed eyes. 'Are you suggesting that I *have* . . .'

'No!' I waved my hands in calming circles. 'Absolutely not.' But I couldn't keep a smile from rising on my face.

Her eyes narrowed even further, then suddenly turned to saucers. 'Are you suggesting that I *should* . . .'

'It would be in a good cause this time. Honest,' I said, putting on my honest face. I had dusted it off specially this morning when I suggested we meet for a drink.

'Honest forgery, eh?' Alison said slowly and held out her empty glass. 'Fill this for me. My listening skills usually improve after the second.'

By the end of her third glass of red Alison was wearing a huge grin, scribbling lists of things she urgently needed on to split beer mats.

Stupid Idea Number One was on the launch pad.

# Chapter Three

'Stop here. I better walk the last few yards, he's a nervous guy. No need for him to see you.'

Alison's Beetle was feeling poorly, which was why I acted as her chauffeur through the suburbs of Bath that night. This was our third stop. However nervous this contact was he wasn't short of a few bob. The houses around here might not have been Georgian but these solid semis with their well-ordered front gardens wouldn't have come cheap. While Alison stepped into a tiny pool of porch light a few houses down from where I had parked, I entertained myself by counting the money that was parked along the street and in the drives. I could see three quarters of a million without having to look around. The poorly lit, leafy street seemed asleep, dreaming of double garages and bobbies on the beat.

The opening bars of Beethoven's Fifth (C minor, Op. 67) got me scrambling to the back seat where my jacket was buried under the stuff we had picked up tonight. The first movement was almost over by the time I got to my mobile.

'Mr Honeysett? John White. Times three. We're ready to deal. Are you?' I had expected the call earlier than this but now that it came I got jittery nonetheless. The voice sounded quite young, with the barest hint of Somerset.

'We're ready in principle,' I said in as bored a drawl as I could manage. 'Naturally we have to establish the authenticity of the items first.'

'Don't fuck us about. Victoria Bridge Road. In one hour. Come alone and –'

'No,' I said simply. It's a great little word.

'You what? Listen, you try fuck with us the pictures go in the fucking bin.'

I didn't think so. Time to spell it out. 'I'll meet you wherever you want as long as it's outside, okay? But (a) not tonight because I'm busy and (b) I will have an art expert with me to look the merchandise over. Clear? I'm free tomorrow. Your call.'

A grunt of surprise, then: 'Hang on.' The mouthpiece at his end was covered. Through the papery crunching noises I could hear a muffled, angry discussion, then he came back. 'We're not happy about there being more than one of you. Send the art expert by himself. Make sure he carries the money. Tomorrow night at ten. Same place, Victoria Bridge Road.' He sounded a little nervous, now that he'd had to change the script.

'Not satisfactory.' I was beginning to sound like Haarbottle of Griffin's, I'd have to watch that. Just now Alison emerged from the house down the road, carrying a large black portfolio. She looked like an art expert. 'The art expert is a she and would never agree to go by herself. Besides, I'm not empowered to hand over the money to a third party.'

A sigh at the other end. A good sign. 'Hang on.' More crunchy noises as more discussion went on. Alison put the portfolio carefully into the back and slid quietly into the passenger seat. She made the sign for stealing, pointed at the mobile and raised an eyebrow. She was good at this. I nodded.

The guy seemed to take forever to come back. The hang-on-I'll-ask syndrome was everywhere these days. Blaggers seem to be no different from any other business in this (and not just this) respect: none of the people you talk to on the phone appear to have the authority to make any decisions, which makes you wonder why they're entrusted with telephones in the first place. Even my plumber gets his wife to answer the phone and negotiations are carried on in a tortuous series of hang-on-I'll-ask-him bites.

Aha, a decision, the paper storm in my ear came to an end. 'All right, here's what you do. Tomorrow night, ten o'clock sharp, by Victoria Bridge. Bring your bloody expert and the money and no one and nothing else. Right? If we see anything suspicious . . .' he added threateningly. I agreed and hung up.

I smiled at Alison and said, 'Eejits.'

'Are you sure?'

'The one I spoke to was. There was a guy in the background he constantly conferred with, but even he's an eejit, so we shouldn't have a problem.'

'What makes the other one an eejit?' Alison asked as I started the engine.

'They'd figured it all out, the place, the conditions and the time. Short notice, one hour, so they could have someone in place watching for unusual activities in case I'd decided to bring in the police after all. Then I changed the conditions and the time and they agreed to meet in . . .' I checked my watch, '. . . twenty-four hours' time. Same location, though. So the place could be swarming with undercover police by tomorrow and they wouldn't know a thing about it.'

'So what was agreed?' she asked brightly, eyes wide awake. I had noticed the change earlier. After weeks of toiling for the exhibition and a constant dullness in her eyes that I had attributed to her dull diet (and rationing of the once free-flowing wine) it was as though she had woken up to find herself on a holiday island in the sun. Alive, sparkling, alert. My proposition had excited her. We were going to do something illegal and Robin Hoodish and perhaps a little dangerous and Alison *absolutely loved it*.

'We agreed to do the handover tomorrow at ten and that I would have an art expert with me to authenticate the watercolours. How would you like to be the independent art expert for the evening?'

'I'd be delighted. My fees are rather high, I must warn you.'

'We'll see about that. Did you get what you were looking for?' I asked, nodding my head at the portfolio behind her seat.

'Kind of. Wrong century of course. Finding seventeenth-century paper would have taken months and cost a fortune. This is early nineteenth, and even that's like hen's teeth these days. I had to make certain promises to get it. Not of an unsavoury kind,' she added quickly. 'So it would never stand up to chemical analysis, but then it's not supposed to, is it?'

'No, as long as it looks like someone has made an honest attempt at forging them that's okay.'

'An honest attempt at forging, I like your turn of phrase, Chris,' she said as we drove off. 'That's me, Alison Flood, the honest forger.'

I found my way out of the little maze of residential streets and joined the steady traffic on Bathwick Street. The little shopping spree SINO (Stupid Idea Number One) had spawned was over.

Or so I thought. I didn't know it then but perhaps I should also have shopped for a rope trick, X-ray vision, full body armour, an elephant gun and an invisibility suit to go over the lot.

I was approaching Cleveland Bridge when the gates of the fire station to our right clattered open and two fire engines, blue lights bouncing off the building, emerged from their pens. Both blasted off a short soundbite of siren. I stopped to let them feed into the road across my path and enjoyed the growl of the big diesels as they accelerated with typical laid-back urgency towards the bridge and the city beyond.

'That's quite eerie,' Alison said as I drove on.

'What, the fire engines?'

'No, dopey, the church,' she said, pointing to our left.

Only the upper half of the building was visible from here, St John's Church being sited much lower than the approach to the bridge and hiding itself behind a shoulder-high wall, but the visible part was indeed weakly though spookily lit from somewhere below. The light was dancing unsteadily. Just then a tall amorphous shadow passed left to right across the dumpy bell tower.

I slowed down to get a better view and was instantly honked at from behind for it. It's tough being a model citizen. I pulled over and stuck the DS on to the wide pavement.

'Looks like a fire,' I said. 'Best place to have one, of course, smack opposite the fire station.' Still, even fire stations burned down from time to time . . .

'Are we investigating?' A little flame was dancing behind the normally cool grey of Alison's eyes. The detective fantasy had struck. Secretly, everyone wants to be in a story. Until they are. Then they want out.

'Irresponsible not to.' We walked across to the wall. Alison was just tall enough to look over the other side. The shapeless figure of a man limped back and forth among a tangle of shaggy-looking pine trees, picking up sticks of wood and what looked like bits of broken furniture to feed a fire that leapt fiercely at us from an oil drum at the foot of the wall. I could make out wisps of grey hair under the woolly hat; the rest of his shape was obscured by a large coat and the unsteady shadows. I was just about to call to him when with a sudden crack the fire sent up a thick shower of sparks. We withdrew our heads sharpish.

'Is that Billy?'

'Could be, can't be sure from here. I'm going down to have a look. But since we're uninvited it's best not to go empty-handed,' I said. I remembered I still hadn't unloaded the crate of Pilsner Urquell I'd bought the other day. I fetched three bottles from the boot. A quick rummage in the glove box produced a full packet of Camels. An emergency ration I kept there for . . . emergencies.

We walked the few yards to where St John's Road sloped up towards the bridge, past a large suffering Christ on the cross, and turned left into the church grounds. It started orderly enough, with a stretch of grass and a few eighteenth-century graves and monuments, but turned increasingly neglected and anarchic the further we went into the tangle of tumbledown headstones, half-sunken tombs and crazily angled crosses. The smell and dance of the fire came from the other side of a particularly thick tangle of ancient fir trees, rampant weeds and brushwood. When we stepped into its circle of light there was no sign of the firestarter.

The jumping brightness of the flames in the oil drum seemed to spread nothing but darkness beyond its immediate reach. I couldn't see beyond the lick of light on the conifers and bushes around us and had no intention of walking into the gloom beyond.

'Let's just wait.' We sat down on a sinking tomb near the fire and waited. After a while I opened a couple of bottles and we drank in silence.

'Did we spook him?' Alison asked eventually. 'How many calories does this stuff have, by the way?' She studied the bottle's label as though it was medicine.

'It's practically a slimming aid,' I said distractedly. A dark shape had materialized just beyond the reach of the light. Whoever it was carried what looked like a table leg and held it like a club.

'Billy? Is that Billy?' I called, putting on what I hoped was my harmless, well-wishing face.

'It isn't. So you can fuck off again. That's my fire. Get away.' He swung the table leg in the direction from which we had come. And he was right. It wasn't Billy's voice. Billy spoke with a deep Somerset burr and this voice had plenty of Scottish grit in it.

'Spare bottle.' I waved the hefty bottle of Urquell and set it on the stone beside me. 'Wants drinking.' I turned half away from him, clinked bottles with Alison and drank.

'Bastards. Bastards everywhere.' He walked past us and flung the table leg into the drum. 'They chucked me out. Bastards. Christian bastard charity at its best, eh?' He swiped the bottle off the tomb. I offered him the bottle opener on my keyring but he wrenched the top off with his teeth. He was also younger than Billy. His short beard still had strands of black in it. His eyes, too, were less guarded than Billy's, had some fire beyond the glow of the reflected flames. 'It was dry down there.'

'Where?'

'The crypt,' he said impatiently, gesturing over his shoulder. 'First he says it's all right, now he says he's had complaints. From the congregation. Gave me a fiver. A fiver! Probably spent more on the new padlock. This is a protest, like.' He gestured at the fire. 'Locked out by the good Christians. No room at the inn, biblical, is it not?' He took a long swig, then looked at the label, then took a longer swig. 'Thought it was wine. Fuckin' big for a beer bottle, but no bad.'

'We came down because we thought you were Billy. Have you seen him lately?'

'You know how to insult a man properly. You telling me I look like that old bastard?'

'Of course not. A trick of the light, that's all,' I placated. I took out the Camels and shared them around. Definitely non-fattening, Alison accepted one. Our Scottish friend snapped the filter off his. He took a light from me and inhaled like a drowning man snatched from the airless depth of the sea. I sucked more delicately on mine. I'd given up smoking a few months ago. Starting again in a graveyard seemed highly appropriate.

'What you want with the bastard?' he exhaled.

'Just a chat, that's all.'

He tapped his forehead with his index finger. 'Not all

there, is Billy. Killed a woman in a brawl, did you know that?' It was news to me. 'Ages ago now, mind. Did his time for it. But it messed up his mind, being inside.' He circled his index finger next to his temple to illustrate his point. 'If it's conversation you're after you made a bad choice. Unsociable wanker. And as I said, not all there.'

'So have you seen him lately?'

'Not for ages. Hang on a sec, he used to be up in Rainbow Woods by a beck, but not for ages now. A few weeks ago I saw him with all his stuff. Looked like he was moving.'

'Moving?'

'Yeah, you know, finding a new hole to crawl into. Always near the river or the canal, our Billy. Billy the water rat.'

'Do you remember where that was?'

'Down by the gas works. Didn't ask where he was going since I don't give a shit and he wouldn't have told anyway.' He got up, emptied his bottle and flung it at the wall, where it shattered. He flicked the fag end towards the fire and missed. 'And this concludes the interview,' he said bitingly, and without giving either of us another glance he walked back into the inky dark among the conifers, presumably in search of more things to burn.

Tim refusing to eat my food momentarily shook my world.

'I went to the Albanian café, next to the bike shop,' he explained. 'Special meatballs. You've got to try 'em, Chris. You get this huge plate of them. They taste like nothing you've tasted before. Secret family recipe. I had two portions, absolutely stuffed.'

Relieved that Tim wasn't ill or had joined Alison on a diet I turned my attention to the gadget he was holding, even though it was Annis who had volunteered to deal with it.

'It's magnetic, right?' Tim waggled the homing bug in

front of her. It looked like a small cigar tube, but black and flattened on one side. 'You've got to stick it right underneath the car. Not a wheel arch, it won't hold there. Do it very gently, or they'll hear it fastening on.'

'That's the least of my worries,' Annis said, pointing her fork at the bug. 'I know how to do gentle.' Both Tim and I gave an involuntary sigh but avoided each other's eyes. 'It's extricating myself from there with the guys right on top of me. If I get out backwards and they look in their mirrors at the wrong moment they'll clock me. But I'll think of something.' She skewered another spear of broccoli on to her fork and shoved it into her mouth, unconcerned.

'What range has it got?' I wanted to know.

'Not much, it's one of my home-made ones, really low tech radio stuff. Half a mile under good conditions. Enough, though. We won't lose them,' he promised.

Half an hour later we were in the yard. Alison was wearing a cream top and navy blue suit. I wasn't happy about the tight skirt and the two-inch heels, since she wouldn't stand a chance of running away should it all go pear-shaped, but she'd insisted she had nothing else posh enough to make her look the part.

Tim laid a hand on my arm and looked across at Annis, who was already climbing into her Land Rover, sensibly clad in a hooded sweatshirt, jeans and trainers, all black as the night. Only her strawberry hair shone as bright as ever. Her luminous hair and the featherlight way she used her body would always make us think of summer. Yet I had also seen Annis in bleak and ashen moods that no one dared try and penetrate, which she would later blame on problems in the studio and refuse to discuss.

'Has Annis recently . . . I mean . . . have you and Annis . . .?' Tim asked.

'Not for weeks. You know what she's like when she's disappearing into her work. Lives like a nun.' We both looked across at her now as she fiddled with something under the dashboard of her ancient conveyance, avoiding each other's eyes. It was last year when we'd found out that our pragmatic friend was favouring both of us with her attentions in more or less equal measure. Annis, who seemed to find nothing odd about this, had made it a condition we didn't 'compare notes' and didn't 'make a big deal' about sharing her appetites if we wanted it to last. And to our lasting astonishment we'd agreed. Being blokes, not talking about our feelings wasn't exactly a hardship either.

'Oh, that's what I thought,' Tim said lightly. We both sighed simultaneously, glad this long and emotionally difficult conversation was finally over. 'Good. Fine. All set then. Let's roll.'

The light was gently fading when our little convoy crept slowly towards the rendezvous. Our opponents weren't completely barmy; the place was well chosen. Victoria Bridge Road was a narrow, sparsely lit and uninhabited street, ending in an iron bridge blocked for traffic by cast-iron bollards. Corrugated iron fencing, eight foot high, ran the length of it on both sides, guarding recently started building sites for office developments from trespassers. Weeds grew out of the broken pavements, piles of builder's sand and litter punctuated the depressing no man's land. No one in their right mind would walk this shortcut between the Lower and Upper Bristol Roads after dark. I had made sure we arrived an hour early, hoping the enemy hadn't. We climbed out of our cars and started nosing around.

'The place is perfect,' Annis acknowledged, sniffing the air.

'For them or for us?' I asked, scanning the length of the empty road.

'Cuts both ways, I'd say. Not many places like this left in Bath. Minutes from the centre yet completely deserted, easily checked over for lurking police cars, rough ground on both sides.' She playfully pulled on a length of corrugated fencing and it scraped away from its neighbour. 'Don't give much for *their* security. They should hire *us*.'

'That's it then,' I decided. 'Alison and I position ourselves just along from this opening. Annis, you lose the Land Rover nearby and then hide on the other side of the fence. Hopefully their car won't stop far from this spot. Tim, you site yourself just outside the entrance to the street so they and their homing bug have to come past you. Let's move.' I shooed everyone along like a stage manager, mainly to make myself feel in control. We had been over the scenario several times already.

Minutes later, Annis came sauntering down the street by herself, hands in her pockets, her curls pulled back into a ponytail, as if she didn't have a care in the world. I cursed the show at Simon Paris which was sucking the woman's sex drive out of her and pouring it into her paintings. Still, the show was imminent now and all would be back to normal soon.

Annis pulled on a pair of black leather gloves, waggled her fingers at us and disappeared through the gap in the fence. Alison and I withdrew to the comfort of the DS. While she checked and rechecked her bag for her 'art expert paraphernalia' I passed the time by trying to find out how quickly I could get back to smoking twenty a day. I was making good progress there. The place made me curiously nervous. I went over and over the proposed scenario yet couldn't see the flaw in it.

By ten o'clock dusk was deepening to darkness. Only two of the street lights were working, one at the entrance to the street, the other close to the bridge. Between the two puddles of acidic sodium light the darkness gathered quickly and colourless shadows hunched their shoulders along the fences on either side.

Five minutes past ten. Pinpricks of worryingly narrow headlights appeared at the end of the road, growing larger very quickly. The flaw in my plan approached at sixty miles an hour. On two wheels.

43

The tomato-red motorbike took only seconds to reach us. It came to a stop level with the DS. The rider was clad in racing leathers matching his bike, his pillion wore a black leather jacket, jeans and trainers. A black portfolio hung on a single strap from his shoulder. He beckoned with a gloved hand. Alison and I exchanged a quick glance and walked over slowly. I slid the case of ransom money between my feet.

Both men wore full helmets and pink-lensed sunglasses, their features completely obscured. The rider half unzipped his jacket and slipped his right hand into it. He constantly scanned the surroundings, his mirrors, the surroundings again, completely ignoring us.

The pillion unzipped the portfolio and opened it out on two plastic-sheathed watercolours, glowing tantalizingly even in this gloom. 'That your expert?'

'I am,' Alison said, cool as the proverbial. 'Shall we proceed?' She stepped forward, pulling a torch and a magnifying glass of Holmesian proportions from her handbag, and started scrutinizing the proffered artworks. She moved the lens slowly and deliberately over the circle of torchlight, felt the edge of the paper between the plastic coverings. She consulted Griffin's notes from her own folder. Then went back to bending over the portfolio.

'Get on with it, will ya? It's the real thing.' Even under his heavy camouflage the pillion looked exasperated. He shifted nervously on his narrow seat.

'Hold still, please,' Alison said in a distracted dentist's voice. The man stiffened and sat still. Eventually she produced a scalpel she normally used for sharpening graphite pens and gently scraped a small area on the back of one of the watercolours and dropped some invisible fibres into a small freezer bag. 'I'm afraid I can't make a positive evaluation. There appear to be some discrepancies. We need to examine these fibres in our laboratory at the University,' she said in a tone that was bored as well as final. 'Thank you,' she added and turned away towards the car.

As expected, the man now zipping up the portfolio in one impatient movement exploded at me. 'What the fuck is that woman on about?! You're fucking us about. The fucking merchandise is the real thing. You fucked up big time with your fucking expert.'

The man clearly needed a thesaurus but I thought it the wrong moment to point this out. Instead I went for my magic wand. I clicked the case open and pulled out a wodge of banknotes. 'I know, mate,' I said chummily. 'The insurers foisted her on me. Here's a deposit. Ten grand. To show I'm not fucking you about.'

He stared at the notes for about three seconds before he swiped them out of my hand and stuffed them in his jacket pocket.

'I'm sure the test'll come out fine. I'll try and hurry things along. In the meantime, let's keep things sweet, all right? You have a number I can ring to get back to you?'

He hesitated. This was not in his script and he had to think about it. It seemed to be a painful process. 'Shit. All right.' He pulled a mobile from his pocket and scrolled through some numbers. 'You got Bluetooth?'

'Blue what?'

'Never mind.' He held the display up to me. I keyed the number into my own phone.

The driver zipped up his jacket, put the bike in gear. The man was no fool. He'd kept the engine quietly idling and never stopped checking around him. He'd never spoken a word. Whether he really did have a gun under his jacket or not, he had given off a quiet air of menace without effort.

'Be seeing you,' said the pillion. The bike leapt forward and shot through the bollards blocking the bridge. Within seconds it disappeared left into the traffic of the Upper Bristol Road. Stupid Idea Number One had just got sillier.

Annis appeared from the gap in the fence. She gave an

expansive shrug and waved the homing device at me. Alison got out of the car. 'Eejits, were they, Chris?'

'How was I supposed to crawl under a racing bike?' Annis added. 'Not much ground clearance, you know?'

Smartarses. 'Okay, okay, I hadn't thought of a motorbike. But neither had any of you. How the hell are we going to find them now?'

My mobile rang. It was Tim. 'Stop wetting your pants, Honeypot, I'm right behind them. Zipped around the block as soon as I saw the bike. They're driving very sedately, I can easily follow them. Whoops, hang on . . .' There was a pause of several agonizing seconds. 'Bloody hell,' came next.

'What?' I near screamed down the phone. The whole operation depended now on Tim not losing sight of them in traffic.

'You're not going to believe this, Chris.'

# Chapter Four

'The lazy bastards,' was all I could think of.

My clever scheme of following our opponents to where they stashed the stolen artwork through one of Tim's gizmos might have been a disaster but as it turned out we might have followed them just as easily with a piece of string tied to their mudguard.

'I take it all back,' said Alison, staring, like all of us, through the eight-foot cast-iron gates that ineffectually barred our way. 'They are eejits.'

'Just pragmatic,' contradicted Annis, herself the most pragmatic of thinkers. If there was a way of simplifying something – life, art, relationships – then Annis would find it. 'Admirable, really. Only they were so sure no one would follow them they didn't even bother to do a detour. Definitely sloppy.'

Right now I was grateful for sloppiness. And Tim's presence of mind. We were standing in front of what, according to a faded wooden sign on the crumbling brick building on the other side of the gates, had once been a small ceramic tile manufacturer. It was only a couple of streets down from our rendezvous in a similarly deserted stretch of urban desert, probably scheduled for redevelopment like Victoria Bridge Road.

'They unlocked the gates and rode in without locking up behind them. By then I was on foot,' Tim told us excitedly. He was our hero of the hour and enjoying every minute of it. 'I hid in yonder bush and saw them come out of those green lock-up gates right at the end of the yard. Without the portfolio. Both were yakking on their mobiles. The pillion has a skinny face and ratty hair, wiry guy. The rider looks like a surfer dude. Seven days a week in the gym. Bottle blond, I reckon. Two natty earrings.'

And just possibly a gun. 'How long were they inside?' I asked.

'No more than five minutes. Then they lidded up, rode out, locked the gates and pissed off back towards the Upper Bristol Road.'

'Are we going in?' Alison asked.

Automatically the three of us looked at Tim, who was snuffling about the gate and the sagging brick wall. 'Mh? Yeah, no probs. But not tonight, I haven't got my gear. Anyway,' he said, consulting his watch, 'the pubs are open and you all owe me a rather large drink.'

Twenty-four hours later Tim and I stood in the same place, suitably tooled up.

'You should be wearing a hard hat, Chris,' he said. 'Remember what happened last time we visited a warehouse?'

I did and I had kept some scars as souvenirs of the occasion, though my hair had grown back nicely over the stitches. 'Don't worry, I learned a lesson there,' I assured him.

'Which is?' he said distractedly. He had that glazed look that came over him whenever most of his mind wandered about inside the lock he was attacking.

'Carry a decent torch.' Last time I got clobbered I had wandered around a dark unfriendly warehouse with nothing but a fashionable pencil light. This time I carried a rubberized torch that swallowed six A size batteries and was heavy enough to do serious damage when applied properly.

The lock slipped open and we squeezed into the yard. Tim relocked the gate behind us. We loped across the potholed yard to the far corner of the building. A wooden cabbage-green double door, bleached to grey in the darkness, was Tim's next target. The doors were old but substantial and large enough to admit a sizeable van. They'd had several locks fitted over the years but only one appeared to be in use. It wasn't the first time I'd found that the bad guys had bad security, probably because they didn't expect the other bad guys. Like us. Tim took less than a minute to defeat the lock.

The doors opened straight into a cavernous space that smelled of damp cardboard, dust and darkness. I had seen a high round window at the front and suspected skylights that might give our torchlight away but in here the darkness was absolute. The windows had been blacked out. With the doors closed behind us we snapped on our torches simultaneously.

The place was a shambles. A shambolic Aladdin's cave. Towers of boxes, rows of flimsy crates, some opened, spilling their wares on to the scarred cement floor. Pallets of shrink-wrapped goodies had been dumped wherever there was space. The wall to my right had been crudely broken through and the chaos appeared to be continuing next door. Babylonic towers of multilingual lagers, crates of French wine, cigarettes and Dutch tobacco; CDs by the thousands; designer jeans, trainers and every conceivable type of perfume. I opened a bottle of Chanel No. 5. Never my favourite perfume but this smelled nothing like it.

'Snide, the lot,' I said. 'Except perhaps the booze and the rolling tobacco. Not easy to fake tobacco. But I bet you the fags were made from undercarpet in Singapore.'

'Multi-talented, then, our friends,' Tim said. 'But remember what we're here for. It's not healthy to hang around too long.' He advanced into the chaos and was soon lost from view amongst the mountains of counterfeit and smuggled goodies.

I played my torch along the mildewed walls and was

about to nose into the adjacent space through the hole in the wall when I heard Tim get religion.

'There is a God after all,' I distinctly heard him say. I went to find him at the back of the warehouse.

'How d'you make that out?' I enquired.

'Look, I found an old friend.'

Next to some collapsing kitchen units covered in crud sat a squat lump of a safe, a dull ton-and-a-half of metal. One dial, one handle.

'You two met before?'

'Not this particular box but look, it's an old Guardall,' Tim enthused, caressing the embossed name on the door. 'American. The new ones are fiendishly good of course but this one looks like it came over in the 1940s as part of the lease-lend scheme. Straight out of a gangster movie. When I open it there'll be a bag inside with "swag" written on it.'

'Easy to open then?'

'They hadn't thought of electronics then. As far as I'm concerned the thing *is* open.'

Perhaps this was as good a time as any to ask Tim some questions I had so far avoided, mainly because I wasn't sure if I would like the answers. 'What made you go straight in the end? Why'd you pack in safe-breaking?' A mildly absurd question to ask of a man who was busy breaking into a safe with the latest electronic gizmos.

'Oh, all sorts of reasons. It doesn't pay, for a start. And I was sick of moving around.'

'Doesn't pay?'

'Not if you're a one-man outfit like I was. Think about it: first you have to find a safe worth breaking into. Then you have to break into the premises and then get out again. It's hard work and I often got it wrong. I didn't have the right connections because I wasn't a criminal.'

Pardon? 'How do you make that out?'

'No, really. I was young, youn*ger*, and a bit mad but I never wanted to be a burglar. I never nicked jewellery or stuff, hence I never used fences and I had no criminal connections. I just wanted cash because I didn't fancy working.' He attached several magnetic gadgets to the safe while he talked. Mr Guardall now looked like an elderly patient having his heart rate monitored. 'But the kind of people who stick money in safes these days are guys who evade tax or do a lot of cash deals, which amounts to the same thing. Haulage people, building firms, bent scrap merchants spiriting cars out of the country. That kind of ilk. And you can't hang around a city and keep ripping off the hoodlums – like we're doing now, incidentally – it's just not healthy. You've got to keep on the move, which is tedious and costs a lot of money. I was sick to the teeth of it. I had a particularly good haul one day and decided to jack it in. Came to Bath and settled down. I'd always been into computers and stuff. So I wrote myself a fantastic CV, started working for the Uni and kept my nose clean. Until I met you, that is.' A digital readout on one of the gadgets showed nothing but zeros. He started turning the safe's dial, slowly, steadily, anticlockwise.

'Are there any safes you can't open?' I asked.

'Yes, plenty. But if I can't open them then I don't want what's in them anyway.' Numbers started appearing on the readout.

'Why not?'

'Think about it. Can you imagine how much a safe costs that I can't defeat? You don't buy one of *them* to keep a few grand in cash and your grandma's baubles in. It'll be full of papers or formulas or some other crud I can't use.'

'What's the weirdest thing you ever found in a safe, Tim?' I asked next.

'You're asking a lot of questions tonight. Can you shut up for a second?' He spun the combination wheel more confidently now, first left, then right, then left again. 'Teeth. A whole safe full of dentures. It completely grossed me out.' He collected his gadgets into his shoulder bag, turned the safe's handle by ninety degrees and the door cracked open. Tim allowed himself a theatrical pause. 'What if it's full of limited edition Kit Kat bars?'

I groaned with impatience.

'Sorry. Don't want you to be disappointed, that's all.'

He swung the door open. The shelves had been removed and the portfolio wedged inside diagonally. The remaining space at the bottom was crammed with small blue boxes. Just as I pulled out the black leather folder with a sigh of relief the sound of voices came from the yard.

Tim quickly closed the safe. 'Now what?'

'When the lights go on try and look like a crate of Chablis.'

We were still scrambling into the chaos of boxes and pallets when the door opened. A lonely strip of neon, the only survivor in a bank of lights suspended on wires from the ceiling, buzzed, blinked twice and snapped on. Its ghoulish glow seemed hellishly bright after the torchlight. I gripped my torch harder. It didn't give me much confidence. I peered through a gap between two stacks of cellophane-wrapped football shirts. Man United, of all things.

There were three of them. From Tim's description two of them looked to be our motorcycle pair. The third man would have needed a very sturdy bike to get around on: six foot something and eighteen stone of saturated fat, his shape was straining the seams of his expensive suit. In this light his fleshy face looked purple with anger and he was having a rant.

'This place is a fucking shambles, how do you expect to find anything in here? I want this fucking place cleared up, I don't care how long it takes.' He experimentally kicked a pile of boxes which teetered but failed to fall over. This seemed to enrage him even more. 'I'm surrounded by idiots!' he bellowed and ducked through the hole in the wall.

'He's just pissed off because of the fuck-up yesterday,'

hissed Surfer Dude. 'Cash-flow problems, has our Roy. He's got people to pay.'

'Yeah, people like us for a fucking start,' the wiry guy hissed back.

'We always get paid. You can trust him like that. But he's made some kind of deal and has people breathing down his fat neck.'

'Jesus Christ!' Roy, too, seemed to find religion here. He heaved himself back into the room where Tim and I huddled, waiting to be uncovered by the clear-up. 'I want all the T-shirts, CDs and other crap next door and all the fags and booze in here so they can be loaded up quickly. There's a pick-up tomorrow. So why are you standing around like the lemons you are? Get a move on. I don't care if it takes you all night. And I want you back at Ashton View afterwards. I need you first thing tomorrow morning. Now get your sad arses in gear.'

'Yes, Roy,' came the sensible reply. 'Ehm, Roy?' the wiry guy added cautiously. 'How are we supposed to get back to –'

'You can fucking walk, for all I care!' was Roy's parting shot as he slammed the door behind him.

A moment of silence, in which Tim and I stared intensely at each other. Then, simultaneously, we started making hand signs at each other. I was trying to signal 'Let's get out as soon as they're next door' and he was signing 'How about a chicken korma?' for all I knew, since neither of us knew any sign language. We ended up rolling our eyes at each other and gave up on it.

'We'll be here all bloody night,' Wiry groaned. 'Can you drive a forklift?'

'Like Michael Fucking Schumacher, mate. Watch me.'

'And then I suppose you'll drive us home on it?'

'Ah, stop whining,' Surfer Dude said as he started up the forklift.

'We should have clobbered the damn private prick

and his expert for the dosh and Roy would be sweet as rain now.'

'Would he fuck. Some sort of understanding with the insurance guys, Roy said. No violence, Roy said. Said it twice.'

I was glad to hear it, though I doubted this arrangement extended to private pricks and their operatives found hiding in his warehouse at night. Surfer Dude hadn't been boasting; the stacks of boxes we were hiding amongst disappeared on to his forklift and into the cavern next door at an alarming rate. Wiry kept himself busy stacking up more stuff for him and piling the slithery packs of shirts into unstable mounds, a couple of feet from where Tim was crouching. What was that film? *Crouching Dragon . . .?* Did that make me a hidden tiger? We'd find out in a minute, I supposed.

'Mind you,' Surfer Dude called over his shoulder as he zoomed next door with the last-but-one pallet in front of me, 'if I ever meet him walking his dog somewhere I'll give him something expert myself! Aaaahshit.'

A scraping sound, followed by a respectable crunch. Schumacher had hit the barrier. Wiry dropped what he was carrying and legged it next door, where he started laughing hysterically.

No sign language needed this time. We were out of our hiding place and to the door before the laughter and swearing had subsided. Once outside we simply ran. The gate was unlocked. We whizzed through it and once on the road just kept on running like a couple of kids who'd kicked their ball through a greenhouse roof.

Back in the safety of Tim's car our mood changed from terrified to jubilant. We'd pulled off the first part of the stunt without getting rumbled.

Tim's diet of curries, doughnuts and secret-recipe meatballs didn't make him the fittest of runners. His breath was still ragged when he put the car in gear. 'Now explain . . . this,' he panted. 'We've got the stuff. You still got most of the dosh. Now why not give the whole shebang to Griffin's and be done with it?' He swung the car into the Lower Bristol Road and drove sedately east. 'Or better still . . . hand over the artwork and keep the dosh. Who's to know?'

I took a deep breath to start my explanation when I spotted a familiar figure by the side of the road. A grey-haired, silver-bearded man, bent nearly double under the weight of a rucksack and several plastic carriers, tottered in the opposite direction. 'Stop! Stop now. Do a U-turn, Tim. It's Billy. I've found the bastard. Stop, let me out.' He didn't react, just kept going. 'What's the matter with you?' I shouted, furious now.

'We've got fuzz-balls right behind us. They've been there ever since we joined this road.'

I shifted a little to sneak a look in the rear-view mirror. Sure enough, a patrol car was hanging back, two car lengths behind, on this otherwise empty road. 'So what?' I was too excited to care.

'What if they decide to take an interest? For a start we've got stolen watercolours on the back seat. Stolen twice, I might add.'

'So? Recovery of stolen goods. They'll be fine about it.'

'Not with a boot full of professional safe-breaking gear they won't.'

'Oh. Damn and . . . what's the other thing?'

'Bugger?'

'That's the one.'

We were nearly three tense miles down the road from where I had spotted Billy when the police car turned lazily away towards the city centre. Tim performed an instant U-turn and screeched back west.

Twenty minutes of crawling along the side streets and nosing around the Oldfield Park area turned up nothing. 'He's got a hidey-hole here somewhere, I'm sure. I'll find him later. Can't be too many off-licences round here and they're bound to know him. Let's get home now,' I said. Alison was waiting at Mill House to work her magic.

'You were going to explain why you're going into this rigmarole of faking the pictures and then making us go back into that damn warehouse to stick them into his safe again. What's his name, Roy's.' Tim drove at a decent speed now, but with more than an occasional glance in the mirrors.

'Yes, Roy Something of Ashton View. Check that out, will you? As for the rigmarole: insurers and blaggers have an unspoken understanding. When insurers get offered the return of stolen goods at an economic price they accept it and no questions asked. The police only ever get involved if the stolen goods in question are extremely high profile, let's say a painting goes missing from the National Gallery or something like that. Or if there was violence involved. Otherwise the insurers pay up and keep shtoom. If they didn't, that door would close. If we simply tried to rip the stuff off then Griffin's would never again have the opportunity to do a deal, no one would trust them again. So I asked Alison to make some flawed copies of them, which we then stick back in the safe. At the next meeting our art expert points out that these are clever fakes. Actually, just bad enough so even they can see it when we show them photographs of the originals. Whoever Roy is he's in the fake business himself. I don't think he bothers with burglaries, so he probably got them off the burglars in lieu of payment for something or other. He'll think he got ripped off by them, not us. And they'll swear blind that they didn't pull a fast one, "Honest, Roy, we wouldn't know how to." Which they probably wouldn't. Everyone's baffled and the whole thing dies a quiet death,' I concluded neatly. 'See any flaws in that?'

Tim scratched his head for a while. 'Can't see one yet,' he said reluctantly. 'But that still doesn't explain why you couldn't for once just do as Griffin's asked, it would be so much easier.'

I took a deep breath. 'Because . . .'

'. . . you've got a thing about art thieves, I remember. Just *you* remember what happened last time,' he said grimly.

We had arrived at Mill House, in time to save me from doing just that. Images of fire and death flickered across my brain and vanished again.

'This one's different,' I said firmly. 'It'll work just fine.'

# Chapter Five

'This is criminal really,' Alison muttered. She was checking the angles for the last time, making sure everything was level.

'Bit late now,' I said lamely. My Accumulated Guilt Quotient was at a seasonal high for involving her in this caper. At the same time I was fascinated by the professional forger I now saw at work. In a half-hearted attempt to keep the operation from Annis, who would not approve, she had set herself up in my attic office.

'Not that, dummy. Well, it is, but it's all in a good cause. No, exposing the watercolours to that much light. They're very vulnerable. I'll try and keep it to a minimum. Just as well I've done the preliminaries from the photographs.' She slipped on a pair of pristine cotton gloves before reverently removing the first painting from its sleeve and laying it face down on the glass of the episcope. Having closed the rubberized lid on it she installed herself on a stool just to the left of a drawing board secured to one of my easels. The nineteenth-century paper was stretched and marked with the dimensions already. I noticed that everything, including the position of the easel and the table with the episcope, was marked in chalk on the floor. Nothing was left to chance, everything double-checked. Gaffer-taped to the floor were foot switches for the various lights, the episcope and a dimmer; clamped to the top of the drawing board was a large magnifying glass with its own light source.

For the next six hours Alison worked like an alchemist who has cast all doubt aside. The lights dimmed to a glimmer, the episcope projected the first image on to the paper. There was nothing tentative about the way she traced the outlines that appeared on the paper; episcope on, a few seconds of pencil marks, episcope off, lights on, a quick check with the enlarged photographs, a tiny correction perhaps, then lights off, episcope on. A permanent frown had clamped itself to her forehead and lines of tension appeared around her eyes as she worked smoothly and silently. The images appeared as if by magic in the slow strobing of light. I was curious about the whole process but kept my questions to myself, simply watching her work from my chair. After some final measurements Alison seemed satisfied with the first stage. The three drawing boards were laid at intervals on a sturdy pasting table where inks, paints and various chemicals were neatly arranged, with the originals, now back in their protective sleeves, taped to the wall above. I drifted in and out of sleep, invariably waking to Alison bent over the table, frowning and humming to herself.

It was after ten in the morning when I woke up properly and with both eyes open. Only a few shafts of light pierced the darkness. I tried to get out of my chair but found that my body had moulded itself into a question mark. It felt permanent. I hobbled S-shaped across the room and tore off the blackout we had rigged up over the skylights.

The finished copies of the John Whites lay on the pasting table, still stretched on their boards, which at first glance was all that appeared to distinguish them from the originals. No sign of Alison, who I hoped was having a well-earned sleep in her room. After a shower and shave I felt ready to take on Mr Roy and his retinue of thugs, provided I could find some breakfast in the kitchen.

What I did find was Annis, glaring at me from behind an empty cornflakes bowl.

'Morning,' I tried.

Her eyes turned into narrow green slits; apparently a good sign in a cat, never a good sign in an Annis.

'Have I got time for a coffee before you have a go at me?' I made a beeline for the kettle, which was singing quietly on the Rayburn.

'I can't believe you're trying to pull a stunt like this,' she began. I hurried with the cafetière. If I couldn't be unconscious, which was the preferred option, I might as well be awake for what was coming.

'And to involve Ali of all people in this idiocy. She's been going straight since she moved in with us and has her first significant show coming up and you make her get back into forgery mode. And I can't believe I didn't ask what you were up to when we all went down to meet those guys. My head must've been somewhere else. But to make Alison assemble another forgery kit . . .'

'She'll be fine. It's a one-off. And in a good cause,' I said lamely.

'Yeah, *your* good cause. What if it goes wrong? What if it backfires, huh? Do you think they'll sit still for this? If they find out it's you who's ripped them off then we could all be in deep shit. Especially if this Roy character is local and has a bit of clout round here.' Annis had caught up quickly. Someone had blabbed. 'I thought we knew all the local bigwigs around here,' she said in an entirely different tone. An interested tone.

'So did I,' I said, grateful for her change of tack. 'But two of them were sent down over the past two years, remember? One of them for six years. Nature abhors a vacuum, there was bound to be someone stepping up to take advantage.'

'So we know nothing about this guy?'

I noted the 'we' with satisfaction. Annis might be mad at me but she was still on board. 'Not a lot. Tim and I heard him mention Ashton View. Probably a house over at Cold Ashton.'

'Oh, great. That's only just over the hill. We're practically neighbours.'

True. Cold Ashton was a village a few clicks north-east from here. 'I didn't know that when I started this.'

'There's still time to call it off, Chris,' she said, grabbing the cafetière from me, the greedy addict. She shoved it back at me across the table half empty.

'Perhaps. Would be a shame though. Who told you, anyway?'

'A sleep-walking Ali. Resistance was futile. I knew you were up to something.'

A sleep-walking Alison shuffled into the kitchen, right on cue, in a fluffy white dressing gown, her eyes bruised and barely open. 'I can smell coffee,' she mumbled. 'Give me some or I'll bite.' I put my mug into her outstretched hand and put the kettle on again.

'You did a brilliant job last night,' I said.

'Piece of cake. It's like falling off a bicycle,' she muttered, 'you never forget how to do it.'

'Why don't you go back to bed? You look like you could do with a bit more sleep,' I suggested.

'Can't. John and Simon are coming up.'

A flat bleep on a car horn confirmed we had visitors.

'Shit, they're here,' said Alison, suddenly alive. 'I haven't had a shower yet, shitshitshit.' She skidded out of the kitchen and hammered up the stairs.

'Simon Paris?' I sought confirmation as we went outside.

'He wants to make up the final list for the show. He's brought John along to rephotograph some of the paintings.' John Gatt, the gallery assistant at Simon Paris Fine Art, who looked after both the Bath and the London branches.

Wait a second. Simon and John, surely. *'John and Simon?'* I repeated meaningfully.

'You're catching up, Honeysett. Alison's besotted. Ever since she first clapped eyes on him.'

'Hence the diet?'

'Hence the dieting.'

Simon, immaculately suited as ever, was inspecting a tiny splash of mud on his immaculate Daimler. 'When are you going to get that jungle track tarmacked, Chris? It's only fit for tractors and horses. Morning, Annis,' he said by way of greeting. John shouldered his photographic gear. He was the fit outdoorsy-looking type, I noticed for the first time, tall, broad-shouldered, with dark, no nonsense hair. Alison probably thought he was good-looking. He gave a cheery, suntanned wave but looked beyond us to the door.

'Ali's going to join us in a second,' Annis said. 'Let's go up. Unless you want some coffee first?' she added hopefully.

An hour or so later Simon steered me away from the studio. We left Alison, John and Annis to discuss the technicalities of hanging the joint show and strolled across the meadow in the general direction of the millpond.

For some reason he had put on his flimsy gold reading glasses and ran a hand over his balding head as if looking for something there. 'How's your own work coming along?'

'Oh, I'll let you know when there's enough to look at,' I offered.

'Bollocks,' he said pleasantly. 'You haven't painted a damn thing since Jenny died.' This was patently true. Only Simon was the first person to bring it up. 'There's a damn cobweb on your easel, you know that? It's been a whole year since you've done any painting, Chris.'

'Ten months, actually,' I corrected.

'Even so. What are you waiting for? Ever since Jenny was murdered you've buried yourself in detective work. You're a painter, Chris. The private eye thing is supposed to be a sideline, remember? You used to tell people to take a hike if the case didn't interest you, now you grab anything that comes up as long as it keeps you away from your easel.' He gestured dismissively back towards the studio.

I didn't have an answer for this at all. I had tried, though not recently, to make sense of canvas, paints and brushes and failed miserably. Somehow I felt starved of images, apart from the one that had burnt itself on my brain – Jenny's bashed-in skull, her features barely recognizable, her blood congealing in the summer heat . . .

'Chris, you're quite well known now. You've got collectors waiting to see what you're doing next. Your last London show got good reviews. This is not the time to drop out of sight.' He flashed his eyes at me above his glasses, then turned away and looked across the valley. 'I had pencilled you in for a September show, as usual,' he continued craftily. 'But I don't see how you're going to make it. I may have to give the slot to someone else. Jack Burns is looking for a new place to show . . .'

'Burns? Bits of hair and used tissue in vitrines? You can't be serious,' I protested.

Simon shrugged and pocketed his glasses. 'I'm serious about September anyway. There won't be another slot for a year unless someone cancels or drops dead. Just want to make sure you realize that.' He sniffed at what he disparagingly called 'country air'. 'Anyway, I'm off. John's getting a lift back with Alison.' He walked down towards the house and his car without another word.

I let out a deep breath through puffed-up cheeks. I knew I had just been 'managed', but all the same – Burns! Bits of rubbish in glass cases and a lot of waffle. Over my dead body. Or preferably his.


Okay, I was going to do the switch alone. Annis was right. I should have talked it over with everybody, weighed up the odds, perhaps even called a vote before I put everybody at risk from retaliation. I had been besotted by Stupid Idea Number One and had kept it from Annis so she wouldn't talk me out of it. I should perhaps never have started it and according to Simon, who was probably also right – and how annoying was that? – should never have taken the case on in the first place. So I was going to do it by myself. Tim had given me an exasperated refresher in lock breaking (and finally suggested I consider ram-raiding the place instead), Alison had packed the forgeries into the sleeves of the originals in the right order for me, and Annis had contributed a few hard stares whenever I came across her round the house.

It was getting dark. Tim had gone back to the futuristic computer den he calls his home in Bath, Alison had gone off for a walk at dusk and Annis was quietly cursing in one of the outbuildings, where for the past few months she had tried to breathe life into a 1950s Norton motorbike. 'Bye. I'm going now. All by myself. See you later. I hope,' a little voice inside me said. Why, I wondered, as I nosed the DS through the gate, did I suddenly feel hard done by?

Because I hated warehouses. Especially dark, dingy, unfriendly warehouses, and especially at night. The word itself made me uneasy. *Storage facility*, now there was a nice, cheery word, conjuring up friendly men in clean, blue coveralls facilitating storage. But not *warehouse* . . .

At the top of the track Alison suddenly stepped out from the gloom under the crack willow and waved. I stopped the car. She slid into the passenger seat.

'I'm just off to plant your handiwork in their safe,' I said.

'I know, let's go,' she said cheerfully, giving the dash-board a couple of encouraging taps with her hand.

'Ali –' I started.

'Not a chance,' she said. 'I've been in it from the start, and you'll need me again for act two of this charade anyway. I'm yer art expert, remember? Anyway, I've nothing else to do, the show is painted, selected, photographed, done. Even Annis has started wrestling with her Norton, that's how ready we are. Drive.'

It was time to prove to Annis how mature and respons-ible I really was. 'Oh, all right then,' I said. With a mixture of guilt and relief I turned the car on to the road towards Bath.

'Piece of cake.' The padlock on the gate had seemed to take no time at all. It sprang open under my ministrations with a little click. A car came by without slowing. We ignored it, trying to look like we belonged here. I closed the gate behind us but didn't snap the lock shut. It would alert anyone entering behind us but I was counting on being in and out of the place in no time at all. The yard with its stacks of broken pallets, its nests of dented oil drums and huddles of detritus lay in semi-darkness. Away from the street lights, in the dark shadows in front of the warehouse doors, I let my eyes accustom to the gloom and got out my picklocks again. The first serrated sliver of steel slid in easily. It always does and doesn't mean a thing. It didn't this time either. For what seemed an age I fumbled around, trying to remember everything Tim had taught me, with Alison losing interest and growing restless beside me. Another car passed the gate from the opposite direction or perhaps it was the same one coming back. I was growing impatient but forced myself to stay calm and continued with my gentle probing. It wouldn't do to leave telltale marks on the lock or ruin my tools.

The lock gave only seconds before I ran out of faith in my abilities to defeat it. We quickly slid inside. The door firmly closed behind us and I found the light switch on the wall. No point fumbling about in the dark this time, we wouldn't be here long. I got a mild shock when a whole bank of neon lights sprang to life. Someone had worked hard in here, replacing the missing lights and mounting a major clear-up operation. There was a lot more space now, boxes and pallets stood at right angles. Even the floor had been swept. The air smelled dusty rather than dank.

'Do you have to break the combination of the safe as well?' Ali asked doubtfully.

'No, thank God, I'd never manage that. Tim wrote the

combination down for me.' I fumbled the piece of paper from my pocket. Nevertheless, I held my breath while I turned the dial. What if it had been opened in the meantime? There was no telling. I had planned to leave a hair stuck to the door, like I'd seen people in the movies do, but there hadn't been time. The boxes at the bottom of the safe looked like they hadn't been disturbed. I opened one: a Gucci lady's watch. It looked real but then I was no expert. I wedged the portfolio into the space above and closed the safe.

Five minutes later we were back in the car, driving towards Mill House, relieved and elated. One more phone call to our adversaries and one more meeting which, admittedly, might turn unpleasant, and we had done it.

That evening, when I rang the mobile number Wiry had furnished me with, it was a new voice that answered, full of gravel and confidence and a hint of Somerset. Roy, the man himself. When I told him that our art expert had 'highlighted some problems' with the John White water-colours he simply said, 'I see.'

I'd had enough of dark streets and blokes on fast bikes. I stipulated we meet at the little Aqua Sulis pavilion in the Botanical Gardens in a corner of Victoria Park, never a crowded place at eleven thirty on a Tuesday morning. To my surprise Roy agreed. Perhaps he was fond of flowers.

We walked into the Botanical Gardens early and separately: Annis and Tim with a picnic hamper, to take up their station near a banana tree within easy sprinting distance of the pavilion; Alison in her art expert outfit with the files from Griffin's and some bogus lab reports; and me minus the briefcase. This was to be the last act.

We sat around on a bench inside the open structure of the pavilion for a while, then got bored and wandered about in front of it. A plaque set into the back wall had informed me that the pavilion had originally been built by the Corporation of Bath in 1924 for the Empire Exhibition at Wembley, then dismantled and re-erected at this site in 1926. A well-travelled pavilion. We chucked coins into the narrow stream that tumbled down into the fishpond below, where large carp and iridescent goldfish negotiated the narrow lanes between choking weeds. We kept our eyes open and, aware that we in turn might be watched, kept a polite distance from each other so as not to look too chummy.

Roy appeared first. In a dark suit and dark glasses he leant against the railing surrounding the pond and started feeding crumbs to the fish from a sandwich bag. He ignored us. We ignored him. Next came the goons. Surfer Dude walked ahead, hands buried in the pockets of a lemon-yellow leather jacket. I noticed with quiet satisfaction that he appeared to have acquired a slight limp since his forklift crash. Behind him trotted Wiry Guy, faithfully carrying the portfolio of fakes.

I got my shot in first: as soon as everyone was in the pavilion I opened up all indignant. 'You've been trying to rip us off and Griffin's don't take kindly to that kind of thing. What you showed us were fakes. Crude forgeries. Those had better be the real ones,' I blustered, waving a hand at the portfolio, 'or this deal is turning sour.'

'What are you fucking nuts what are you fucking talking about this is the real fucking stuff. Where's the money?' Wiry looked round for the briefcase.

'Perhaps I may shed some light on the matter?' Alison offered. She opened her file and spread the photographs along the bench. 'If you'd be so kind,' she asked. Wiry huffed but dutifully unzipped the portfolio. Alison continued in her dentist's voice: 'The laboratory tests show quite clearly that, although some effort has been made to disguise the relative youth of the paper, it was clearly manufactured two hundred years after John White. But I don't expect you to take my word for it. While superficially competent, the forger made several mistakes in the execution itself. Probably a rush job. Please compare the arm of the dancer in the photograph of the original,' Alison pointed to it, 'and in the forgery. Here it is half raised, there raised to above shoulder height. Please observe also the flocking of the paper. It is level with the spear tip while here the blemish has slipped below it. Done with diluted coffee, we believe. Probably instant,' she added with disdain. For a moment I thought she had blown it but the goons' puzzled expressions didn't change. In the next instance a row was missing from one of the seed heads, and so it went on, like one of those Spot Ten Differences competitions in the back of a TV guide. Wiry muttered obscenities but didn't interrupt. I heard slow, heavy footsteps behind us. I ignored them. They moved away. Surfer Dude had looked over his shoulder though and now straightened up. 'It's a fuck-up,' he said resignedly.

'That is the technical term, yes,' Alison concurred.

'No it isn't,' I contradicted. 'It's a rip-off. You owe us ten grand.'

Surfer Dude patted Wiry on the shoulder, who zipped up. 'It was a gamble. We all lost, it seems. It's not your fucking money, is it? So forget it. Shit happens. And I know someone who'll have a lot of shit happening to him soon. We might be in touch again. Let's go, Spurv.'

They marched out. Wiry, aka Spurv, in a stroppy strut, Surfer Dude in an attempt at a cool limp. There was no sign of Roy.

Alison and I looked at each other and both took a deep breath. We still felt watched and tried not to show our relief too obviously. As we sauntered off towards the banana tree I scanned the gardens discreetly. The opposition had melted away.

Tim was sitting alone, munching on an onion bhaji. It took him only two munches before the thing had gone and his speech was relatively unimpeded. 'Did they swallow it?' he asked, swallowing.

Just then Annis came jogging from the direction of the exit. 'Gone off in a 7 Series Beemer, Surfer Boy driving. Big

Man in the back. He called Surfer Boy "Wakey".' She tapped a finger to her temple. 'I've got the registration.' Excellent. I knew a man who would soon put a name to that number plate.

'Okay, party-time!' announced Tim and flipped open the hamper. One half was crammed with bottles of Pilsner Urquell, still icily beaded with condensation. He handed each of us an opened bottle. 'Right then, who's our designated driver today?' We looked at each other, shrugged and drank.

# Chapter Six

I sat on it for another couple of days before announcing the successful exchange to Griffin's. Haarbottle seemed to appear within minutes of me making the call. This time he was the passenger in a large car driven by a middle-aged man with a salt-and-pepper beard who turned out to be a real art expert from Bristol University. He didn't say much but seemed unimpressed by finding the famous John Whites in a portfolio sticky with quince jam on my kitchen table. I hadn't finished my breakfast yet and I wasn't going to take my eyes off them, so what did he expect? He took a good fifteen minutes to satisfy his expert mind that I had brought back the real thing while Haarbottle slurped coffee and tried to quiz me over the exchange.

I gave him inanities like 'The less you know, the better,' but did make much of the fact that the guys were armed. Haarbottle paled visibly and his officious façade crumbled. 'They didn't . . . oh dear. I mean, I didn't . . . have any idea. I assumed . . . well, no harm done.' He gulped up the last of his coffee and since the art expert appeared to have finished his examination I got up to guide them to the door. Hadn't I forgotten something, Haarbottle asked, a little bemused.

Ehm . . .? I'd clean forgotten to ask for my fee. Which under normal circumstances was quite unlike me, but considering I was sitting on a hundred and ten grand of Griffin's money perhaps pardonable. I waved them out of the yard with the drying cheque. Magnanimously I hadn't insisted on danger money for having to deal with armed villains.

I should have.


Damn it, Simon had been right, there really was a cobweb on my easel.

I was alone in the studio. The girls had disappeared into their wardrobes back at the house, no doubt trying on every single outfit they owned, even though it was a good few hours yet before their presence at the private view was required. There was also no doubt in my mind that eventually they would be facing this important night wearing the first outfits they'd pulled out this afternoon.

Not being afflicted in that way, nor blessed with anything like the same amount of clobber, I knew I had the barn to myself for the afternoon. For a while I just stood and remembered the devastation I had wrought while exploding my anger at Jenny's murder over a large canvas, now long burnt, its ashes kicked into the grass outside. All I could hear was a faint scrabbling noise. Field mice. It was much too quiet in here for my state of mind. I wound up the paint-spattered clockwork radio, found some acceptable jazz and turned the volume to full. Right. Cobwebs first. That was the easy bit. My large glass palette was so encrusted with last year's paint it took twenty minutes of scraping with a palette knife before I had a vaguely level surface again. Though a fistful of brushes had died in jars where the turps had evaporated, all my tubes of Italian oil paints were stoppered and in their wooden trays, saved by Annis I'd no doubt. The shadowy back of the studio where a hedgehog liked to overwinter yielded several stretched and primed canvases. I placed a modest three by three foot square on my easel and fastened it down.

Damn. I had somehow hoped it would take longer to get the place in working order. I shredded an old bed sheet for oil rags, you can't have too many of those, and spiked a wad of newspaper on the nail in the supporting beam to the left of my easel. Then I recovered my stool which the girls had appropriated to balance their interminable cups of coffee on and sat down. Never in the history of art had a blank canvas looked so empty. And talking of empty, I was hungry. Yes, I was sure I could manage a little something. Suddenly much happier I trotted back down the meadow to the house.

Upstairs two conflicting sets of dance music mingled with excited chatter and the girls' footsteps as they end-lessly traipsed between bathroom and bedrooms. Down-stairs in the kitchen I rummaged around for sustenance. There was a large cut of lamb in the fridge I was going to roast for Sunday lunch tomorrow. Hell, we didn't need all that, did we? I carved off enough for a decent kebab, threaded it on skewers and chucked olive oil, thyme and some chili flakes at it and shoved it under the grill. After I'd wolfed it all down with a mountain of salad the kitchen was in a fine mess and naturally needed cleaning . . .


'Excellent turnout, quite a few people here I recognize,' Eva said, scratching names on to the screen of her palmtop computer. She had already managed quite a bit of publicity for the show and was hoping to do features for the West Country press. Bath was used to premieres at the Theatre Royal but art shows that opened here before going to London were a rarity. 'When's your next show coming up?' Stylus poised above the screen.

I hesitated for a fraction of a second before saying, not entirely untruthfully, 'This autumn, I hope.' I considered Eva a friend but she was a journalist after all. Perhaps it was not a good idea to give her chapter and verse and possibly column inches on my painting troubles; why test your friendships?

Tim joined us, handing glasses of wine to Eva and Jerry, her long-suffering, red-haired gentle giant of a boyfriend. 'Is it always like this?' Tim whispered. I'd forgotten this was his first time at a private view. He'd dug out a suit for the occasion and looked a little uncomfortable, holding his glass of wine as though he was afraid it might break in his hands.

'You mean is it always crowded with people more interested in looking at each other than the paintings?' Jerry said in a voice that suggested Eva had dragged him to one function too many.

'No, not that. But everyone's talking in really low voices, I feel I have to whisper in here. Why don't they turn the music up a bit?'

'That comes later,' I promised. 'At the moment it's not really a party, it's a business meeting. There's fifty grand hanging on the walls and several million standing about chatting.' I recognized some collectors and several regulars who might or might not be here to buy. 'This is where Simon earns his commission.'

'How much does he get?' Jerry wanted to know.

'Fifty per cent,' I said with an involuntary sigh.

His face suddenly came alive. 'That's outrageous!' he said, loud enough for a few heads to turn in our direction. 'I'm in the wrong job.' Jerry worked as a cranial osteopath from a clinic in Bath and was doing very well indeed.

'He's very good. Fifty is low these days. And fifty per cent of profits is better than a hundred per cent of nothing,' I said with conviction born from experience. 'Selling the occasional painting is easy, making a living requires a specialist like Simon.'

Simon was a master at managing exhibitions and artists. The meticulous, military-style planning of every detail, from the guest list to the amount of sheen on the hardwood floors, made sure the show rolled along seamlessly while the strings he pulled all night remained invisible. As he worked the rooms crowded with the fashionable, the decorative and the wealthy, steered Annis and Alison into conversations with the people that mattered and married people with paintings, I was glad I had no more arduous duties to perform than nurse a glass of excellent red.

It was a good-looking show, we all agreed. Annis's hard-edged abstracts were beautifully complemented by the loose brushwork that characterized Alison's more accessible canvases, where more than a hint of the sea- and landscapes of Cornwall remained visible. Both girls were dressed in regulation darks (never compete with your paintings), Annis in a little black dress and long black boots, Alison in a charcoal trouser suit and heels. Simon kept them busy, steered them around the rooms, made introductions, directed conversations. Annis played the game easily, creating animation and laughter in the clusters of punters around her. Alison had to work harder. She seemed distracted, did more listening than talking, her gaze straying often to her paintings as though she was checking to see if they behaved themselves.

Eva handed her glass to Jerry and slipped away to take photographs of paintings and people, not necessarily in that order. Jerry drained the glass, plonked it on the nearest surface and shrugged. He was often required to escort Eva to openings, concerts and literary dinners only to find himself abandoned while Eva furtled about for a story. We made our way towards Ali's little group. John Gatt was standing supportively by her side while pretending to listen seriously to a man in his late forties, with greying, shoulder-length hair and a pedantic voice that grated across the room. Alison's smile, when she spotted us coming, had more than a hint of relief in it. But the relief was short-lived. The bulk of a large, blue-suited man heaved out of nowhere and inserted itself into the small circle. The man with the grating voice fell silent. I grabbed Jerry and Tim by the arms and steered them aside before we got to Alison. I'd recognized the straining suit before I recognized the face of the hulk: Roy, he of the warehouse full of snide goods and recently cheated out of £110,000 by an art expert's opinion on his merchandise.

'This is not a good moment,' I informed Jerry.

He shrugged again. 'I need another drink anyway,' he said flatly and pushed off towards the bar.

Tim had clocked Roy too. 'What the hell is he doing here? Will he recognize Ali? He saw her at the Botanical Gardens.'

'I don't know, but he doesn't seem to have seen me yet. Have a shufti round the place for his goons. I'll keep an eye on Ali.' I fortified myself by emptying my glass, depositing it on a marble mantelpiece and, keeping behind Roy's broad back and inside Alison's sightline, I edged closer. Roy stood, feet wide apart in an effort to keep his balance. When I got close enough to hear the rumble of his voice I realized he was drunk. I fervently hoped he'd be too sloshed to recognize Ali, whom he'd only seen briefly and from a distance.

'Love it. Really love your stuff,' he intoned heavily. 'Don't usually go in for this heavy oil stuff, more into watercolours myself. But this stuff of yours is great.' He swept an arm towards the paintings, narrowly missing a passing waiter's head. 'Now I'm no art expert of course, but you did well there. I'd love to buy one, really, would love to.' He reached out an arm and laid a heavy hand on Ali's shoulder.

John stiffened. 'Now look here . . .'

'Relax, boy,' Roy said to him, reaching out a fleshy palm as if to pat him on the cheek. John jerked back his head. 'Just having a friendly chat, nothing for you to worry about. As I was saying, I'd love to buy but I had a little financial setback lately,' he growled at Alison, who semaphored wildly with her eyebrows at me. 'But I have every intention of making good my losses and then, you never know, I may look you up.' He made as if to drink, found his glass was empty and thrust it at John, then turned. Startling two elderly couples next to me by diving through their little gathering, I circled around a pillar, keeping an eye on Roy's progress towards the door. He stepped out into Margarets Buildings, vigorously hiked up his trousers and walked unsteadily in the direction of Catherine Place.

Ali poured wine down her throat with a shaky hand. 'That was horrible. Do you think he knows, Chris?'

'Knows what?' implored John impatiently. 'Will someone tell me what all this is about?'

'If he hadn't left when he did I'd have thrown him out. He was definitely drunk,' said the long-haired man indignantly. It was no idle boast, he had the muscles to back it up, I noticed.

'This is Keith, by the way,' John introduced. 'He's a friend from the re-enactment group.'

'Re-enactment?' I asked distractedly.

'Yes, we're both in the Somerset World War Two Re-enactment Group. We meet twice a mo –'

'Can you get me another drink?' Ali interrupted.

John gave both her and me an exasperated look but took her empty glass and reluctantly pushed his way towards the bar.

'Fresh air,' I suggested. Leaving Keith to re-enact indignation I steered Ali out of the place into the quiet and cool of Margarets Buildings. Alison shivered, whether from cold or the fright of being confronted with a drunken Roy I couldn't tell. I put my jacket around her shoulders in a gesture of care and protection that seemed ironically feeble considering it was me who put her in the firing line.

'God, that man gave me the creeps. What was he doing here?'

'Did you feel he recognized you?'

'I'm not sure. He could hardly focus he was that drunk. And I'm wearing a different outfit and my hair's up. That's usually enough to confuse men when they're sober.'

One thing convinced me that Roy had probably not known who he was talking to: his sort was usually too straight to bother beating about the bush. If we were rumbled then Roy and his goons would have confronted me directly. I'd no doubt that any argument we might have had would swiftly have gone their way.

The door to the gallery opened and Annis and Tim tumbled out, followed by Simon Paris who was wearing his best frown. Tim shook his head: no goons at the show, so perhaps we'd have nothing to fear for tonight.

'You all right, Ali?' Annis asked. 'Tim told me about Roy turning up. Did he recognize you?'

'Girls, please,' Simon interrupted. 'You can chat to your friends later, you have clients to talk to. This is business, not a girls' night out.'

'Simon, did you invite someone called Roy?' I gave a quick description.

'Yes, Roy Hotchkiss. Bit of a rough diamond. Not really his kind of show, more a watercolour man, but a good client. He didn't grope you or anything?' he asked Alison, who was quickly recovering.

'He'd be unconscious on the floor now if he had. No, just a bit leery, that's all.'

'Then please . . .' Simon gestured towards the brightly lit gallery.

'You coming back inside?' Tim asked after the girls had left.

'I'd better not. Gotta go and think this through.'

'Want me to tag along?' he offered.

'You stay and keep an eye on the girls. I'm going for a walk.'


Walking is how I think best. When things get tricky a leisurely inspection of my neglected three acres at Mill House or a ramble through the valley normally puts things into perspective, gives me new ideas. Here in the city nearby Victoria Park would have to do. The green in front of the Royal Crescent was deserted. Apart from the odd dog walker and cyclist the Royal Avenue too was empty. Not a sound came from the aviary; once I had passed it I was alone and felt it. The light of the few street lamps that reached the heart of the park bleached the colour of the grass into greys and blurred the outlines of shrubs and trees. Strange how a place so friendly during the day could become desolate by the mere subtraction of light and noise.

The sequence of recent events turned over and over in my head yet I couldn't see how Roy would have concluded so quickly and firmly that we had switched the merchandise. Perhaps we'd just been unlucky. How he might have found Ali was no longer a mystery once I remembered that her picture had appeared in a feature by Eva in the *Chronicle* about the forthcoming show. Eva had come up with Jerry and taken pictures of the girls posing in front of their paintings. That didn't mean of course she couldn't have also been Griffin's chosen art expert. It made no difference, I told myself, to what was going to happen next. I might as well stop beating myself up about getting it wrong since Roy and his mates would surely offer to do it for me if they caught up with me.

I passed the children's playground, found myself in Park Lane and kept on walking. I'd been worse than useless, I realized, as a painter as well as a private eye. Another few minutes of stomping about in wine-fuelled self-pity had brought me along the Upper Bristol Road to Windsor Bridge. Once on the other side I kept on walking. I could look for Billy at least, now I was in this neck of the woods.

Half-heartedly I described Billy to a thin shopkeeper with neon-grilled skin behind the counter of the first off-licence I came to.

'Could be the old bloke who just left, well . . . half an hour ago maybe. I noticed the chewed-up ear. He didn't seem drunk,' he said defensively, 'so I sold him what he wanted.'

'It's all right,' I assured him, 'I'm not interested in what you sold him. What *did* you sell him?'

'Carton of Albanian Red. Special offer.'

'I'm sure. Which way did he leave from here? D'you remember?'

'Left. He went left,' he said without hesitation.

'Thanks. Did he carry anything? Apart from the wine. Bags or anything?'

He shook his head.

If Billy didn't carry any of his gear, I calculated as I followed his footsteps back towards the main road, then he had found a hidey-hole and it was probably close by. I was half an hour behind him, which meant, surely, that he had disappeared off the streets for the night, halfway through a carton of wine by now. The effect of the couple of glasses I had sipped earlier had worn off and left a metallic tiredness behind my forehead which only sleep or more wine could cure. It was unlikely Billy would offer me a drink when I found him.

The pubs were closed by the time I passed the Golden Fleece and the New Trams Social Club. I had left the Oldfield area behind and drifted into Twerton now, exploring side roads leading towards the river, spying into fenced-off wasteland and nosing around half-finished developments. The sky had cleared. Despite the orange street lighting a few stars were visible and the temperature had dropped steadily. I wasn't dressed for spooking about at night. At least I knew now where to look – within a reasonable radius around the off-licence where I had started. I turned to walk back towards the centre where I would join the queues for taxis by the Abbey when I heard a faint clanging noise. I looked back but saw nothing. Fifty yards or so from where I was standing the arch under the railway bridge lit up briefly with the pinkish glow from a car's rear lights, then fell dark again. I heard no engine noise.

Out of the stonework of the railway bridge beside the arch grew a tall Victorian building which began at the level of the now-deserted street and finished multi-gabled and spiked with chimneys high above the level of the railway line. It was unlit. The old Twerton railway station.

It had been years since trains had stopped here. As I walked closer I could see by the advertisements, posters and flyers festooning the walls and boarded windows that it was empty and falling into decay. A fly-posted wooden door at ground level was firmly locked though the wrought-iron security gate that once protected it was open. A steep flight of stairs ran up the outside of the building. I carefully climbed the damp steps strewn with crumbled masonry and rubbish to a landing covered with the mouldering remains of old posters, under yet another boarded-up window which now sported a bright green invitation to visit a nearby garden centre. Another few steps led to a final platform and an iron door, heavily barred and padlocked. I gave the lock an idle pull: it was secure. Just then the metallic clang repeated itself, only much closer. Quietly stepping down to the lower landing I peered below. There was movement in the dark shadow that fell across the pavement from the direction of the ground-floor entrance. I slowly descended the last steep flight. The shadow stopped moving, another tinkling sound. 'Billy? That you?' I rattled down the slippery steps, nearly came to grief at the bottom and skidded on to the pavement. There was nobody at street level. Had I imagined it? I ran the few yards to the railway arch. The short tunnel was empty apart from the echo of my own footsteps. And its emptiness made me shiver.

Getting jumpy, mister, I told myself and was ready to call it a night when a tiny detail in my peripheral vision contradicted me. I stared at the door. It was shut as before, only the wrought-iron security gate, although still ajar, now had a padlock on its hasp, identical to the one upstairs but dangling open on its latch.

The wooden door behind the metal gate which had before been firmly locked now yielded grudgingly in its warped and weather-swollen frame to a firm push. I took a tentative step inside and was instantly swallowed by the darkness. Instinctively I patted my pockets for my Mini Maglite which lived in my leather jacket. This was stupid, there was no way I could do anything here without a torch I told myself, even as I got out my old Ronson lighter. It illuminated just enough of the narrow corridor to stop me from stumbling over the bricks, bottles and bits of timber that littered the floor. I could see however that someone had roughly shoved the obstacles to the side to clear a path through the mess. Bits of glass and sand crunched under my leather soles as I advanced. Through a further door, this one hanging drunkenly off its upper hinge, I stepped into a larger space my wavering flame could not completely illuminate. I circled around clockwise: more debris, some large metal lockers, their doors bent and beaten up; a broad passageway, bricked up, and on the final wall another door. It felt sweaty to the touch. I withdrew my hand quickly, loath to touch it again. Like the outer door, it had a large padlock, hanging open in a brass latch that looked new, incongruously shiny in all this dinginess. I stared at it for a moment wondering why it made me so uneasy. The heavy door opened smoothly as though on recently oiled hinges. Immediately behind it I could make out worn stone steps leading down and curving round to the left. It was damp down there; dark, clammy and cold. Why was I doing this, I asked myself as I followed the stairs below, why was I spending my Saturday night in this ridiculously Gothic pursuit?

The answer came with the smell.

# Chapter Seven

A sickly, flowery scent at first, just as though someone had emptied an entire can of room freshener into the cavern. Its sweetness failed to entirely mask the other, stronger smells however, the acrid bite of stale urine, the darker stench of accumulated faeces, the wretched odours that only human filth can produce. Beyond the scents that register in the membranes of the nose were other, more unsettling notes too, the terrifying exhalations of fear, of despair, and the reek of insanity. I knew I was not alone down here, felt more than saw that the narrow space I had entered was crowded with shapes. Something was alive in here.

I nudged a table with my thigh. It took me a while to dare take my eyes away from the darkness beyond the light of my single flame, expecting to be jumped at from inside the jittering shadows. The lighter had become unbearably hot in my hand but letting go of the flame, which now began to sputter and turn blue, was impossible. Someone or something besides myself was breathing in here. On the table, amongst detritus of takeaway meals and plastic bottles, stood a propane storm lantern. A frantic, one-handed fumble got it lit and gratefully I dropped the superheated lighter. The shadows jumped back and the pathetic light seemed painfully bright in my eyes. The glare revealed no attackers. Much worse.

I didn't at first register the shambles of the room, the mouldy cardboard boxes, empty cans of air freshener, the split binliners and festering carrier bags of garbage. My eyes were nailed to the cage.

A doorway really, the door replaced by a grey metal grille; a small room behind it, vaulted like the one I was standing in, no more than four by six feet. In it, on what looked like a wooden pallet, lay a shape, a creased bundle. The shape retreated towards the furthest corner with agonizing slowness. I could make out a foot, blackened, twisted like a claw, pushing at the filthy stone of the floor. I could hear the rasping, laboured breath even above the hiss of the storm lamp as I approached the iron bars. And still I didn't act, didn't speak, held back as if spellbound by the strangeness, the enormity of it. Then I began to struggle to my senses. I gripped the bars and pulled. They were locked with yet another shiny brass padlock. The shape gave a strangled groan. Even with the lamp pushed through the space between two bars I struggled to make out any definite features. Finally I found my voice. 'It's okay, I'll get you out of there. It's all right.' The bundle lifted a head and took on human shape, though only just. It was dressed in what looked like a simple cotton shift or a nightdress with some kind of pattern on it, though stained beyond recognition. I could see now that it was a woman's face that stared through matted strands of hair out of blackened, sunken eyes across the few feet of space. The face was haggard and stupefied. Grime further dulled her creased, emaciated features, her cheekbones so sharp they appeared to have bruised her skin into black.

'It's all right,' I repeated idiotically. I had never found a situation less all right. 'I'll call for help.' I made to turn so I could put down the lamp on the table and use my mobile. The woman, whom I still only registered as some kind of pathetic creature rather than a fully human being, made me jump when she flung herself at the bars, sticking filthy, starved arms through the gaps, scrabbling at my jacket. Her first words were lost in a croak, then she found her voice. 'For fuck's sake get me out. Get me out. Open this thing. Get me out quickly. He'll be back.'

I set the lamp on the floor and put my face close. Her eyes were dull and bloodshot, but sane. 'I'm calling for help.' I didn't have my picklocks with me, they too were in my leather jacket. There was a lesson there I quickly filed away as I punched the emergency number on my mobile. Nothing happened. There was no reception in this tomb. 'I'll have to go outside, I can't get a signal down here.'

'No!' she said in an urgent whisper. 'Please, no! Don't go. Don't go away again, don't go away. He might be up there. He's coming back. I know he's coming back.' She grabbed my arm through the bars. 'He hadn't finished.'

With the lamp held high I searched the room for a metal bar, a length of pipe, a key, even. There was nothing useful, just an accumulation of filth and bare, sulphurous walls.

'I can't see anything to break open the lock with. I'll have to go upstairs and call the police.' I spoke in a hushed voice, aware that he, whoever he might be, might be close, might be on his way back.

'Don't go. Don't leave me here!' she begged, her eyes flickering with terror. 'No. No no no!'

'I'll leave you the lamp,' I said soothingly. I was speaking as though to a frightened child while she shook her head, her eyes boring into mine. 'Here, I'll leave you my watch, too.' She grasped it in a bony fist. 'You can check, I'll be . . . three minutes. I'll come back immediately. Then we'll wait together.'

I glanced back from the foot of the stairs. She was retreating into a corner of her prison cell, crawling on all fours, pushing the lamp in front of her. She didn't believe me.

My lighter was running out of gas at last, halfway up the curved staircase. The last few steps I negotiated by feel, sliding my hands along the rough walls. After the light of the storm lantern the darkness was thicker than ever. My steps seemed to echo in the room above. Then I realized there were other footsteps, speeding up now, in the corridor. I stumbled into the room. My foot connected with an object on the floor, sending it glassily whirring away. I reached the unhinged door and ran along the corridor towards the narrowing chink of light as the door to the street was being pulled shut. Then it went completely dark. I shouted; no words, just a sound of panic and anger. I collided with the door, scrabbled for a hold along its edges, found a bolt and yanked at it. It gave. In two frantic jerks I had the door open and gasped air as though returning from the bottom of the ocean in a single breath. The iron security gate was shut but the padlock was not engaged. I flung the gate aside and ran on to the pavement. A car sped by full of kids shouting. An empty drinks can clattered then the road was quiet again. I ran the few steps to the railway arch. There was nobody. My hands shook as I dialled the emergency number.

I got through immediately. 'I think I found Nikki Reid,' I shouted into the phone. By the time I had finished the call I was shaking all over. I groped my way back into the darkness of the tomb below the railway station.

This time I took both padlocks with me.


'Constable, search that man.' Superintendent Michael Needham pointed a podgy finger at me as soon as he heaved himself out of his car. The surprised constable, who had been standing near where I was sitting on the outside steps of the railway station, came to life. 'Ehm, he's the one who made the call, sir. He says he's a private detective.'

'I know what this long-haired geezer thinks he is, Constable, and I want him searched for concealed weapons,' Needham barked at him. 'Do I have to do it myself?'

Still wearing a puzzled expression the young officer patted me down. I held still for the procedure with my arms spread wide like a suffering Jesus, among the urgent toing and froing of people lit by the blue flashes from police vehicles and the ambulance, which still hadn't left.

I'm not in the habit of carrying a gun at private views, the public is never *that* hostile. It was safely hidden under the dashboard of the DS. If Needham was disappointed he didn't show it. 'What the hell is going on, Chris? You've got a lot of explaining to do.' I always seemed to have a lot of explaining to do with Needham. 'She's alive then,' he added quietly. After all this time, over three months if I remembered it rightly, nobody had really expected it, least of all Mike, perhaps. Nobody had expected it after three days. 'She's a goner' was the jaded opinion I had heard expressed more than once when her disappearance had been announced so soon after the body of the first missing woman had been found.

Arc lights had already been set up; the pavement was snaked with cables that disappeared into the bowels of the station; Scene of Crime Officers in their moonwalk outfits were waiting to go over every square inch of the convoluted building; a forensics team would follow later. At last the ambulance team reappeared with the still form of Nikki Reid on a stretcher; a WPC was holding the drip aloft and disappeared with the stretcher into the ambulance. Without sirens but with its blue lights flashing it finally drove off at speed. 'Right, let's have a look at it then,' Needham invited.

'No thanks, Mike. I've seen all I ever wanted to of that place, I've no desire to go down there again,' I said and really meant it.

'I don't really care about your desires, Chris. I want you down there with me and after that you and I will have a nice long chat about how come you just happened to wander down there on a Saturday night and find a kidnap victim we've been trying to find for months. Until then I'll not lose sight of your scrawny arse for a second. After you.'

While we wriggled into the regulation papery body

86

suits, Needham struggling to fit his circumference inside his, DI Deeks, Needham's cadaverous sidekick, appeared. Tall, gaunt, horse-faced and utterly humourless, with a guilty-until-proven-innocent attitude to policing, he was to be avoided even more assiduously than his boss. His halitosis alone would have made sure of that. 'Morning, Super, I . . .' He recognized me. 'What's *he* doing here?'

'Our friend here found Mrs Reid. *Stumbled across* her,' Needham said sarcastically, 'on his Saturday night out.'

'Stumbled across her? When he does this stumbling-across thing,' he jerked a thumb at me, 'it usually means withholding evidence.' He stepped closer. 'It usually means interfering in police business. Isn't that so, Mr Honeysett?' Deeks grated at me.

I made as if to undo the body suit again. 'Look, it's a bit late. Perhaps you could just take your undertaker friend on this potholing jaunt instead. I suddenly feel like a lie-down, all right?'

'Hold your horses, Chris. Deeks?' Needham raised his eyebrows at him and the DI made himself busy elsewhere. I noticed not even Needham called him by his first name. He had to be very good at something though or Needham wouldn't have teamed up with him. Whatever it was, his charms eluded me. 'All right, Chris. Take it easy. We're going to have a little look-see together, then we'll go and have a lovely chat over a nice cup of coffee at the station and you can tell me exactly what happened here.'

I groaned. 'I remember your cop shop coffee and I'm sure it breaks the Geneva Convention on the treatment of prisoners.'

'Oh, we'll make a special effort for you,' he said with an avuncular chuckle, giving me a gentle but irresistible push towards the now brightly lit entrance.

I just hate it when he chuckles.

Eva was there, snapping away and loosening off some flashes in our direction as Needham and I climbed out of our suits once we had resurfaced. 'Can I have a few words Superintendent is it really Nikki Reid you found and can you confirm that she's bloody hell Chris what are you doing here?' she said, punctuation optional.

'Eva Keen, always first on the scene,' was all Needham offered her while propelling me towards his car without stopping.

'Thanks but I heard all the jokes. How about it, Mr Needham?' she said sweetly, trying to dodge a WPC who was guarding the cordon of police tape.

'Wait until the press conference,' he said over his shoulder.

'I can always ask Chris here, I'm sure he'll talk to me,' she said, keeping pace with us.

'Mr Honeysett is helping us with our enquiries and doesn't have time for a chat,' he pronounced. He held the car door open for me. 'Get in and keep shtoom.'

I simply nodded at Eva and got in. Not that I felt like talking much anyway. The second tour of Nikki Reid's prison had done nothing to endear the place to me or make this night any cheerier. In the glare of the arc lights and with SOCOs at work it no longer felt frightening but the miasma of insanity down there had if anything been enhanced by the contrast of controlled, rational activity. Needham had made me go through all my actions in the vaults but had asked no other questions. That joy was still ahead of me as we drove through the near deserted Sunday morning streets to Manvers Street police station.

Three hours later we were still at it but we had shifted from an interview room with its camera and twin tape recorder to Needham's own office. Mike had satisfied himself that I had not been investigating Mrs Reid's disappearance, that he had the events of the night nailed down in his methodical mind, and I had signed my statement.

A wide-awake PC brought up sandwiches and takeaway coffee from the nearest sandwich bar. Needham folded a ham and cheese triangle into his mouth. He had put back on all the weight he had lost so heroically the previous year when our paths last crossed though he'd also lost a bit more hair than he could afford to. The decaf and sweetener days were over, it appeared. He looked more comfortable on it. But Mike was not as happy as he should have been, considering Nikki Reid had been found, and found alive at that, and it wasn't just because I had stolen his laurels.

'We have to nail this bastard and nail him fast before he takes the next one,' he said bleakly.

'You think the two are connected then? The dead woman in Rainbow Woods and this one? Same guy?'

'We know it's the same guy. He told us so.'

'He told you? He contacted you?'

'Almost straight away.' Needham held his breath for a moment, perhaps wondering how much he should tell me, then let out his breath noisily.

'Ransom?' I prodded.

'Amusement. Sick amusement. A note arrived. Bath postmark, cool as you like. Said he had another one. But this time he was giving us a chance to get her back. All we had to do was follow *the clues*.' Mike put bitter emphasis on the last two words. 'Most of it was rubbish. Just cryptic ramblings. Some of them made sense eventually . . .'

'You got more than one note?'

'We got plenty of them. Meanwhile he was starving the woman. "Slimming her down", the sick bastard called it. Nikki Reid, as you might remember, was quite a big woman when she disappeared. So was the woman in Rainbow Woods. He kept that one imprisoned in one of the old World War Two bunkers up there. Ironically it had been "made safe" because drug addicts were using the place. A steel door was fitted and heavily locked. It was perfect – out of the way and pretty secure. He cracked the locks and fitted new ones. Pretty handy with tools is the Doctor. It wasn't as safe as his latest venue though and it was probably his first time so he didn't have the confidence he has now. Perhaps that's why he strangled her in the end. But Nikki Reid he was going to "starve into perfection". And he challenged us to find her. All we had to do was solve his little riddles. Had us running round in circles.' He twisted his coffee beaker round and round in his hand while he spoke as though to illustrate the point.

'Now let me get this clear. He set you riddles to solve and you couldn't do it? And if you had cracked them . . .'

'Ah, bullshit,' he growled. 'It was all bullshit. We had a team working on his notes, including a linguist and a trick cyclist from Bath Uni. We solved some clues. They always referred to a location in Bath and when we got there all we'd find was another snooty note, ridiculing our efforts. He was taunting us. And we had to sit on it. If that had got into the papers the Doctor would have had a right laugh. He could easily have sent them to the papers himself of course but it was a private game, between him and the police. And he enjoyed every second of it, the sadistic swine, while I've been living on burgers and caffeine and three hours' sleep. All of us, the whole team, I promise you.'

I'd never heard Needham so defensive before. The last months had to have been a nightmare, the fear of failure ever present. The pressure to find her alive before she starved to death must have been unimaginable. 'I've no doubt, Mike. He must have fed her something though, she couldn't have survived on air all this time.'

'He said he would and we had to believe him. He refused to furnish us with proof that she was still alive. She might of course have been dead ages ago but as long as he was playing his game we had to keep playing ourselves. And all the time the normal course of investigation, of trying to trap him, of finding a profile that might lead us to him continued.'

'Is it sexual? I mean, did he assault the women?' I asked.

'Yes, it's sexual. It's *also* sexual. But there was no rape. Sally Dixon, the first victim, was not raped although there were semen stains found on her and her nightdress. The pathologist thought some of the sexual activity happened *post mortem*.'

'A kind of necrophilia then. And Mrs Reid was also wearing a sort of nightdress when I found her but she was snatched off the street I seem to remember.'

'Identical nightdresses, size 20, Marks and Spencer's, very pale blue with tiny violets on them,' Mike reeled off. 'He seems to get his kicks watching them starve, watching them shrink, watching them die.'

It was enough to put you off your sandwiches. It didn't seem to have affected Needham's appetite however, he had long finished his. He had won a reprieve, after all. But for how long? 'You said something weird earlier, you called him "the Doctor". Is that what you think? Medical profession?'

Needham shifted uncomfortably in his chair. 'Naah, although it's possible of course. He's certainly well enough educated, we can tell that from his notes. No, some of the boys started calling him Dr Atkins, you know, after the diet fad. I stamped that out pretty quickly. Can you imagine if anything like that had leaked to the press? What a nightmare. We kept security dead tight on this one; I threatened instant dismissal if anything got out, only the name seems to have resurfaced as "the Doctor" somehow. And, I'm ashamed to say, that's how I've come to think of him now.'

'Did you ever have anyone in the frame for it? Any suspects at all?' I wanted to know.

Impatiently he pushed back his chair on its castors and walked over to the window from where he had a view of Manvers Street and bits of the Abbey. It was early May, the tourists were out in force, the weather had turned mild and bright. Needham however was standing under his private cloud of doubt and anguish. I doubted if he saw anything out there. 'We had no one in the frame. We got plenty of DNA from the first crime scene and pulled in every likely lad, all the usual pervs and nutters, and came up empty-handed.'

'Any connection between the two victims at all?'

'Apart from their body shape none we could turn up.'

'Any boyfriends, husbands?' I seemed to remember Nikki Reid's husband from a television appeal, soon after she disappeared. A pale, stunned, shaky-voiced man reading a prepared script with fluttering voice and hands.

'Long eliminated. Sally Dixon was also married. Her husband attempted suicide a month after her body was discovered. Messed it up. Suffered severe liver damage, still in hospital now. Not that it means anything. Only that the destruction continues. And he's out there, looking for his next victim as we speak.'

The thought hung in the room for a while, neither of us speaking, with hardly a noise penetrating off the street through the plate glass windows. I broke the silence with what I thought was a ray of hope. 'You'll have plenty of new material to work on now.'

'Yes, we're pinning all our hopes on getting a decent description of the Doctor from Mrs Reid as soon as they let us interview her. Even if he wore a mask or something, there'll be his height, weight, voice, an accent, a smell, *some*thing.'

'Now his hide-out is blown it'll take him a while to find a new one anyway.'

Needham snorted with disbelief. 'In this warren?' He gestured at the Georgian city beyond the window pane with its rising ranks of eighteenth-century houses. 'Finding another rat hole out there is no more than an afternoon's work.'

Needham personally escorted me downstairs, a four star service that contrasted markedly with the usual treatment I got from him. On the ground floor we encountered a PC in charge of a small, middle-aged man, drowning in a grotesquely large puffa jacket. The unhappy-looking PC was also in charge of a carrier bag he held with two fingers and as far away from his body as possible. 'Oh, yuck,' said Mike once we had passed the pair.

'Yuck what?'

'Another local perv. The place is full of confuseniks.'

'What's he in for?'

Needham sighed. 'You'll wish you hadn't asked. Get this: he chucks a loaf of bread into the trough of public urinals. When it has soaked up fifty types of piss he likes to take it home with him.'

'And do what exactly?' I asked, though I could guess by Mike's sour face and puckered lips.

'Don't make me say it. We're trying gentle dissuasion at this stage, mainly because we haven't got a clue what to charge him with.'

'I wonder what kind of bread he uses . . .'

He gave me a look of utter disgust. 'Only you would. Now get out of here.'

The wave of media attention my discovery of Mrs Reid had aroused was at this moment breaking on the front steps of the station. Needham let me out through a back door near some blue wheelie bins. 'Thought you might want to avoid that lot as long as you can. I'll have to face them in a few hours. Press conference.'

'Cheers. I'm grateful.'

'And Chris,' he grabbed my arm, 'so am I. So is Mrs Reid, I'm sure. But this is where it ends, right?' I opened my mouth to protest my disinclination for further involvement but he went on: 'I know the way you're wired up, Chris. You just can't leave shit alone. So here's a friendly warning. Don't stick your oar in this murky pond. If I see as much as a ripple I'll have you and your whole crummy outfit in front of a magistrate before you can shout "local hero".'

Oh good. Things were back to normal then.

# Chapter Eight

The absence of a parking ticket surprised me for a moment until I remembered it was Sunday. I had every intention of making it a day of rest too. I felt tired beyond belief, the kind of hollow feeling you get when you keep yourself awake with tea and coffee all night and talk until there's nothing left to say and nothing interests you except how to stop doing what you're doing. I drove home on autopilot. The girls' cars were there but I saw no sign of life, which suited me just fine. The shutters closed and barred to keep out the May sunshine, I let myself fall backwards across the bed and zonked out.

There was still a bright crucifix of light burning through the shutters when I woke, dressed in yesterday's clothes and spreadeagled where I had fallen unconscious. I undressed then showered for a long time, trying to ease the kinks and creases out of my body, perhaps hoping that some of the imagery I had soaked up in the dungeon below the railway station would fade along with the aches and pains. But really it was the smells that I wanted to forget, that I felt I had inhaled and absorbed through my skin, thought I could still detect in my nostrils as I towelled myself, as I put on freshly laundered gear. I went downstairs in search of food and distraction.

The kitchen was full of women. Annis, Alison and Eva sat around the table, which was bestrewn with the debris of what looked like several meals or perhaps just one Eva had had a hand in dispatching. 'Who's a clever boy, then?'

she said. They were all grinning at me until I could feel an idiotic grin rising on my own face.

'Saving damsels in distress, how unbearably romantic of you, Chris,' Annis mocked.

'Wanna coffee?' Alison offered. 'There's some cold chicken left, too.'

'Sit down and tell us all about it.' Eva patted the seat next to her.

'My body clock's still on breakfast time,' I protested and shoved a couple of croissants in the oven. 'Yes to the coffee, no to the chicken and definitely no to telling all about it.'

'Oh, you must,' Eva pleaded. 'I was the first on the scene and I got zero apart from the pictures. The press conference was crap as usual; Needham said, "Yes, no, not at this juncture and no comment," don't know why he bothers. But you were there. So tell.'

'Give the man a chance,' said Annis wisely, sharing as she did my pre-caffeine dysfunctionality on a daily basis.

'How did you make out last night?' I changed the subject as the coffee unfogged my brain.

Alison was near bursting with suppressed excitement. 'Annis sold four and I sold . . . wait for it . . . six! Three of them to the same couple. And that's before the show goes to London.'

'Told you Simon was good. Any sign of Roy or his gorillas?'

'Nope. Forgot all about him, in fact. I don't think he actually recognized me. I think he was just pissed.'

Eva got up. 'I'll see what Jerry is up to, he's gone for a wander. Back in a tick.'

'Jerry here too?'

'Yes,' said Annis once Eva had left the kitchen, 'they've been here for two hours. Jerry has gone for a walk round the grounds. I think he's fuming. Sunday is supposed to be the day they keep free for each other. First he got dragged to the show, which I know he wasn't too keen on, now he's been made to hang around here until Eva squeezes the story out of you.'

I felt for Jerry. Their jobs were worlds apart: the steady, supportive world of alternative therapies, where everything happens slowly, and the hold-the-front-page mentality of journalism, where getting the story or even just getting on with the mundane stuff of local news means dates postponed, arrangements broken, weekends disrupted. They had tried living together and given up on it again and were splitting up and getting back together on a six-weekly basis. When Eva found a flat in Bristol she could afford Jerry had stayed put in Bath where his client base was.

'Why don't you give Eva a quick spiel so they can get away together and salvage something of the day?' she encouraged. 'And it's not like we're not curious,' she added.

'Even if I wanted to, I can't really. Ongoing investigation and all that. Needham would kill me, for a start. If details of this get into the press they'll have every crank in the area claim responsibility.' I heaped quince jam on a croissant and stuffed some in my mouth so I wouldn't have to talk. Even if Needham hadn't warned me off there was something else that stopped me from wanting to relive the moment; guilt, shame, call it what you like. When confronted with the wreck that Nikki Reid had become in the course of her imprisonment I had felt no sympathy, no pity. Only revulsion. I didn't feel like revisiting the moment.

However, after breakfast and a vague description of my Saturday night to Annis and Ali I did go outside to look for Eva and Jerry. They were deep in what looked like another argument on the far side of the millpond yet Eva skipped towards me as soon as she saw me approach. 'You ready to talk to the press, mister?'

I supplied her with the same shorthand version I had already given them in the kitchen: I walked in, there she was in a kind of cage, I called Manvers Street, end of story. Eva was not impressed. 'Come on, put some meat on that for me,' she said in an unfortunate metaphor. 'You always were stubborn,' she added when I refused. 'This here girl needs to make a living, you know.' But she didn't press me any further.

I had a question of my own. 'How did you get there so quickly? You seem to have a reputation for that.'

She tried for an enigmatic smile but couldn't keep it to herself. 'Police radio. Always have it tuned to their band.' She cocked a thumb over her shoulder at Jerry who was wandering towards us with his hands buried in his pockets, the picture of boredom. 'Mr Radio here fixed me up with a decent receiver.' Jerry's only hobby was surfing the airwaves, the obscurer the transmissions the better. 'Not exactly legal and I'm sure they suspect but, as I said, the girl's got to make a living. Right, country pub, since we're out here,' she said to Jerry, who immediately came to life and even found a smile. 'I'll buy you the biggest steak this side of the Mendip Hills. You drive, I'll phone this in and then I'm all yours.'

Until your mobile goes off, I thought.

As I walked them to their car I made the fatal mistake of rolling my neck which had felt stiff and painful for days. Jerry suddenly fixed me with his preternaturally blue eyes. 'I can hear that crunch from here. Any time you want me to do something about that let me know. Free of charge.'

'Cheers, Jerry, I'm sure it'll sort itself out, it usually does.'

'Well, if it doesn't, call,' he offered, unoffended.

I lit another cigarette as I waved them off, filled my lungs with smoke and exhaled noisily. If Eva remained the only example of press harassment I was going to experience I'd be extremely lucky. I knew Needham ran a tight cop shop but someone always blabs in the end. Until that moment I had work to do and for that I'd need a car. Tim had pestered me for ages about getting better vehicles for the business. All our cars are conspicuous in their own ways. The ideal accessory for the private eye is a souped-up shopping trolley that blends in, poses no visual threat but has enough hidden horsepower to hold its own against the GTIs and XXRs out there. I was finally convinced but had done nothing about it. There wasn't time now. All I could think of, late on a Sunday afternoon, was a visit to Jake's.

Jake had bought a smallholding not far from nearby Chippenham with the intention of breeding ponies. It hadn't worked out. So he had swapped pony power for horse power. Brake horsepower. His first love had always been vintage cars and he turned his erstwhile hobby into a lucrative business, restoring and repairing classic cars. Preferably British, naturally, but he would make an exception for my black Citroën DS 21 because of its undeniable classic chic. I hoped.

'If you think you can slip your Froggy rust bucket amongst these fine examples of British engineering and expect me to save it from the crusher you've got another think coming!' was how he greeted my arrival. 'What's more, it's a pig to work on and I don't have time to spend hours on the phone with a French dictionary tracking down the bleedin' parts, so turn around.'

'There's nothing wrong with my car,' I lied as I got out.

'Well, that makes a change,' he said brightly. 'Also unlikely,' he added, giving it a suspicious look. 'So how you doin', Chris? Muggotea?'

Tea made, we sat on a beer crate each in the late sunshine, breathing in the spring air laced with petrol fumes. Jake shook his head and scratched his shiny baldness, scarred with welding burns and streaked with grease. 'You want something less conspicuous than that and you come to me? Look around. You think you'll blend in with an E-type Jag, not that I'd let you near it?' A sparklingly pristine Jaguar gleamed in the gloom of one of the converted outbuildings. The barns and yard were crammed with cars, some under tarpaulins, some just wrecks to my eyes, standing on blocks; body parts, axles, engine bits everywhere.

'There must be something I can drive for a while in this lot . . .'

'Yeah and bring it back looking like yon French coffin. Can't you at least wash the thing from time to time or are you afraid there's no actual bodywork under the mud? It is supposed to be black, isn't it?' He snorted his disgust then turned his attention to a blackened, broken fingernail for a while. 'Who are you after this time, anyway?'

'Just checking out a local villain, lives out Cold Ashton way. Roy Hotchkiss. Seems to specialize in snide designer gear, smuggled tobacco, that kind of stuff . . .'

'Roy bleedin' Hotchkiss . . .'

'You heard of him? How come I haven't before?'

'Probably because he's too clued up. He does the respectable citizen bit, successful self-made businessman, pillock of the community and all that. He bought Ashton View, big Gothic pile at the top of the valley overlooking Cold Ashton, a couple of years back. Churchgoing too, with bodyguards! Donations to the church roof fund and I'm sure he helps old ladies across the road, whether they want to go or not. He's the guy behind half the discount shops in the West Country. You know, everything costs a quid? Makes accounting real easy, I imagine. If you can count on your fingers you can work for Roy. But you better count your fingers after you shake hands with him. It's all a front, though. He's a nasty piece of work and smuggling is probably his most charming activity. Take my advice: stay away from him. I've met him.'

'Socially?'

'What? No. He came up here looking for a motor. Had two gorillas with him, standing around covering points of the compass like they expected a bloody ambush.'

'Did he buy?'

'Nah. He was looking for a Cadillac, you believe that? No taste. Bit like you. So what you want with him?'

'I diddled him out of a hundred grand and I think he twigged.'

Jake gave me a long, hard stare.

'What?' I said when it got uncomfortable.

'Just trying to memorize your face in case he catches up with you. You mess with Hotchkiss you won't need a car, you'll want a tank.'

'He knows my car. I just want a motor for tonight so he won't spot me a mile off. Tomorrow I'll rent something.'

'With your driving record and Roy's habit of flattening the opposition it would have to be something I don't want to see again,' he mused. 'All right, follow me.'


If you've not heard of a Morris Minor just imagine your gran's sofa with a wheel at each corner. It has about three buttons on the dash (Jake: 'Best not touch any of them'), just enough horsepower to overcome its natural inertia and drives like a bread bin. This one was baby blue on the outside and rotten on the inside. A getaway car it wasn't but I didn't really mind. I shoved my telltale shoulder-length hair under a baseball hat so from a distance I might be mistaken for an ancient local in his ancient runabout. Approaching Ashton Vale from the Chippenham side meant I could drive to a spot quite close to Ashton View. I had looked it up earlier, it had been there long enough to be marked on the Ordnance Survey map. I let the Morris grind to a stop under some trees on the verge of the narrow road just as it was getting dark. The house was nestling in an acre or so of woodland, set well back from the road. Nestling was more an estate agent's term though. It didn't so much nestle as loom through the trees behind a ten-foot stone wall which appeared to surround the entire property. Though its design of ornamentally wrought iron seemed in keeping with the fanciful archi-tecture of the house I suspected that the gate was in fact a later, automated, high-tech addition, adorned as the entrance was with no less than two CCTV cameras, an intercom and an infrared box mounted on the stonework. I kept well away from there.

Instead I pushed into the trees along the southern edge of the wall. I hoped the security might be less formidable further from the road and my trust was repaid in the shape of a pile of old builder's rubble sloping up the side of the stonework where it had been repaired. Teetering on this I could just pull myself up. As I crouched on the top all I could make out on the other side was a leafy gloom pricked with a few lights emanating from the tall bulk of the house, a black silhouette against the darkening sky. The thing even had a couple of Addams Family turrets and crenellations in its skyline. I let myself slither off the other side of the wall into what turned out to be a dense thicket of holly and other spiky growth, lost my baseball hat and got thoroughly scratched on the way down. Crawling on all fours I found the dried holly leaves under my hands were, if anything, even pricklier. The whole thing suddenly appeared just a little ill conceived. For a start I had no clear idea of what I was going to do here. I had simply followed my maxim of finding out as much as possible about the opposition but as I finally made it out of the undergrowth and into a stand of tall pines I was no longer sure this was the way to go about it.

To the left the tree-lined drive curved from the gate into an oval of gravel in front of the house with its self-important porticoed front door. Leaded windows on either side were dimly lit. Two dark Mercedes were neatly parked at the edge of the gravel area. More twenty-first-century Gothic, I thought. Further on, a high gabled coach house was presumably where Roy's BMW lived. Another window above the front entrance showed light behind drawn curtains but most of the light spilled from the back of the house, illuminating some of the trees there. I advanced cautiously between island flower beds across

101

the lawn towards the back, aware that each of the dark windows at this side could have a pair of eyes behind it. At the back I found a terrace running the entire length of the house, dotted with stone urns planted with fleshy foliage. Light spilled brightly on to it from three sets of french windows.

I edged around the corner, using the first mossy urn as cover. It was a large reception room I looked into. Someone had gone to town on it with a lot of dosh and very little sense. Two life-sized porcelain 'Moors' with gold turbans flanked the enormous in-your-face fireplace. The wallpaper was a velvety maroon flecked with gold. I could see a large black china dog of some description, also life-sized, sitting to attention next to an ornate drinks trolley.

Roy was playing host to four men sitting two by two in white leather sofas ranged around a gold-edged green marble coffee table loaded with glasses around a white, lacework china bowl with porcelain fruit. Nearly disappearing into a third sofa was a silver-haired, fifty-something, bony woman with sharp features in a knee-length gold dress. The man himself was seated in an enormous white armchair, filling it to capacity with blue-suited heaviness. Heaviness seemed the order of the day. While I couldn't hear what was being said I nevertheless sensed that this was not a joyful gathering. Roy was talking, but first one, then another of the men shook their heads. All four of them were dark-haired, immaculately groomed in white shirts, sober ties and dark suits, and had the kind of complexion you get in the Eastern Mediterranean and beyond. All of them appeared relaxed whereas Roy leant forward, straining his waistband, looking from one to the other while he held forth. What had Wakey, the surfer dude, said at the warehouse? Roy's got people to pay, he's got cash flow problems. Over a hundred grand of Roy's cash was parked in the cupboard under my stairs, next to the shotgun locker, flowing nowhere.

I watched the silver-and-gold lady rise with a mute sigh and carry her glass towards the window closest to me. I shrank further into the shadows. Go on, lady, open the windows, it's a mild night. For England in May, that is. But instead she turned round again just as she got to the window and started shouting. Well, almost as good as opening the windows, except I didn't understand a word of what she was rattling off until she put down her glass with a bump on to a spindly bit of furniture and shouted the last two words twice: 'Iki haftá, iki haftá!' Then she walked away from the window and everyone suddenly rose. Meeting over. Roy continued talking at their backs while his guests filed out of the room but didn't see them to the door. Instead he scratched his close-cropped hair, swiped his empty glass from the table and replenished it from a bottle of vodka I was certain was the real article and not one of the cleaned-up methylated spirit concoctions from the warehouse. Then he opened the middle pair of french windows – a little late for me, unless he was in the habit of soliloquizing – and stepped out on to the terrace. I just had time to sneak back around the corner and take shelter behind the sparse foliage of a buddleia. Fortunately I was still able to keep an eye on him from there. Far behind me car doors slammed and engines started up. Roy half turned and made a clicking noise in his throat and out trotted the big, black china dog. Time to go home. Any minute now and the two china Moors might follow him out. Almost immediately the dog stiffened its stance and sniffed in my direction then, predictably, growled.

In all directions there were yards and yards of lawn between me and the wall I had to scale to get out of here. It only now occurred to me that I had foolishly omitted to bring the pile of builder's rubble with me to help get up it again from this side.

The dog growled again and started towards my buddleia when Roy kindly helped me out. 'And you can shut up and all. Here! Get inside.' He grabbed the mutt by the collar, yanked it towards the open doors and followed through with a kick which sent the dog inside with a yelp. My breathing calmed down, just in time to hear a padding footfall behind me. Someone was approaching across the lawn. I squeezed deeper into the shrubbery making as little sound as possible. It was Surfer Dude.

'They've gone, boss.'

'And thank fuck for that,' Roy said heavily. He took a gulp from his glass and kept staring into the trees.

Wakey just stood and waited on the grass below the terrace until his boss carried on.

'It was a mistake. I don't need this shit. Bunch of foreign wankers giving me ultimatums in my own house. I've been my own boss since I was seventeen and I'm not gonna change now. Not for a whole warehouse full of Natashas. If I can't raise the two hundred quickly I'm gonna back out.'

'Can you do that? Won't there be trouble?'

Roy seemed to be considering this, staring into the dregs in his glass. 'Could be, with that self-styled mafia lot. I'll get Cannon and Ball over for a bit of extra muscle.' A noisy intake of breath from Wakey. 'I know they're a couple of psychos,' Roy said forcefully, 'but if they scare *you* they might scare *them*. They scare *me* sometimes,' he added with a joyless chuckle. 'Right, lock up, see to the alarms, no phone calls. I've had enough for tonight.'

Wakey padded off again towards the front of the house and was soon swallowed by the darkness. Roy stayed on the terrace for a few moments longer, breathing noisily in the still air and clenching and unclenching his big hammy fists around the empty tumbler. Then at last he turned back inside. I could hear him lock up behind himself.

I had of course no idea what kind of security the grounds themselves might have but since I got in rather easily I expected to get out again somehow. From this side I had a ten-foot wall to climb. The ground floor of the house soon fell dark and I set off deeper into the grounds at the rear. Only a few yards into the trees at the back I spotted a low structure shimmering in the thin starlight. It turned out to be a long, derelict greenhouse, many of its glass panes missing. Ideally I was looking for a ladder but when I approached the stone wall near the sad structure I found something nearly as practical: thick wires, stretched horizontally at regular intervals between tensioners, where plants had once been trained to grow against the wall. All rusty now but sturdy enough to hold my weight. Two minutes of scrabbling about got me over the wall again. I took my time wading through the damply fragrant leaf mould and half-seen undergrowth on the other side of the wall, making as little noise as possible. When I at last gained the narrow lane I was almost happy to spot my baby-blue conveyance, though as I spent a tense minute coaxing its tiny engine into life I guessed I would never become fond of it.

So what had Roy got himself into that he now regretted having started? Those stony-faced blokes with their trendy suits and the angry gold lady with her neatly sharpened elbows had made podgy Roy look a little desperate and almost homely by comparison. I had never learned the language properly but had picked up enough of the lingo in the months I bummed around Turkey to know that *iki haftá* meant 'two weeks'. And Roy had mentioned a warehouse full of 'Natashas'. Almost universally that meant prostitutes, sex workers brought in with or without their consent from former Soviet republics or eastern Europe. The resorts along the coasts of Turkey were awash with them, smuggled across the long borders that country had with Bulgaria, Georgia and Armenia. Brought in and run by the Turkish mafia, their lives were miserable and their usefulness short and so was the tourist season. There were no seasons for the sex industry in Britain.

Was this how Roy made his real money or was it a new departure for him? Somehow I had Roy down as an old-fashioned hoodlum, a type I had met before, who ran a personal little empire like a family business and eschewed cooperation with other gangs and especially the mafia, where very soon the reins of power might slip from his hand even if the money might be good. Had I felt any guilt at all at having diddled him out of a hundred grand before, by the time I bumped the Morris into the yard at Mill House I was certain I had done Roy a favour, though I doubted he would quite see it that way.

Sunshine had returned to the valley. Standing on the grass beyond the verandah I drank it in as greedily as I did my first mug of coffee. The olfactory hallucinations had gone, I no longer had the acridly insane smells of Nikki Reid's prison in my nostrils but all the smells of spring, of sunshine on warm stone, of the kitchen herbs that miraculously revived each year outside the kitchen door, of the meadow in which more wild flowers seemed to appear with every new season. Alison, who knew about these things, had tried to teach me their names but I was hopeless at remembering (Bastard Toad Wart? Stinking Goat's Retch?) and was simply glad they were there.

I was also aware that this idyll had a flaw. It was an illusion. It wasn't safe. Roy had surrounded himself with high walls and I had got close enough to him to hear him breathe. Here all I had were hedges and bits of rickety fence to keep out my neighbours' livestock. You can't hide in the countryside. People in the country are as visible as cows in the city.

I sniffed again. This morning the air was laced with a definite tang of petrol which cut sharply across the rural smells. Following it I was carrying my mug past the herb patch by the kitchen entrance on my way to the yard when the first explosion shook the air. Two more bangs in quick succession, followed by an ear-splitting roar. When I reached the yard I could see blue smoke billowing from the old stables. Alison was standing a few feet from the entrance, covering her ears with her hands, then jumped back as Annis barrelled out of the smoke astride a growling, rust-coloured contraption which at five-second intervals backfired like an elephant gun with puffs of sooty smoke. In her army shorts and vest and covered in oil and muck she looked like she had driven the Norton all the way through hell. She bombed past me in a wobbling circuit round the potholed yard with an insane grin, shouting her delight: 'It works!' Another wild circuit and her expression had somewhat changed. 'Eek! No brakes!' Sensibly she pointed the monster at the gentle rise of the meadow, cut the engine and let it bounce to a stop in the tufty grass. I gave her a hand wheeling it back to the workshop. 'Hey, Chris, is that why they call it the Roaring Fifties? Can't believe you were actually *there*,' she said in mock amazement.

'It's the Roaring Twenties and I was only a baby in the Fifties,' I defended myself lamely, knowing that in our gentle age war eventual defeat was as inevitable as surrender was out of the question.

With the Norton returned to the work stand Annis wiped her greasy hands on her chest. Sweat glistened on her oily arms and in the down on her temples. She turned the green headlamps of her eyes on mine. 'I need a shower. Perhaps several.' Stepping close she pressed her face into my neck and sniffed. 'Have you had your shower yet, Chris?' she mumbled distractedly as she munched on my earlobe. 'I could use some help getting the grime out of all the creases,' she added, pushing me backwards to the door.

I had got dirty, then clean, then dirty again and was definitely in need of another shower but I had no inclination to quit this lazy sun-streaked tangle of limbs and duvet in a hurry. Neither did Annis, it seemed. Not that she could easily have done so since I had unchivalrously parked a glass ashtray on her bum. I was relieved things appeared to be back to normal and tried not to wonder whether she had broken her fast in this bed or in Tim's.

'So whaddayagonnado with the mummy?' came from the tangle of red hair half-buried under a pillow.

'The *mummy*?' Perhaps I had more problems than I realized.

'Mon-ney.' Her head surfaced. 'Pounds, shillings and pence, in a case under the stairs. Stuff, folding, for the use of?'

'Oh, that mummy.' I hadn't really thought about it. The important thing had been that art-thieving blighters didn't get to spend it. 'Don't know. Rainy day? Stick it in the business? Buy some paint?'

'Helluvalot of paint, Chris.'

'Tim's been on at me about getting a van for surveillance stuff, for ages. Cameras, computers, tapes, fridge, the lot.'

'Wigs and false beards,' Annis said dismissively. 'Shouldn't the money really go back to Griffin's?'

'Why should it? They stumped up the dosh to get the artwork back because it saved them paying out a larger sum to the policy holder. They got what they paid for. Should be happy enough.'

'But Roy presumably isn't. You think you got away with it then?'

'We'll see.'

Annis took the ashtray off her posterior and turned to face me, propped on one freckly arm. 'What worries me is what we'll see if you *didn't* get away with it.'

'That's why I'm in no hurry to spend any of it, just in case someone comes calling.'

'And if he's twigged, do you think Roy and his firm are just going to ring the doorbell and say, "Excuse me, Mr Chris, sir, can we have our lolly, please?" and you're going to say, "Oh, all right then, no hard feelings I hope, Mr Hotchkiss"? Is that how you envisage the transaction?'

I had tried hard not to imagine that scenario in too great a detail but before I was forced to admit to that fact the old

108

1940s dialler by the side of the bed gave its old-fashioned alarum. I picked it up gratefully.

'Honeysett?' Through the ancient handset Needham's voice sounded tinny and remote as though he were calling from the 1940s with a zinc bucket on his head. 'Have you seen today's edition of the *Chronicle*? Bar your gate, disconnect this phone and batten down the hatches. Your good friend Eva hasn't done you any favours. She's only gone and named you as the local hero and both our mugs are on the front page. You'll have a press circus camping on your land in a few minutes. Hope you've got enough food in the fridge to last you a while. And the same rules apply, you talk to no one. Especially now.'

'Especially now?'

'That's why I'm really calling, didn't think you'd like to read about it in the papers: Nikki Reid is dead. She died during the night. Heart failure. A direct result of what that bastard did to her. That makes it murder, Chris. We're looking for a serial killer.'

I was sitting bolt upright now. I tried to push away the image of Nikki Reid, starved into a ghost and clinging on to my sleeves, and tried to remember the picture I had seen on posters around Bath instead. It wouldn't come. 'Two killings don't make a series. Did you get to interview her?'

'I didn't,' Needham said grimly. 'Not a word about her abductor, no description, nothing. We haven't got anything new, we're back to square one. This isn't over, Chris. He's out there looking for his next victim, building his next dungeon, preparing his next paper chase. I've got work to do, so take care. And Chris? I'm sorry.'

I put the receiver down slowly and very carefully. I repeated the news to Annis, who hugged me briefly, then got dressed silently and slipped out of the door.

I'd been too late. I had achieved precisely nothing. Nikki Reid's abductor had been there, had been close, and I hadn't even managed to catch a glimpse of him. Nikki

Reid hadn't been saved that night. She hadn't died under the hands of 'the Doctor' so much as the doctors. There couldn't even be the consolation that she had died with dignity, knowing as I did what indignities the frantic efforts of resuscitation visit on a frail body. Her death had been violent, violated. Was it grief I felt? Or was it the selfish sadness and anger that I had been cheated of my newly acquired hero status? Had I cared about the woman in the cage? The impressions of the last two days were still too fresh and confused to tell one emotion from the other but as I dressed I felt something shrinking inside me and hardening into a small and urgent ball of hate for a man I had never met. Yet.

Needham's warning had been apt and timely. The tortured sound of a car being driven badly down the still muddy track made me throw open the shutters. Looking to the right I saw Annis closing the five-bar gate to our first uninvited visitors. By the time I made it to my front door there were three cars blocking the track and Annis was walking away from five or six people all calling after her, waving tape recorders or pointing cameras. I heard my own name being called, Mr Honeysett, only a few . . . and Mr Honeysett, can you just . . .

Inside the phone rang without pause, even my mobile chimed continuously in my jacket on the chair by the hall table.

'I told them you wouldn't talk to them but I doubt they'll simply turn round and head back home,' Annis said.

'Let's just leave them to it, they'll get tired of it,' I said, not really believing it. I closed the door, then, on an impulse, locked it. I switched off my mobile and took the phone off the hook in the sitting room. After a short while a siren sound warned me to replace the handset. I disconnected it at the socket.

'They're so damn excited, that's what gets me about it,'

Annis fumed. 'They think it's their God-given right to demand answers to their moronic questions.'

'What's all that palaver?' called Alison, coming in from the meadow through the kitchen door. 'Who are all those guys by the gate?'

I told her.

'How long are they gonna be there? As long as they're there we can't leave by car, they're blocking the road. Idiots. Ehm . . .' She hesitated while she looked at Annis, then her feet, then me again with a frown. 'I just had a look in the studio. The painting on your easel, Chris, it's . . . none of my business but . . . you're not seriously going figurative, are you?'

'Certainly not. Tell you the truth . . .' I noticed Annis stiffening. Here was the thing we had avoided mentioning for nearly a year. 'I'm finding it hard to start again. Ever since Jenny. I've been thinking about it these past few days, farted about in the studio and got as far as putting a prepared canvas on my easel but . . . When it came to it I didn't do any painting.'

Alison's frown deepened. 'Well, someone did. Of a sort . . .'

We traipsed up the meadow to the studio, ignoring the long-lensed cameras and half-hearted calls of the reporters. I was the first in through the door. And I understood why Alison looked worried. The pristine canvas I had left on the easel the day of the private view was a mess. It was hardly painting, more a crude drawing done in paint. It was meant to be a crucifixion. Only the figure on the cross was recognizably a woman. A naked woman. Large circles for breasts, dotted in the centre for nipples, the curvaceous body indicated in outline, a furious welter of brushstrokes indicating a jungle of pubic hair. All of it was done in the same unbroken colour, cobalt violet, straight from the tube, and with the same filbert brush which lay encrusted on my muddied palette.

'Definitely not my new style,' I assured them. 'Don't think it'd go down well with Simon.'

'Glad to hear it,' said Annis. 'So someone came in and did a doodle on your canvas.'

'Expensive doodle.' Alison pointed to the maltreated brush and the squashed tube of paint on the palette. 'Cobalt violet, most expensive paint around, forty quid a tube.'

'Was anything taken? Anything damaged?' I wondered.

We took a good look around and found everything in order, or rather the usual creative mess we all favoured. I took the hideous thing off the easel and chucked it into a corner where other debris was waiting to be taken outside and burnt. There was no great mystery as to how someone had managed to get inside. We were notoriously lax about locking doors, especially the studio, and anyone could come across the neighbouring land and hop through a hedge to find the place invitingly open. Vandalism wasn't a huge problem in the countryside. It was beginning to creep into the villages, though, where there was nothing much to do for teenagers not old enough to spend their evenings in the pub. If their village was lucky enough to still have a pub.

I locked the studio now and we trundled back to the house and spent a few hours busily ignoring the press guys outside. Annis spotted one of them at the top of the meadow thinking he was being clever and went up to disabuse him of the idea. Eva herself wasn't out there. I rang her mobile from mine but there was no answer. I left a thank-you-so-much message.

As the afternoon ticked away a feeling of unease took hold of me that had little to do with a bunch of reporters at the gate. I had the odd sensation that something was coming at me from over the horizon, a threat I hadn't even thought of, and like a V2 rocket it wouldn't bother to whistle before it hit. Remaining at Mill House suddenly felt like sitting in the middle of a giant bull's-eye and all

I could think of was escape for myself. I could of course slip into the narrow strip of woodland behind the studio, strike out over my neighbour's land and make it to the road that way on foot, but then what? No, the only way out of here would be through the huddle of by now bored reporters and their column of cars.

'I'm going out,' I announced.

'Thought you might,' said Annis from the sofa without lowering her book. 'You've been fidgeting for an hour. You realize of course the track's blocked and they've got nowhere to turn round unless we let them into the yard? All of them? We'll never get rid of them once they're in here.'

'I'll give them a chance to practise their reversing skills,' I said vindictively.

She snapped her book shut. 'Oh goody, I'll watch.'

Leather-jacketed and booted I approached the gate and the whole lot of them came alive where they'd been lounging on car bonnets and the strip of perpetually damp grass by the millstream. And all surged forward and started talking at once, fiddling with their little recorders or pointing their cameras. It didn't feel real. It felt so much like the movies that I couldn't take it seriously any more. I lifted my hands to get some quiet.

'I have a short statement for you: Piss off! Get those cars off the track because I need to use it. Do it now or I'll get the tractor out and push every one of them into the ditch.' I hooked a thumb over my shoulder at the outbuildings when I mentioned the tractor. I didn't have one of course but Mill House looked enough like a run-down farm to warrant one. The reporters all started talking at once again when the sound of Annis's Norton exploding into life turned the lot of them into mime artists. It sounded nothing like a tractor of course. It sounded like a Sherman tank starting up and that got them moving fast.

Annis switched off and opened the gate for me. It was getting dark and from inside the baby-blue Morris

I enjoyed watching them make a pig's ear out of reversing the 150-or-so yards over the rutted track back on to the road. Even there they started getting into each other's way, gesticulating and blaring their horns at each other. I took the opportunity to floor the accelerator and grind past. Not that I had any hope of shaking them if they decided to follow. You can't shake anything in a Morris Minor, except perhaps your fillings loose.

At first I thought no one had bothered. There was nothing in my rear-view mirrors except darkening countryside until just before I reached the main road, then headlights appeared far behind, and that could have been any one of my neighbours from the valley. By the time I drove along the London Road into Bath there was no telling, there were so many cars on the road. I felt so relieved to be moving, to be going somewhere, I didn't really care.

# Chapter Nine

If by tomorrow I'd be portrayed in the press as an ill-tempered country bumpkin driving a baby-blue wind-up toy so be it. Right now I didn't mind. The wind was in the south. It was an exceptionally mild night for early May. I tried the handle for the window. It opened a couple of inches and stuck. I pulled it down by hand and it disappeared with an ominous bang below, possibly forever. With my elbow out of the window I discovered what this car was made for – pootling. I pootled through the familiar streets of the centre of Bath just for the sensation of it: the gentle curve of the Vineyards with its high pavement; Milsom Street, where sober banks had been turned into not so sober bars and restaurants; an illegal right turn brought the floodlit Abbey into view. I got happily stuck behind a horse-drawn hackney carriage full of self-conscious tourists taking pictures of each other and followed them all the way across Pulteney Bridge and restaurant-encrusted Argyle Street and past the Laura Place fountain. The carriage decided to circle it so I tookled on along the ridiculously grand Pulteney Street towards the Holburne Museum. As I took a right turn I could see where all this pootling and tookling was leading me – back to Twerton station. This I didn't want in tomorrow's papers. A quick check in my minute mirror showed a couple of cars. I'd taken no note of the makes of cars at Mill House, so there was no telling. A lazy full circle of the roundabout by St Mary's Church brought both in front of me as I rejoined

Pulteney Road heading west, but only one accelerated happily away. The second car, a claret-coloured Volvo, seemed to be pootling also. I waited until the road narrowed and an impatient queue had built up behind us, then ducked into a narrow side street without warning. There was nowhere for the Volvo to stop for hundreds of yards without causing chaos. I cranked the Morris around in a muscle-building seven-point turn. There were other roads to Twerton.

A single bobby still guarded the taped-up entrance to the station. I stayed in the car, contemplating the building and the railway arch, now made ghoulishly Gothic by recent events. The police constable was beginning to show an interest and prepared to cross the street, presumably to tell me to move on. I moved on. I had no business here. The business that had brought me there in the first place, however, might still be in the area, so I turned off into Oldfield, crossed over the railway line and rattled about the Moorland Road area. Twice I had come close to finding Billy by pure chance, perhaps I'd get third-time-lucky. Quite a few people were about. I asked in a couple of off-licences, including the one Billy had used on Saturday, bought a litre of reconstituted orange juice and sucked on that while I hung around for an hour without much enthusiasm. The coming and going of police in the area might well have put Billy off his Oldfield domicile and induced him to find something quieter. The man in the off-licence might have tipped him off. And the place felt all wrong; too far from the river, on the wrong side of the railway tracks, too far from the centre. I turned the Morris around and clonked through the gears towards St John the Baptist in Bathwick. Perhaps the irate Scotsman would give me another, no doubt reluctant, pointer to Billy's possible hiding place.

I parked in St John's Road directly in front of the church. As I'd feared the driver window remained stubbornly submerged in its housing despite my effort with the handle. Anyone insane enough to steal this chariot got all he deserved, I decided, and left the thing unlocked. I took the same route through the neglected churchyard amongst the sunken graves to the spot where the Scotsman had fed his fire of defiance. No flames shed any light under the high wall now. This time I had brought my torch and played its beam over the area between the wall and the east side of the church. The oil drum was still there, now lying on its side in a scatter of cold ashes. A few broken bottles glittered here and there among other debris, charred pizza cartons and Tesco carrier bags. The lack of a fire did not guarantee the absence of short-tempered winos waiting in the gloom to defend their turf, so I listened carefully after every few steps through the dark wilderness behind the church. Perhaps the clergy had since relented and the fiery Scotsman had once more taken up residence in the crypt, which by his description of it had to have an outside entrance. I found a small side door. It was locked. A few more steps over broken paving stones brought me to a dank and mossy stairway leading down to a door heavily strapped with iron and set back into a darkly arched recess. This had to be the outside entrance to the crypt. A shiny brass padlock as large as a fist secured it against my trespass. The sight of it made me shudder. I'd seen too many padlocks lately. The picklocks were in my pocket this time but there was no point. The Scotsman wasn't here. I turned to ascend the steps and heard a noise. A scraping noise, of foot on pavement I judged. I snapped out the light and tiptoed up a few steps until I could cautiously raise my head above ground level. The occasional noise had become firm footsteps and the corner of the church turned sharp and black in the backlight of a powerful torch beam. Then the light turned the corner and found my eyes with uncanny swiftness. I ducked.

'There's no point hiding down there, my lad, none at all. So let's have no nonsense. Come on. Up! Up you come!'

The voice grated right above me now in a pedantic sing-song that seemed vaguely familiar. Reluctantly I took the last few steps to put myself level with it and turned on my own flashlight to illuminate the man behind the glare.

'Ill met by torchlight, I might say, Mr Honeysett.' The beam diverted to the church wall. In its reflection I could make out a broad-shouldered man with thinning, shoulder-length hair. I still couldn't quite place him but he came to my rescue. 'I see you are baffled, yet we have met, if briefly. At the private view, last Saturday. I am Keith Ward.'

The penny dropped. John Gatt's mate from the historical re-enactment thingy. 'Pleased to meet you again, Keith,' I managed.

'I'm not so sure it's mutual until you tell me in what capacity you are trying the doors of St John's at night. Let's have that conversation in the light around the corner, shall we?' he said and walked off.

I followed him into the gloaming of streetlights that reached the courtyard on the other side of the church where we extinguished our torches. I recognized his features now; the curiously broad face that matched his wide shoulders, the thin-lipped mouth under the strong, straight nose.

'I take it you are wearing your detective hat tonight. I'm curious to know what you were hoping to detect.'

I suddenly felt like simply running away. Something about Keith Ward aroused schoolboyish impulses in me, but I answered sensibly: 'I'm looking for a tramp who used to hang around here, Scottish guy, big, loud, likes lighting fires. He used to doss down in the crypt, I believe, but was turfed out.'

'Ah. Yes, turf him out we did. I'm caretaker for St John's and I made sure he looked somewhere else for lodgings. He was making a nuisance of himself. What did you want with him?'

'To ask him about another tramp I'm looking for. Looks

in his sixties, steel grey hair and beard, chewed-up ear. Name's Billy. Ring any bells?' I asked, hoping for a non-campanological answer.

'From that description, no. But then it would fit most of them, wouldn't it? Apart from the ear. I don't recall anyone called Billy. I won't ask what you want with him, I suppose it's covered by client confidentiality. But I suggest next time you creep around a church in the dark you first obtain the vicar's permission. We've had so many break-ins and attempted break-ins, we're a little bit nervous.'

It seemed to me that there hadn't been even the smallest hint of nervousness about the way he had approached me in the dark, without knowing who I was or if indeed I was alone.

'Well, Mr Honeysett, I'm afraid I must leave you to it. My wife will be wondering where I've got to,' he said without moving. It was an invitation to leave and apparently he was going to make sure I did.

I said goodnight and walked off to the Morris. It hadn't been nicked but someone had given it their attention. The bonnet was scratched. I stood in front of it to assess the damage and realized that the broad scratches added up to a message, executed in that curiously cuneiform script which scratched writing takes on all by itself: YOU OWE M.

The message was either cryptic or incomplete but from the position of the last letter in the left corner of the bonnet it looked like the messenger had been interrupted, perhaps by Keith and myself appearing at the front of the church. YOU OWE M . . . Money? The beginning of a name? Had it read 'YOU OWE R' I'd have guessed that Mr Hotchkiss's goons were catching up with me.

Jake would be pleased: so far I had managed to lose the driver window and get the bonnet redecorated. But I wasn't worried about Jake. It was the feeling that someone who didn't mean well seemed to be always just around the corner, watching. Someone knew where I went, following close behind. I had come across messages scratched into the paintwork of clients' cars before and it had always been the prelude to more unpleasant happenings.

Cars are easy targets, not just when they're stationary, I reminded myself as I drove home, the feeble headlights of the Morris illuminating only a few feet of track ahead and the tiny vibrating mirror showing nothing but a dancing blackness behind.

In the kitchen I found Alison drinking some herbal concoction at the newspaper-strewn table. My mood instantly blackened even further. Next time I got hold of Eva I'd give her a short lecture about not exploiting our friendship for a by-line.

'Have you seen the papers?' Alison asked.

'No, and I don't want to, either,' I said, picking one up and scanning the article. Second victim . . . serial killer . . . private detective's discovery . . . and my name. I threw the thing back on the table. Alison took a sip of her infusion and pulled a painful grimace, either from sympathy or the taste of the evil-smelling stuff.

'Your office answer machine's been going all day. I think your tape is full. I had a listen. Sounds like everyone in the country wants you to find someone: children, wives, husbands, confused grandparents, dogs, cats, and an iguana called Knut. You'll never be out of work again.' She pulled the appropriate face, knowing that missing persons was my least favourite assignment, which I often referred to a much larger agency in Bristol with better resources and a good track record. They in turn seemed to shove anything my way they found simply too screwy to handle.

'Yeah, yeah, everyone's looking for somebody. Where's Annis?'

'She's at Tim's.'

I opened the fridge, pulled out a Pilsner Urquell, yanked the top off and took a long icy draught straight from the bottle. I opened the fridge again and grabbed another two. What the hell. One wasn't going to do it tonight.


'What in heaven's name is that?' Alison stared into the saucepan with undisguised horror. It was late afternoon and I was working off my frustrations in the kitchen. Ali wouldn't eat a regular meal, full stop, Annis was still not back from Tim's where she probably got fed on Indian takeaways, so I could indulge myself by cooking whatever I liked.

'Octopus braised in its own ink. You're welcome to have some when it's ready.'

'Eargh! Not if I was starving to death. Just make sure that thing is properly dead, I don't want it to come squeezing under my bedroom door at night.'

'I think you're safe there, it's been cooking for an hour already.'

'You can never be sure. Are you still driving the piece of junk you borrowed from Jake's?'

'That's a bit rich, considering the parlous state of your own conveyance.'

'Beetles are considered cool again, I'll have you know, mine just needs . . . a new clutch. And engine, apparently. And some other thingy I don't remember. And a lot of welding, they said. And new tyres. Otherwise it's fine. Can I borrow the DS?' she fluted. 'I've got a class, it's at the other end of town.'

'It's left-hand drive and the gear shift is tricky if you're not used to it.' Not that I was trying to put her off.

'That's cool, left-hand drive is cool. Honest. The pedals are the same way round though, aren't they . . .?'

Half an hour later I nervously waved her off as she sped out of the yard.

I returned to the kitchen, chucked together a green salad, ladled octopus and night-black sauce over a mountain of linguine, poured myself a glass of fuliginous Italian red to match the colour. The house was quiet. Very quiet. The

121

main phone was still disconnected, the office phone set to silent. It was so quiet I could hear the food on my plate steam. I twirled some pasta round my fork. Somewhere in the house something creaked. Somewhere upstairs. I held the fork still and the linguine slowly unravelled. Something always creaked at Mill House. It was that kind of house. I stabbed the fork back in the pasta and twirled. There was that creak again. Perhaps a bit louder, or else I was listening harder. I put the fork down, got up quietly, walked into the sitting room and looked up at the stairs, listened. Not a sound anywhere. I put my foot on the bottom step, then changed my mind. I was getting spooked in my own house on a sunny evening in May. I went back to the kitchen and my Italian feast, but somehow my heart was no longer in it.

When I woke it was to a gentle rocking and the subtle aroma of cardamom laced with the less sophisticated one of lager. Before my dreamy mind could complete the pleasant picture of a dhow carrying spice and Pilsner across the Indian ocean Annis's voice spoilt it for me: 'Wake up, Honeysett.'

I tried to pull her into bed but got nothing but a handful of unyielding leather jacket. That made me open my eyes at last. Her welcome silhouette was outlined against the light coming through the open door. I turned on the bedside lamp. The clock showed three in the morning. 'Are you awake, Chris? Tell me you're awake.'

'I'm awake,' I lied.

'Where's Ali, Chris?'

My brain worked slowly. 'Don't know. Went to a class. She borrowed my DS.'

'Well, she's not back. And I'm worried.'

I sat up. 'What's to worry? Perhaps she's staying the night at John's.'

'Their relationship's not progressed that far. And John's in London.'

'So she went to a nightclub or something.' I was clutching at straws. Ali hated nightclubs. 'Or perhaps she pulled.'

'At the slimming club? You're not really awake at all, are you? Come on, get your togs on, we're going to look for her.' She pulled the duvet off me and dumped it on the floor to speed up my progress into the land of the alert and vertical. 'I'll make you some coffee. You're driving, I'm over the limit.'

I walked straight into the shower and gave it thirty seconds of ice cold followed by thirty seconds of piping hot and was awake. While I dried off in record time and jumped into my clothes I got a bad feeling. I knew Ali wouldn't borrow my car, then decide to hang on to it overnight without calling. But the phones were switched off, so there was always the possibility that she had tried but failed.

We downed the hot black coffee wordlessly standing up by the kettle. Annis looked grimly at the walls. She put her mug down, took mine out of my hands and gave me a shove towards the door. 'If it turns out this has anything to do with the watercolour stunt you pulled then you're a dead man, Chris.'

The Morris didn't like the cold night air but I persevered because the alternative was Annis's nightmare on wheels. She stared into the dark without comment while I coaxed the engine into sputtering life. 'Where's this slimming class held?'

'St Mark's Community Centre. In Widcombe.'

'I know it.' St Mark's was next to a school converted to artists' studios where I'd given a talk once.

'Can this thing go any faster?' We were doing a teeth-rattling forty along the deserted London Road. The permanently open window produced a freezing gale inside.

'Not without losing the wheels, I think.' But I put my foot down. The speedometer crept up to fifty. The result was a hand-numbing vibration on the steering wheel and an exhaust note that suggested the engine ran on soya beans. At any other time I'd have found this hilarious. Right now it sounded like a fanfare to failure as it echoed off darkened houses along hollow canyons of night-grey streets. I slowed as I reached Claverton Street and dog-legged into St Mark's Road. There were no parking spaces. We left the Morris in the middle of the street and checked the cars on either side of the road. There was no sign of a black Citroën DS 21 in the short cul-de-sac. St Mark's lay dark and quiet. A sign high up on the church wall pointed an arrow to the right towards a broad wrought-iron gate: *St Mark's Community Centre, Entrance.* Through the bars of the gate I could just make out a ramshackle churchyard but beyond the marble sculpture of an angel I could see nothing in the gloom. I pointed my torch through the bars of the gate and let it sweep along the paved area by the side of the church. Right at the back two round, old-fashioned cat's-eyes reflected in the feeble beam.

'It's in here.' I tried the gate. It was locked. Its structure provided plenty of footholds and we were over and down the other side in a few seconds. Once there though, we approached slowly. The car was parked awkwardly in the furthest corner, the driver door hard against the side of the church. I was glad I was not by myself just now; the feeling of standing on a giant bull's-eye returned, making me want to run as far away from this place as I possibly could. I snapped the torch on again and played it over the car's bodywork. It was just as I remembered it, in need of a wash and of patching up here and there. Nothing out of the ordinary. Under the windscreen wiper was stuck a damp, folded piece of paper. I pulled it free and unfolded it. It was written in pink felt pen and read: *Please don't leave cars inside after classes have finished. The gate must be locked after 9.30 and won't be unlocked until 10 in the morning.* It was signed: *L. W.*

I handed it to Annis but she'd already read it over my shoulder.

124

'She could of course have wandered off somewhere after the class, not realizing that the car would be locked in, then come back and found she had no transport. But why didn't she call?'

'The phone at home is still disconnected and she might not know my mobile number. Or she might not have had change, or any money at all.'

'She could have walked the distance three times by now. I don't like it, Chris.'

I didn't like it either. But I didn't say so. Because I had pointed the beam of my torch inside the car and what I saw went beyond not liking it.

# Chapter Ten

The keys were in the ignition. Placed neatly on the driver's seat lay an envelope. The passenger door was open. I slid in and picked up the letter. It was standard business stationery. A printed address label had my name on it, nothing else. The envelope was gummed shut and I sat there, not wanting to open it, somehow wanting to postpone the moment. I suddenly thought I knew what I would find inside and a dreadful heaviness settled on me, a paralysis of the will. Annis snatched open the rear door and got in the back. 'Well? Open it! Oh, give it here . . .' She tried to grab it from me but I put it out of her reach, then slid my finger in and ripped it open. It contained a single sheet of A4 paper, precisely folded and typed in capitals.

DEAR MR HONEYSETT. AS YOU WILL HAVE GUESSED BY NOW, I HAVE YOUR GIRL. IT'S ONLY FAIR, DON'T YOU THINK? SHE IS ALIVE. HOW LONG SHE STAYS ALIVE DEPENDS ENTIRELY ON YOU. DO NOT INVOLVE THE POLICE. IF YOU DO, I WILL KNOW ABOUT IT. GO HOME. YOU WILL RECEIVE FURTHER INSTRUCTIONS.

Annis grabbed the sheet from me, gave it one glance, then thumped me. Once, twice, with the heel of her hand, hard, ill-aimed blows at my shoulder. She slumped back for a moment, then gave the back of my seat a few savage kicks and subsided again into motionless silence. I also sat still, but my mind was racing with useless images, imagining Alison's abduction, and my chest ached with a mixture of outrage and fear. *How long she stays alive depends entirely on you . . .*

'Get the engine started, get us out of here, Chris.' Annis's voice was hard, cold and flat.

'The gate's locked, we'll have to go back in the Morris.'

'Oh, for fuck's sake.' She got out and walked off, leaving the door open. I locked the car and followed her. When I got to the Morris she was already sitting in the passenger seat, chewing on her lower lip, eyes swimming. I reversed all the way to the main road and pointed the car east.

'What price your little schemes now, Honeysett? You prat! I told you it was a shit thing to do, involving Ali in it. And before you even knew who the guys you scammed were. I wish I'd paid more attention and put my foot down earlier. I can't *believe* I helped you. If anything happens to her, if Roy as much as bends one hair on her head I swear it's you not him I'm going to kill. Why the hell are you slowing down?'

I hadn't noticed that I had, but now I slowed down even further and eventually pulled in under a streetlamp opposite the Holburne Museum. I turned to Annis who looked ready to hit me again.

'What?'

I took a deep breath. 'If Roy Hotchkiss has Ali, then we're very, very lucky. Read the note again.'

Annis closed her eyes and a silent 'Oh no' formed on her lips. Then, with heavy movement as though the letter was written in lead, she lifted the crumpled note to the light.

'That's not a ransom note,' I said gently. 'There's no demand for the money. This guy's not interested in money. You see? I stole his girl, he thinks he stole mine. *It's only fair.* Roy hasn't got Ali. The Doctor has.'

Annis turned to me and invited me into her arms. We hugged hard. Then we disentangled, sniffed, coughed, and I got out my mobile.

'You ringing Needham?'

127

'No. No police. You read the note. I'm calling Tim.' She made to protest but I dialled and let it ring until I heard his surprisingly wakeful voice on the other end. 'It's Chris. Some bastard snatched Ali. See you at Mill House.' What else could I possibly have said?

Tim got there only minutes after us. Soon the three of us were arguing around the coffee table in front of the unlit fire in the bleak pre-dawn hour. I had reconnected the main phone, willing it to ring and dreading it at the same time.

'They always say don't call the police,' Tim said dismissively. 'But we'd be stupid not to.'

Annis nodded her assent. 'Exactly. Call Needham. They're looking for him anyway, they must have some sort of lead by now.'

'They've got zero. Absolutely nothing,' I said vehemently. 'They couldn't get a bead on the guy after months of trying. Apart from some DNA they have nothing to show for it. He was playing games with them and they lost spectacularly. Read the note again. *If you do, I will know about it.* What if he has an ear in Manvers Street somehow?'

'I'd say he's bluffing,' Tim maintained.

'This isn't a game of poker. At least it isn't one we can afford to lose.'

'It isn't one we can afford to play in the first place, not with Ali as a stake,' Annis said fiercely.

'Then what if he's a police officer? Or a civilian working in Manvers Street? Computer operator, SOCO, caterer, cleaner? All civilians, all going in and out of the police station. He'll know the moment we make the call. Then what?'

We all chewed on that thought silently. Dawn lightened the sky but it would be a while yet before the sun reached us down here in the valley. I opened the verandah doors and sucked sharp, joyless morning air into my lungs. *You will receive further instructions.* The wait seemed unbearable. Yet after Needham's description of the police hunt for the Doctor I knew that the tough times were just beginning. After finding Nikki Reid in her prison I knew we were the lucky ones. Whatever might happen to us in our lives, we'd forever be the lucky ones.

The ringing of the phone made me move so abruptly that I grazed my forehead on the door frame in an effort to get to it quickly. Tim slipped on his headphones, clicked on the reel-to-reel tape machine he had connected to the phone line, then gave me the sign to pick up. My hands were shaking as I lifted the receiver.

It was a noisy connection with lots of interference, perhaps from a mobile with a bad signal. The voice I heard was distorted, mechanical in its tinniness but very human in its gleeful, spiteful inflection: 'Good morning, Honeysett. It's time for bed.' The line went dead. I put the receiver down.

'What did he say?' Annis asked impatiently. Before I could answer Tim had rewound the tape and played it back to us. We listened, spellbound, to the four seconds of recording.

Tim pulled a face and shook his head. 'He's using some kind of device to distort his voice. You can buy them in novelty catalogues. Illegal to use on the phone but legal to buy. We won't get anything from that.'

'Yeah, all right, gadget boy, but what does he mean?' Annis said with emphasis on mean.

*Time for bed*. Nothing cryptic about it. I took the stairs two at a time and flung open the door to my bedroom. Tim and Annis hammered up the steps behind me. I had expected to find the duvet on the floor where Annis had thrown it. Instead the double bed was tidily made, the night-blue duvet straight, the matching pillows neatly in place. On the one nearest the window lay an envelope. On the other a set of raspberry-coloured women's underwear – bra and panties. Annis and I exchanged glances and she nodded heavily.

'Shit, he got in here,' said Tim, but his voice was unastonished. He checked my bathroom, shrugged. I ripped open the envelope and extracted two sheets of A4 paper. My voice shook when I read out the message.

'THE GAME HAS STARTED. THESE ARE THE RULES. YOU INVOLVE THE POLICE AND THE GIRL DIES. IT'S A GAME FOR TWO PLAYERS ONLY. WE PLAY FOR KEEPS. YOU FAIL, I KEEP THE GIRL. I GIVE YOU DIRECTIONS, YOU FOLLOW THEM. I GIVE YOU A CLUE, YOU SOLVE IT. AT THE END OF EACH SUCCESSFUL TASK PERFORMED THERE'S A REWARD: THE GIRL GETS FED.'

I turned to the second sheet and read on.

'FOR YOUR BAPTISM SEEK INSPIRATION FROM THE MOTHER OF GOD, HER HOLY WATERS NOW BREAK ONCE REMOVED.

REWARD: ONE SLICE OF BREAD.'

'He's starving her and we have to solve those clues and all she'll get is one slice of bread?! The insane . . . sadistic . . .' Words failed him. Tim kicked the door shut so hard it slammed open again. 'How long can you live on one slice of bread?'

'Quite a while, actually.' Annis's voice was steady and matter of fact. 'As long as you have water you can hold out several weeks, depending on your fitness.' She looked at both of us in turn and all three of us probably thought the same. Ali's fitness regime only started three weeks ago and even then she had managed to put away more wine every day than was good for her. 'We're going to play his game, we're going to solve the clues and keep her alive.'

'And we're going to get her back. We're going to nail this bastard,' I added grimly.

Tim looked up from where he'd been staring a hole into the floor. 'Too fuckin' right.'

'Okay, that's the Three Musketeers stuff out of the way. Now let's solve the clue.' Annis picked up the sheet and we followed her downstairs.


The moment we sat down round the kitchen table with a pot of coffee I felt better. The buzzing dread I had felt in my insides was quieted and submerged under the illusion of activity.

'Right.' I smoothed out the second sheet of the message. It was bog-standard printing paper, the typeface looked like Courier to me, printed off on a computer. There was nothing extraordinary about it yet it seemed to ooze evil intent. Having seen the work of the Doctor first hand it screamed madness at me. I shivered as I touched it again. 'What the hell have we got then? Let's take it line by line. *For your baptism*? He probably means our first clue. Seek *inspiration* seems obvious. *From the Mother of God*?'

'Mary, Virgin Mary,' Tim said impatiently.

'Okay, seems obvious too,' I agreed. '*Her holy waters now break once removed*? Should I get the bible out?'

'Didn't even know you had one.' Annis screwed up her face in concentration. 'I never heard mention of her waters breaking, so that's definitely something else, some kind of clue.'

'There isn't a Book of Mary or anything like that in the bible, is there?' asked Tim hopefully.

'No, there isn't.' My knowledge of the bible was pitifully scant but I was sure of that.

'There's hardly anything about Mary in the bible. Apart from the annunciation bit and the nativity stuff. She turns up again at the crucifixion and that's it, I think. And she doesn't make any big speeches.'

'So we're almost certainly talking metaphorical here.'

'In that case "her holy waters breaking" has nothing to do with the birth of Jesus. Not amniotic fluid, but holy

131

water. Holy water – Catholic Church . . .' I let my mind drift. 'Something like Lourdes? Healing, baptisms . . .'

Tim groaned and grabbed two handfuls of his woolly hair, elbows on the table. 'We're not going to get anywhere like this. It could mean a million things or a million places.'

'Wait a second, that's right.' Tim and Annis stared at me, expecting instant enlightenment. 'The question is . . . are we looking for a word, a sentence, some kind of answer to a riddle, or are we looking for a place? There's nothing in the letter that says "When you find the answer let me know." For a start we can't contact him. So is he going to ring every day to see if we've got it yet? I don't think so.'

'So . . .?' Annis invited me with round eyes and arched eyebrows to come across with any earth-shattering conclusions I might have.

'Well, it's a place. That's what Needham got when they were looking for Nikki Reid. It's a paper chase. He said the notes they got always referred to a location somewhere in Bath. But they were hoping to find Nikki at one of those locations. All they got were taunts and more notes. That's what we can expect, only the game has changed a little. There's the reward of food.'

'He just wants to draw out his sadistic game.' Annis chewed savagely on a fingernail, something I had never seen her do before. Tim absentmindedly took her hand from her mouth and covered it with his on the table. The gesture hit me like a collapsing ceiling: they looked like a couple.

'The longer the game the more of a chance we have of finding her,' I quickly continued. 'Let's get back to the message. We're looking for a place in Bath.'

'Mother of God – Mary – St Mary's. We're looking for a church, then.'

'And I know where it is,' said Tim brightly. 'Just around the corner from where I live, Julian Road. I'm sure it's St

132

Mary's. Catholic, too. What are we waiting for? Let's go.'
He was on his feet.

Annis squinted at the wall clock by the fridge. 'It's
twenty past seven in the morning. It won't be open yet,
will it?'

'We'll set off at eight,' I pronounced. 'Let's have some
breakfast.'

'No thanks, I'm going for some fresh air,' said Annis and
slipped out of the door into the herb garden.

'Tim?'

He looked out through the door at Annis's retreating
shape, set rigid against the weight of the day. 'Do we have
a chance at all, Chris? Getting Ali back. Alive.'

The Three Musketeers stuff had worn off quickly. Tim
seemed to have shrunk to half his normal size. Looking at
Annis's motionless silhouette I was glad I had kept my
descriptions of Nikki Reid in her prison to a minimum
since I was sure Annis's imagination was already furnish-
ing her with all the nightmare scenarios she could want.

Right now Ali would be frightened and feel alone, but
would only have missed breakfast. It had only just started.
Did Ali know? Would he have told her about his game of
starvation and death? Of course he would. Each time
I failed, which I was supposed to, he could supplement his
revenge by showing Ali how useless a detective I was.
'I don't know, Tim. He doesn't intend us to find her, I'm
sure of that. It's just a sick game. But for us it's the only
game in town and if we don't play then the consequences
for Ali could be bad. Very bad. On the other hand I read
somewhere that criminals who taunt the police or leave
messages have some hidden desire to be caught. But then
Needham and his team tried for months and couldn't find
Nikki Reid.'

'But you did.'

'That was an accident. I wasn't looking for her. I was
looking for Billy.'

Tim gave me a simple look. 'So keep looking for Billy. And yes, I'll have some breakfast.'

Annis drew the short straw and had to cram herself into the back of Tim's TT. Normally this would have elicited a torrent of good-natured abuse about blokes and their toys in general and pseudo sports cars in particular. Not now. Annis restricted her conversation to the task in hand; 'Turn left here,' or 'It's quicker that way.'

'There we are, I remembered it right, it is St Mary's.' Tim swung the Audi off the road on to the broad pavement next to a Co-op convenience store opposite the small, red-roofed church. We crossed Julian Road, took the few steps up and shouldered impatiently through the door.

The cleaner was in. A middle-aged woman with a grey, utilitarian crop of hair was pushing a wheezing vacuum cleaner around the altar. Dust motes danced in a slant of morning light. Not knowing what we were looking for, the three of us spread out, looking, searching for anything, a hint, a clue, a pointer but, most of all, another letter. The cleaner, or most likely a volunteer from the dwindling congregation, stopped pushing the Hoover about and watched us for a moment or two, then decided enough was enough. She switched the machine off, waited for the noise to ebb away, then tried a cough, followed by a sturdy 'Can I help you?'

'No thanks, we're all right,' I said in the friendliest tone I could muster, but it wasn't enough. The poor woman knew we didn't have a Catholic bone in our bodies simply from looking at us. For a while she tried to keep an eye on all three of us at the same time, then gave up with an annoyed little sound from her throat and disappeared through a side door. Tim started sniffing around the bases of the columns like a dog about to relieve himself, Annis walked systematically along every aisle, while I snooped around the little area dedicated to Mary. Next to a small window, surrounded by vases of simple white flowers, stood a brightly painted statue of the Virgin. Mary was wearing a gold crown, a blue mantle with gold lining over a wine-red dress and she was holding a baby Jesus. With his arms and fingers outspread the infant looked as though about to take his first unaided flight, tree-frog style, but I knew that the gesture was meant to symbolize his embrace of the world. Below Mary's feet a gold scroll proclaimed *Our Lady, Help of Christians*.

'Can I help you at all?' The voice did not come from above and wasn't female but it was enough to make me jump. It was a sonorous voice belonging to a pale bespectacled man, late middle-age, whose dress sense proclaimed him to be a priest and who had soft-shoed up without me noticing.

'Are you . . .'

'I'm Father Joseph. You and your friends . . . appear to be searching for something other than . . . spiritual support? Anything in particular? You have perhaps lost something during your last visit? Although I don't recall having seen any of your faces before . . .?' All this in a rich singsong, possibly the politest way of asking 'What the hell are you up to?' I'd ever come across. Tim and Annis had joined us now by the statue of the Virgin and our congregation might easily have appeared a little sinister to Father Joseph, but if it did he didn't show it.

'No, we didn't lose anything,' I lied. I hadn't really thought about how to explain to a stranger what we were engaged in without telling the whole story. 'We came here following a kind of clue in a kind of game, like a paper chase.' *Kind of*? What had happened to my vocabulary all of a sudden?

Father Joseph appeared to have noticed it too. 'Kind of game. Three grown-ups are playing *a kind of game* in my church. This is a place of worship, not a place for playing games,' he reminded us gently but firmly.

'It's rather more important than a game. I'm a private

135

investigator and we are following a clue we were furnished with.' I dug out the second sheet of the message from my jacket and handed it to him. 'Does this mean anything to you?'

He gave the paper one quick glance, shook his head and offered it back to me. 'Nothing at all. I don't see how these lines brought you here, apart from the fact that the Mother of God is, without a doubt, St Mary.'

'Are there any references in any religious texts to water breaking, in connection with Mary?' Annis asked him.

'Not to my knowledge, though I don't claim to be a mariologist.'

'Where would I find one of those if I needed one?' I mused.

He gave me an exasperated look. 'Rome, I believe, is still your best bet. Lovely this time of year.'

I didn't blame him. He probably had better things to do than talk to three hungover-looking characters playing games in his church, frightening the cleaner. 'Can you think of anything that might help us solve this clue?'

'You think it points to a church building?'

'A place in Bath, anyway.'

He sighed. 'Well . . . you could always try St Mary the Virgin in Bathwick. Though I suspect you'll find much the same there.'

'There's another St Mary's? I didn't know that,' Tim said apologetically.

I took the paper back and folded it into my pocket. 'Thanks, Father. Sorry to trouble you.'

He followed us outside into the morning sunshine. 'And when you finally solve your clue you will receive a slice of bread as a reward?'

I'd forgotten it said so at the bottom of the page I had shown him. 'Yeah, I'm the breadwinner in this family. Come on, children,' I said, more cheerfully than I felt.

It was my turn for the cramped back seat, from where

I issued new directions. 'Right, St Mary's, take two, in Bathwick. Know it?'

'Didn't know it was called that, never paid any attention. It's smack by the roundabout at the bottom of Bathwick Hill, isn't it, must have driven past it a million times on the way to Uni without taking it in. I'll drop you off.' He did a U-turn in Julian Road and accelerated back towards Lansdown Hill.

'Drop us off? And where are you going?'

'Work. I've got a job at Bath Uni, remember? That's the one that pays the bills.'

'You're going to work now? With Ali disappeared and us working against the clock you're going to work?' I got myself worked up.

Tim's eyes found mine in the rear-view mirror. 'Chris, I'd take leave if I could but I've already used up all the holiday I had during the last big thing we had on. And I can't pull another sicky. If I go AWOL one more time they'll fire me.'

'I don't believe this,' I said obstinately.

'I told you what I think about getting Ali back. Call the police, do it discreetly, then we'd have all the resources of Avon and Somerset's finest behind us.'

'We've had this conversation and we decided –'

'No, Chris, *you* decided. As per usual. *You decide* and we get to pull the chestnuts out of the fire when it all turns to shit.'

'So quite apart from mixing your metaphors you're now trying to blame me for –'

Annis hit the dashboard with both fists. 'Shut up, both of you!'

'Careful with that, there's a lot of electronics behind that,' Tim said foolishly.

'Yeah, and a fat lot of good they're going to do us in getting Ali back,' she said icily. 'Stop here.'

'Here?' We were rolling down New Bond Street towards the traffic lights by the post office.

'Here.'

Tim stopped and Annis got out. 'Got your mobiles? If you find anything at St Mary's let me know, Chris.'

'And where are you off to?' I asked, irritably.

She waved her arms around her head. 'Just . . . off,' she said helplessly. 'I'll stay in touch.' She slammed the door and disappeared around the corner. From behind, a car horn urged us to catch the green light, which Tim did. He screeched the Audi around the next few corners in grim silence, touched fifty down Great Pulteney Street, then calmed down again and delivered me gently to St Mary the Virgin.

'Call me as soon as there's any news, right?' he said with a joyless smile and rejoined the morning traffic at the roundabout, leaving me in the ambitiously sized and empty car park. This St Mary was superficially a more impressive affair than the church we had just left, a Gothic Revival job with a tall tower and a forest of pinnacles and crenellations. I counted five entrance doors. All of them were painted bright blue and were firmly shut. I walked on to the annexe on the west side. The door here was also closed. I rang the bell. I couldn't hear it ring and got no answer. Through the glass I could see a deserted office of some kind but it appeared God did not expect to do any business in Bathwick this morning. Despite the carefully tended patch of garden with its rose beds and sundial the place gave the impression of being dead, defunct, shut up for good like a bankrupt business waiting for the official receivers to decide what to do with it. Did churches go bankrupt? I had no idea and didn't care. Right now all I felt was irritated by the obstinately unyielding doors, the uncaring air of the deserted, traffic-swept building.

Now what? I hunted in my jacket pockets for my packet of Camels. I found I had one cigarette left. Judging by the feeling in my throat I had probably smoked most of the packet that morning. I lit it, had a little cough, and puffed away while I dodged cars across the geranium-chased roundabout and struck out along Pulteney Road. This was basically the A36 and smelled like it. All distances in Bath are negligible, the town is so compact, but when you're impatient and narked off and on foot when really you want to fly, a mile or so can drag on forever; under a railway bridge, past a funeral parlour and into Widcombe, where I replenished my stock of Camels at a newsagent's and bought some chocolate to keep me going.

The gate at St Mark's was open, the DS still where we had found it, parked against the mossy north side of the church. I could hear faint noises from the other side of the door marked *Community Centre* and pushed in. Across the uninspiring and, despite the time of day, neon-lit hall another door stood open. The clanking of crockery came from there. In a square, spartan kitchen a woman was arranging cups and saucers on a couple of trays. On the stove an enormous brown enamelled kettle sang quietly on a low heat. I knocked on the door frame.

The woman whirled around. 'Oof, you gave me a start. Didn't expect anyone so early, half an hour yet.' Then she frowned, put down the bag of sugar she'd been opening and scrutinized me with lively grey eyes. She wore no make-up. Her hair was pulled back from her narrow face and severely skewered at the back. Together with the grey skirt, white top and grey cardigan the ensemble conspired to make her look ten years older than the barely forty I gave her. 'You're not here for Intermediate Pilates, are you?'

'I've no idea who they are so I'd have to say no.'

'It's a form of deep muscle exercise. Improves your postural strength, flexibility and co-ordination,' she rattled off.

Standing quite still and upright on the other side of the kitchen table she certainly demonstrated postural strength. 'Do you teach it?' I asked.

'Oh no. I just organize the classes at St Mark's. We have

a Pilates Institute qualified instructor to lead the session. So . . . why are you here?'

'You do run a slimming club here, is that right?'

'We do. Every Tuesday evening. Last night, in fact. I do take part in that.'

'You run it?'

'I organize it. It's not a class, as the name says, it's a club. Look, what's your interest and who are you? I feel I'm being interrogated here but I've never seen anyone look less like police than you do.'

I decided to take that as a compliment. 'Oh, I'm Chris. Chris Honeysett,' I said, as though that explained everything.

'I'm Linda Ward. Pleased to meet you. I think.'

'I'm a friend of Ali's. Alison Flood? She comes to the slimming club, doesn't she?'

'Does she?'

I described her. 'She certainly went last night.'

'She only came the once. Last week. She didn't come last night.'

'She wasn't at the club?'

'Not last night.'

'Are you sure?'

'Would you mind telling me what this is all about? And, yes, I'm sure. Attendance last night was bad, there were only five of us and Ali wasn't one of them. Why are you asking me these questions?' She gripped the bag of sugar harder.

'Oh, it's just that I lost contact with her and thought you might have an address for her,' I said casually.

Linda Ward smiled a cold, suspicious smile. 'You must have lost contact very recently if you know she joined the slimming club last week. Even if I had her address I'm not sure I'd give it to you. Something about your story doesn't seem quite right, Mr . . .'

'Honeysett,' I resupplied. She was right on all counts, of course.

140

'I think I would like you to go now, Mr Honeysett,' she said firmly.

'Sure,' I agreed. 'Goodbye, Miss Ward.' I turned and walked across the drab hall to the exit. She followed a few paces behind, to make sure I left, followed me all the way outside. I unlocked the DS.

'Oh, so it was you who left his car here overnight. My husband said we should have it towed away but I said, no, it's bound to be one of the slimmers.' She put both fists on her hips in a caricature of crossness. 'So you were here last night. Curiouser and curiouser. I think there's something very fishy about all this,' she said shrewdly. 'Keith!' She called the name so suddenly and loudly over her shoulder that it made me jump, which Linda, now mentally amended to *Mrs* Ward, probably took as a sign of guilt. She certainly never took her eyes off me until there was a rustling in the tall shrubs near the entrance and first a garden fork and then the gardener attached to it emerged from the foliage.

My heart sank when I recognized the broad face and the matching shoulders. His hair was tied back into a ponytail today but his nose and mouth were as sharp as before. 'Ah, Mr Honeysett. Now why am I not surprised to see you here? Do you have a secret passion for churches? Or are you still looking for Billy the tramp?'

Keith Ward seemed to have a thing about churches too. If he was caretaker of St John the Baptist in Bathwick then what was he doing here? Moonlighting?

'You know him, Keith?' Linda Ward pointed an accusing finger at me.

'Yes, it's Mr Honeysett. He's a private detective. Pops up everywhere. Detecting things.'

'It's beginning to look just as spooky from my end, I assure you.' I smiled at both of them, though I had taken a quick and easy dislike to Keith. 'Are you the caretaker here too?'

'More or less,' he said, leaning stiffly on his fork now.

'My wife Linda, who I presume you have met, organizes classes and courses here. I'm just employed to look after the bit of ground they have here, but naturally if anything else needs doing and I'm around . . .' He shrugged. 'So that's me explained. What's your interest in St Mark's?'

'Oh, I was just looking for a friend. Someone I thought had joined a class here. A club, I should say,' I amended, hearing Linda's intake of breath. Then, despite my irrational dislike of the man, I pulled out the Doctor's message. 'But quite apart from that, you might be able to help me with this, since both of you spend so much time in churches. I must admit it's taxing my unecclesiological mind a bit.' This time I folded it so that the part promising the reward of a slice of bread didn't show and held it out to Keith and Linda, who had moved into easy husband-and-wife-team proximity.

'Some sort of riddle.' Linda showed an amused interest.

'I think it refers to a place in Bath. A church, perhaps. But I don't really know. I've just come from St Mary the Virgin in Bathwick.'

'No luck, eh?' Keith tilted his head at the paper. 'I don't really go in for crosswords and puzzles. Too obscure for me.'

'This has to do with a case you're working on?' Linda asked. 'Maybe what you want is a Catholic church, like St John's, by the police station. They have a Lady Chapel. Ask there, perhaps?'

I thanked them, climbed into the DS and reversed out of the churchyard before they thought of asking questions about how the car came to be there in the first place. I had just decided to take Linda Ward's advice and drive across to St John's when my mobile chimed Beethoven at me.

When I first got the thing I thought it a fabulous idea to have some classical music as a ring tone. But now, just two months later, I had gone off Beethoven in general and his

142

Fifth in particular. I stopped at the end of St Mark's Road and answered it.

It was Eva Keen, my favourite reporter. 'Now before you scream at me and I know you want to, say you'll have lunch with me, on me of course, and then you can do all your shouting in person, much more satisfying, at the George, I'm already here, it's a great day for it, okay?' She didn't wait for an answer and hung up before I could draw enough breath to bellow down the line that it was extremely brave of her to call me after naming me in the paper and that if she thought I was going to lunch with her she was right, I would. I was starving.

# Chapter Eleven

I gunned the engine and drove to Bathampton. I hadn't thought about the George Inn for a long time. It's definitely a summer place, sitting right by the towpath along the Kennet and Avon canal, with a stone bridge and a little church opposite to set it off picturesquely. It's a Sunday morning, why-don't-we-walk-along-the-towpath-to-the-George kind of place. And Eva was right, it was a great day for it, if by that you meant fluffy white clouds, a warm breeze and the promise of summer just around the corner.

Eva was sitting by herself at a wooden table in front of the pub. As soon as she spotted me scowling up the road she grabbed her shoulder bag and started rattling away, 'You sit down I'll get us some beers unless you want something else and I'll get the menus be right back.' She disappeared inside with an angelic smile which I struggled not to return. I've got a real problem holding on to grudges. They seem to run through my fingers like silver sand, like money. The question was: would Ali still be free if my identity had not been revealed in the paper? Would the Doctor have found out anyway? If he did have an ear inside Avon and Somerset Constabulary then the answer had to be *yes*. Whatever the answer, I couldn't blame Eva for what had happened but I didn't need my privacy compromised any further. Which meant that from now on I would treat her less as a friend and more as a journalist who could be trusted to always put the story first.

She reappeared with a couple of pints and the menus. 'All right, if I have to get bollocked get it over with but I tell you now that I had no choice, it was all or nothing, I had a big palaver with the editor about naming names but he was adamant and let's face it I'm broke and really, really needed the money so I sold you down the river. Sorry, Chris. I'm an unprincipled bitch and a rotten friend.'

'Hey, that's my line,' I protested. 'And why are you so broke you need to sell your friend's privacy to the local rag?'

'Going freelance wasn't the cleverest idea I ever had. I didn't do the maths – mortgage, car, bills . . .'

'Beer, food,' I completed, flipping open the menu.

A goat's cheese and tomato tart (me) and a beef and ale pie (Eva) later the two of us sat with more pints on the bit of grass by the canal, arguing. As soon as she had sensed that she'd got away with her little betrayal without being ritually dismembered she had gone on a new offensive. Her latest idea was a detailed profile of me, in several instalments. The thought made my hair stand on end: 'Not bloody likely!'

'But think of the business you'd pick up. It'd be done really well, over a number of weeks . . . painter and private eye at work . . . and people would get to see a side of Bath that's normally hidden, it'd be really good.'

My idea of what would be really good had changed just lately. The temptation to tell Eva about Ali's kidnap was burning on my tongue, and not just because it would shut her up and give her a massive guilt trip which would deliver her into my debt forever. With her contacts and her knowledge of Bath she would be a useful ally in the search for Ali and in trying to solve the clues the Doctor had given us. I searched her eyes, which were all excitement and urgency for her latest idea, wondering. But the Doctor's message remained in my pocket. I didn't trust her enough, could not trust her with Ali's life.

'Look, you can ghost-write my memoirs for me when I decide to pack it in but while I'm still working as a private eye – no way. End of story. Thanks for lunch.'

'Ooooh.' She let herself flop back into the grass with a groan. 'Ah well, I'll just have to think of something else. Quickly. Either that or let out the flat and move back in with Jerry.'

'And that would be such a bad idea?'

'I don't know how long it would last.' A bleeping noise in her bag made her sit up. She pulled out a pocket PC, glanced at it. 'I'd better go, I have an appointment.' She got up, hoisted her bag over her shoulder and slid her sunglasses on. 'See? Perfect illustration, this. Jerry says I have a more intimate relationship with my computer than with him. Perhaps he's right. But then my iPAQ never tells me that I've let it down or don't spend enough quality time at home. See you around, Honeypot.'

As soon as she'd rushed off it was my turn to flop back on to the grass and let out a long groan. This was complete madness. A kidnapping, for pity's sake, a goddamn abduction, and I wasn't going to tell the police? If a prospective client had come to me and given me this scenario would I have taken it on? Not bloody likely.

I sat up and lit another cigarette and sucked up great gulps of lager and scared myself witless. Tim was right. What if I failed, what if between the three of us we didn't have the resources, the tenacity, the knowledge, the intelligence to bring Ali back? I had to risk it. I had to tell Needham. Was this really what my fretting was about, though? Would going to the police merely mean I would not have to shoulder the guilt alone if Ali died? What, precisely, was I doing, sitting here? How was this cosy, beer-fuelled weighing up of moral niceties going to help Alison?

Ludwig van again. I answered my mobile with a sigh of low expectations but sat bolt upright as soon as I heard the voice: tinny, menacing, harsh, robotic.

'What do you think you are doing? You don't have time to lie in the sun, Mr Honeysett. You should be far too busy saving your girl.'

I was on my feet now, looking around me. He could see me. He knew where I was, what I was doing. *He was here.* There were two couples and a group of three cyclists sitting on the lawn. Another cyclist had just passed right to left on the towpath.

I panicked and talked drivel into the phone. 'Look, whoever you are . . . let Ali go. Please. She's done nothing to harm you. It's me you really want, and I can . . .'

The metallic staccato of his laugh stopped me. There was movement behind a window on the nearest houseboat. I walked towards it.

'No shit, Honeysett. It is you I really want. And it is you I'll get. Only first we'll have a little playtime. But don't worry, I'll give you every chance to die nobly while trying to save her.'

Through the window I could see a young woman washing up in a minute sink. She looked up at me, then drew flimsy net curtains across, shutting me out.

'I hope you're not thinking about going to the police again? Because that would have disastrous consequences, I assure you. I know who you talk to. I'm so close I can almost hear you think. Best of all, I know where you'll go next.'

As I drew breath to shout my answer the phone went dead. I felt like throwing it into the canal. On the opposite side of the sluggish waterway a flat-capped man was pushing an old-fashioned lawnmower across a narrow strip of grass bordered with garden gnomes. An angler carrying his gear upstream trudged by. A waitress from the George was collecting empty plates and glasses from the seating area below. The bastard was here somewhere but I wasn't going to give him the satisfaction of seeing me run around like a panicked chicken. Without moving from the spot I scrutinized every person, scanned every

147

possible hiding place – there were too many. The row of chocolate-box cottages along the towpath, the blind windows in the houses opposite, the church with its tower and graveyard across the lane; he could be anywhere. Or perhaps he had long left and had made the phone call from a safe distance.

Wherever he was now, somehow he had managed to follow me here, watch me eat, drink, talk to Eva. Warm, friendly sunshine had suddenly taken on the cold, menacing, exposing glare of the searchlight. Rather self-importantly I had thought I was going to hunt down a killer. It hadn't occurred to me that I might become the hunted. *I'll give you every chance to die nobly while trying to save her* . . Worst of all, anyone he might see me with could wind up on his hit list.

As I drove towards the private bridge over the Avon I dug around in the glove box for some loose change to pay the toll with. I couldn't find any. What I did find was a year's worth of parking tickets, sweet wrappers and fistfuls of petrol receipts I should have filed somewhere for my tax return. It seemed symptomatic somehow. I was unprepared. Disorganized. My methods were haphazard. I even found Nikki Reid by accident, had blundered into the Doctor's lair and come to within the click of a padlock of becoming a victim myself.

I had to hand over a ten pound note and wait while the bloke who collected the tolls got change from inside his booth. The Doctor liked to play games. The game had only just started. If the Doctor killed me then this game was over. I had probably little to fear from him as long as he didn't lose interest in making a fool of me. Or as long as Ali was alive.

I poured the change impatiently into my jacket pocket and drove off fast. Every vehicle was suspicious now, every glimpse into the rear-view mirrors became a search for a shadowing car, every van with tinted windows was driven by the Doctor. Of course the greatest menace on

148

the road was probably myself; I didn't devote more than two brain cells to driving the car, the rest were busy with paranoia.

I double parked at the end of the cul-de-sac in front of St John the Divine Roman Catholic church. I'd always been impressed by the tall, elegant spire of this St John's; it seemed to dwarf the rest of the building, which wasn't exactly puny either. But I'd never been inside. The door was open.

Through the ancient wooden doors I stepped into an empty church. It didn't seem credible. The town was heaving with people, the pavements thronged with tourists, the streets were choked with cars and coaches, diesel-belching tour buses and taxis, crisscrossed by bicycles and prattling scooters. And here was silence. Of all the hundred thousand people out there not one had thought of coming in here, if only to admire the glow of the circular stained glass windows, the sheen on the pink marble columns, the proportions of the place; not one felt the need of quiet or contemplation or rest or refuge. There was something astonishing about the mere existence of a place like this in the very heart of the city.

Here on the east side was the Lady Chapel Linda Ward had mentioned. By the half-open door in the gilt iron screen that separated the chapel from the rest of the church stood an iron votive stand, with space for close to a hundred offerings. There was a tray of candles and a money box. One small candle had been lit very recently; it had hardly burned down at all. The aroma of incense hung faintly in the cool air, like a fragile memory. On a sudden, unexamined impulse I took a candle and lit it on the flame of the other one, planted it next to it. A small noise echoing from the back of the church made me hastily plunge my hand in my jacket pocket and produce some change which I funnelled uncounted into the money box. When I turned I caught a glimpse of a man dressed in black disappearing into the shadowy back of the church. I'd spotted the flash of a white collar and set off in pursuit. Instead of running – I was sure one didn't run in church – I followed in a ridiculous kind of speed-walk and not wanting to call out I tried a very noisy stage whisper: 'One moment please . . . Father?' I just couldn't get used to calling people that. I had called my own father, who disliked being called 'Dad', by that sober appellation, and fifteen years after his suicide the word tasted bitter and strange.

I had been right. The black-dressed man turned out to be a priest, a Father Simon. He took in my appearance with quick, wide-awake eyes behind ultra-modern, rimless specs and responded to my request for advice with an invitation to sit down. 'Take a pew.'

'Cheers, Padre.' I think Father Simon also had no trouble identifying me as a non-Catholic.

I briefly explained that the clues pointed to a place in Bath, unfolded the by now fairly crumpled sheet of paper and handed it to him, leaving the clincher at the bottom visible. He creased his high forehead while reading through it, then narrowed his blueberry eyes at me. 'Some kind of game?'

I tried to size up the priest who easily held my gaze. The hair round his temples was greying though he had to be a good ten years younger than me. Most of the lines on his face looked like laughter lines to me, though what a priest with an empty church had to laugh about I couldn't guess. What the hell, I thought, if you can't trust a priest.

I nodded. 'A deadly game. Is this,' I fanned the air between us with one hand, 'confidential?'

'As confidential as you like.'

It was all the invitation I needed. I started rattling off the story but he stopped me, gently patting my arm. 'We'll find somewhere more private.'

A few minutes later I was sitting in a comfortable leather armchair in a comfortable study, sipping a generous measure of Jameson's, talking talking talking. If anyone had told me that confession was like this I'd have joined ages ago. And it was a kind of confession; I confessed my feelings of guilt at the revulsion I had felt when I was confronted with Nikki Reid; my guilt at having brought Alison into this deadly game; my doubts at my ability to save her; my suspicion that it might be pure arrogance that made me want to play the game and free her without the involvement of the police. Father Simon was horrified at this more than anything else I told him.

'But you must. You must go to the police. They will help you. That's what they're there for, surely.' He gestured helplessly at the leaded window. You could see the brutal bulk of Manvers Street station from here. The temptation to unburden myself to Superintendent Needham, to abdicate responsibility, was strong enough to expel me from my chair and draw me to the window. But the Doctor's phone call at the George had scared me more than anything so far: he knew where I went. He knew who I talked to. I shook my head. He pulled a pained grimace. Father Simon, for one, did not believe I could bring Ali back.

'I will pray for you,' he said gravely. 'All of you.'

'Can't hurt, I'm sure.' I was desperate to lighten the tone because I knew I had to leave in a moment and I really didn't want to go out there.

'No, it can't. I wholeheartedly recommend it. Don't look at me like that. I know you said you don't believe but I did see you light a candle earlier. There's perhaps a part of you that wants to believe?'

I don't know what pastoral duties Father Simon neglected while I ranted in his study but coffee had replaced the Jameson's and the sun was in the west when we finally got back to the clues and the crumpled message on the low table between our chairs. He read aloud: *'For your baptism seek inspiration from the Mother of God, her holy waters now break once removed.'* He shook his head. 'The last christening we had was last week. Our font is locked when it isn't in use but I suppose someone might manage to slip a written message past the lid.'

151

'Would you mind if we had a look at it? Just to set my mind at rest?'

'Not at all.' He armed himself with a key tied to a lump of wood from a drawer in his desk. Three minutes later I was standing in the back of the church, staring down into the beautifully carved, hexagonal stone font. It was empty and devoid of messages except perhaps the unwritten one that I was looking in the wrong place. Under different circumstances I might have quizzed my host on the significance of the creatures and letters carved into the side of the thing but at that moment I hardly noticed them.

'I can't think of anything else, short of searching every square inch of the church,' I concluded flatly.

'I have to say, the more I consider the message the more I'm convinced it has nothing to do with St John's. I think your first instinct was right, you should go back and take a look at all the St Mary's in Bath. And if you think the word "baptism" in the riddle is a reference to a font then I'd start with St Mary the Virgin in Charlcombe –'

'*Another* St Mary's?'

'I'm afraid so. And an ancient one. Bits of it are eleventh-century. It's their font I was thinking of, though. It's very old, definitely Norman. Worth seeing in itself, I should think. Yes, I'd go there first.'


I'd collected a parking fine, which was predictable, but hadn't been towed away, which was surprising. I hadn't planned on spending this long in St John's and was profoundly relieved at the sight of the old Citroën.

St Mary's at Charlcombe . . . Somewhere among the crud on the back seat had to be an *A–Z* of Bath. I was preparing to dive in when my mobile chimed.

'You anywhere near the Bell?' Annis's voice had an uncertain tilt. 'I need a lift. Possibly a fireman's lift.'

'Be there in five,' I promised rashly. I could probably have legged it to the Bell in five minutes but driving there was another matter, especially at this time of day. 'Rush hour' seemed to start around four nowadays and lasted into early evening. Even with a couple of illegal turns it took longer than five minutes to snake to Walcot Street and find a place to abandon the DS where it wouldn't attract the attentions of a tow truck.

I had no problem finding Annis in the Bell, though. She was slumped on a bar stool not six feet from the entrance. According to the barman that was as far as she had made it when she got in and that's where she had stayed and slurped vodka until he refused to serve her any more of the stuff.

'Taxi for Annis Jordan.'

She needed surprisingly little support for someone that cross-eyed with alcohol, but she was not a happy drunk. She fell heavily into the passenger seat of the DS and shrank deep into her suede jacket. 'She's dead, isn't she? As good as, I mean. We'll never see her again, will we. *Will we*, Chris?'

I leant over to fix the old-fashioned seat belt for her. There was nothing left of our early-morning bravado and determination. 'I don't know. We're going to try very hard, though.'

'What's the matter with you?' she gurgled. 'You're blurred.' A couple of minutes later she started to gently snore while I insinuated the DS back into the traffic on Walcot Street. I had no intention of joining the five-mile-an-hour processional clutch-burning on the London Road. I zipped up Margaret's Hill alongside Hedgemead Park, then Gay's Hill into Camden (I don't know why I'm telling you this, you'll all be doing it now) and from there dropped down through Larkhall. Here I took to a narrow lane which eventually spat me out on to London Road West, a world away from the multitudes inching towards the Batheaston bypass. Two more minutes and I had turned off into the sanity of the valley and set course for home.

# Chapter Twelve

The house lay in quiet shadow when I rolled into the yard and switched off the engine. The DS settled gracefully on its sighing suspension. Annis's snoring had stopped but if anything she was even more soundly asleep now. I gently brushed the red curls off her face. I was glad she'd found the oblivion she had sought in the vodka bottle all day. Her jacket gaped open and a snow white sliver of paper shone from the top of an inside pocket. I pulled it out gingerly and unfolded it. In Annis's large, spiky writing it said:

*Another Mary! St Mary the Virgin in Charlcombe Lane. Norman Font!!*

I turned the paper over. It was a library request slip. So Annis had managed to get exactly as far as I had but had also found time to drown all her pain and worries in vodka.

I managed to extricate her from the car and carry her inside and up to her room without banging her head too much against the furniture. She grimbled and grumbled but didn't bother to open her eyes until I dropped her on her unmade bed. She started fumbling inside her jacket.

'You looking for this?' I held up the paper.

She nodded. 'Another Mary. You going?'

'On my way now,' I assured her. I leant down to kiss her forehead but she closed her eyes and turned away. It was time to go.

Dusk was settling in the valley when I stepped back into the yard. I locked the front door, something we don't do very often at Mill House. I walked along the side through the herb garden and checked the kitchen door, continued round the next corner, tried the verandah door. I had checked them from the inside, now I was rechecking them from the outside. I turned my back on the black silhouette of the studio at the top of the meadow. It appeared miles away and irrelevant now.

I hadn't found a St Mary's on the map but there was a Charlcombe Valley on the edge of Bath and it had the little black mark of the cross, denoting a church, nearby.

It was completely dark when I picked up the steep hill of Charlcombe Lane on the other side of Larkhall. It soon disappeared into an unlit tunnel of foliage as it narrowed, twisted and rose even further. On my map this bit of countryside was littered with names like Woolley, Batstone and Dead Mill, all of which suited my mood. My headlights picked out a road sign, a toad in a red triangle: beware of toads crossing. The next sign would probably have a vampire bat on it. At times the road became ridiculously narrow but I appeared to be the only one using this dark funnel tonight.

When it came I nearly missed it. The headlights swept so quickly across the wooden sign by the side of the lane that I had to reverse to illuminate it again: *The Church of St Mary the Virgin, Charlcombe*. From here a steep track doubled back up the hillside into inky darkness. I squeezed the DS into it and drove up slowly. Trees silhouetted darkly to my right and as I drew up on to a piece of almost level ground I could see the church some way ahead.

I stopped. As soon as I cut the engine and the headlights went out the little church became no more than a dark smudge in the starlight. I hadn't for one moment forgotten the Doctor's casual offer: *I'll give you every chance to die nobly while trying to save her.* No thank you: under the dashboard my hand found the Webley in its magnetic holder and unclamped it. I stuffed its reassuring weight into the left-hand pocket of my jacket and got out of the car. Instinctively I tried to make as little noise as possible. However quiet the DS's engine, I had almost certainly advertised my arrival, yet a little subtlety might give me advance warning if anyone was lurking out here. This was an idiotic time to try and look around a church but if necessary I was going to try my picklocks on the door.

I had brought my torch but hadn't switched it on yet, which was just as well: a tiny glimmer of light winked behind a narrow window and immediately disappeared again. A few breathless seconds later, it reappeared, dancing feeble and ghostly through the interior of the church. Completely on cue an owl hooted nearby. I tiptoed closer to the blind entrance porch. My eyes were getting used to the dark now and I could just make out that the heavy old door was ajar. I laid a hand against the smooth wooden surface: if it creaked spookily when I pushed it open it would serve me right for ghosting about churches after dark. It swung open silently on well-oiled hinges. I stepped inside the cool, musky fragrance of the interior. To my right a tall figure whirled about in an arc of candle-light and promptly disappeared in complete darkness, letting out a startled cry. Training my torch in that direction I picked out a man in his sixties clutching his chest in mock horror.

'Blimey, you gave me a fright but whoever you are, as long as you have a torch that works you're welcome. Unless you're a thief of course, in which case I'm going to clout you with a spanner, have no fear.'

'Ne'er cast a clout till may is out.' I walked over to the spirited little guy who stood dressed in grey trousers, white shirt and tight waistcoat among a mess of tools by an odd-looking little organ that was shoehorned into an alcove on the left wall. He still held the stump of a candle which had gone out when he turned round too quickly. 'Go easy with the spanner, I'm friendly. Just visiting,' I reassured him. 'What are you doing here in the dark?'

156

'I was trying to effect some repairs to this fine Harrison and Harrison organ when somehow the lights went. The fuse box is probably in the vestry, only I don't have a key to that. I found myself a candle but I'm just packing up my tools now, can't do a thing here by candlelight. Do you mind shining your torch for a bit while I collect my stuff?'

I didn't; it gave me time to give the man the once-over. He looked in his mid-sixties. Only a thin crown of silver hair remained on his liver-spotted head. Everything about him looked thin, from his bony nose to his skeletal hands. But he moved with a vigour that gave the lie to his fragile looks. 'Bit optimistic, weren't you?' he said while he dropped his tools into an old Gladstone bag. It was monogrammed A.B. 'Coming up here at this time of day to visit the church?' he added with just a hint of suspicion.

'I know. But I was visiting someone in the area and they mentioned the church so I took a chance. They mentioned a Norman font. I wanted to take a look at it.'

'You walked past it when you came in. I'm done. Let's go. You can look at it on the way out.' He gave me a friendly but irresistible push up the aisle towards the exit. 'There it is.'

I picked out the font in the concentric rings of light from my torch: a goblet-shaped lump of stone with a carving of leaves around the base. It stood on a stone plinth with an unadorned astragal at the bottom. The wooden lid was heavy but unlocked. I lifted it and shone my torch inside: it was empty.

'Well, that's it, but you'd better come back in the morning.'

'I'd quite like to have a little look around . . .' I started, knowing it sounded unreasonable and suspicious.

'In the dark? With a torch? No, no.' He pushed me out through the door and locked it noisily. 'I'm going now and I think you should do the same, mister. Come back tomorrow if you want to see the inside of the church. You're free

157

to wander around the garden and visit the holy spring in the dark, of course, if you have a mind to.'

'Holy spring?'

'You haven't heard about it? Most people come to visit the spring, you know. Even after they moved it, the cheeky buggers.' The old guy had lightened up now that the church was safely locked.

'Moved it?' *Her holy waters now break once removed.*

'Yup. Oh go on, I'll show you, I can get back to the lane from there.' He led through a gate in a wrought-iron fence that separated the path from a dark and steeply sloping area planted with trees. 'Couple of fine old quince trees here. Apple, too, of course.' He waved an arm at indistinguishable shapes in the dark. 'Keep left. Yes, the spring. For thousands of years it sprang over there.' He pointed into the dark beyond some fir trees. 'That's the rectory garden. No one paid that much attention to it until a few years back some daft bishop declared the thing "holy". But later, when the church wanted to flog off the rectory they had a problem, didn't they? Can't flog a "holy" spring, can you now? And the new owners wouldn't want the faithful having to traipse past their barbecue to drink from it. It gave them quite a headache for a while but with a goodly amount of cement and a bit of fancy pipe work the spring soon sprang somewhere more convenient, beyond the boundaries of the rectory garden. Still holy, mind. Here we are.'

There had been some attempt to make the thing look natural but whoever had done it had probably had more expertise in fish-pond than holy-spring construction. At one end of the little pool water trickled from below a tombstone-shaped stone carving.

'Do you mind shining your torch in this direction a minute? There's a gate into the lane there. Once I'm in the lane I'll be all right, I know it well enough.'

He refastened the latch behind him and disappeared

into the dark without another word. I turned back towards the soft splashing of the spring.

But what was I supposed to look for? The spring was surrounded by evergreen foliage and grasses. The carved relief looked to be a modern thing made to look old, or perhaps a copy of an ancient sculpture. From what I knew of Christian imagery it probably depicted the baptism of Christ. There were waves of water and the statutory dove, representing the holy spirit, as well as two figures that might be Jesus and John the Baptist. This had to be the right place: St Mary; the baptism; the holy waters 'removed'. But I could see no other signs, no tokens or omens. The whole pool was no more than eight feet long. I knelt down where the water spouted forth and took a long draught from my cupped hand. It tasted clean and was ice cold. As I shook the drops off my left hand and got ready to rise a little movement nudged my peripheral vision. I swung the torch to my left but illuminated nothing but grasses, trees and shrubs. The quiet splashing of the spring now sounded strident as I strained to hear any noise beyond it. I switched off the torch and took a few quick steps sideways into the dark, then stood still and listened: beyond the trickling of the spring nothing but the rustling and breathing and hollowness of the night. I returned to the little pool, walked around it slowly, examined the ground. It was easy to miss something in the dark, by torchlight. Only when I had completed the full circle did I see it.

A boat. A little folded-paper boat, floating lopsidedly in the slow current that rippled across the dark surface. Its whiteness glared at me in the torchlight. It couldn't have been there a minute ago. Surely I'd have noticed it. I snatched it from the water, afraid it might disappear down a drain hole somewhere. Even though I could see it was folded from the same kind of paper and had typed words running across it nothing was going to make me read it here by the side of the pool. Because if I was right, then the Doctor had dropped the evil little thing on to the water while I was here, stumbling about in the dark.

I followed the old guy's example and exited the garden through the gate. A few steps brought me down into the lane. It would be easier to get back to the car this way, I told myself, than to slither up the dewy grass through the garden. I would read the note in the car, I decided. With the paper boat gripped tightly in my fist I fell into a trot, trying to get there quickly. That's probably why I didn't hear it until it was nearly too late. As I reached a particularly narrow part of the lane an engine roared and a car leapt towards me; dark, large, no headlights. Something, probably its wing mirror, clipped my elbow as I pressed myself flat against the steep, unyielding bank. The car roared off into the night. I stumbled back on to the track, rubbing my painful elbow, and could just glimpse its tail lights coming on before it disappeared. I had only taken a few shaky steps towards the turnoff to St Mary's when my mobile rang.

'You really ought to be more careful on dark country lanes, Mr Honeysett. I nearly had you there.'

'You stupid bastard!' I shouted back. 'D'you want to play games or d'you want to kill me? Make up your sodding mind!'

'Oh, but I'm not at all sure. Both, really. Preferably we'll have a game first and I'll kill you later, when you've lost the game. But then I hate you so much I might not be able to restrain myself. You'll just have to watch out, won't you?'

'You're a sick bastard. When I –'

'Is that so? Now shut up and listen. That wasn't a bad performance, in fact you found that far too quickly. Perhaps the next clue will exercise you more strenuously.'

'Will Alison get fed? You will keep your promise?'

'Trust me.'

Despite the metallic distortion of the voice I imagined I could hear the stupid smile that accompanied his last words. The line went dead in my ear. If only there was some way of tracing the calls but anyone clever enough to pull this stunt would use a stolen mobile, probably more than one.

The little paper boat with its message was burning in my hand but I didn't feel like staying in the lane any longer than was necessary. Only when I was back in the imaginary safety of the car and had lit a soothing cigarette did I fumble the paper open and read the message. And hoped Father Simon had started praying.

# Chapter Thirteen

'Naah, no hope, mate. I've always been crap at crosswords. And this is worse.' Tim pointed an accusing bit of Thai fishcake at the Doctor's message and dribbled sweet chili sauce all over the sheet. He then looked at the fishcake on his fork like he was seeing it for the first time, popped it into his mouth and kept on talking. 'I mean, with a cross-word you know how many letters and all that and you might already have one or two. But this could refer to anything. What's Annis make of it?'

'Nothing. She hasn't seen it. Still sleeping off the hang-over from hell.' Which was one of the reasons why I'd asked Tim to meet me at the Bathtub Bistro in his lunch hour. I had to show it to someone. The new message had kept me sitting and brooding in my attic office until the small hours. Several angry bottles of beer had refused to help make sense of it. When I woke up in my chair halfway through the morning with a crick in my neck and a fuzzy outlook on life it had taken several seconds to remember why I was there. Then I had grabbed the mes-sage off my desk and stared at it again and it still didn't make sense:

THE ART OF SERIAL KILLING IS DEAD AND BURIED. BY GEORGE, IT'S ALL A BIT SICK!

'Is it a message in a message sort of thing? Have you tried making a sentence just from the first letters or something?'

'I tried that for hours last night. There are all sorts of words you can make from the first letters. Disk, Abba, kiss, said, boast and so on but nothing that makes sense and certainly no sentence, unless you're fluent in baby talk. I'm sure it's not that.'

'But the language is odd. Who says "by George" these days?' Tim pointed out.

'I agree. Even though . . .' I turned the crumpled piece of paper over and exposed the second, painful part of the message.

REWARD: 1 OZ CORNFLAKES.

'He says "one ounce". Do you use grams or ounces, Tim?'

'Both.' He shrugged off my round-eyed look. 'What? Not at the same time of course. When I go shopping I do kilos and grams because the shops do but when I'm at home I think in pounds and ounces. I thought everyone did that, unless they were born yesterday.'

'I always think in pounds and ounces but then I also think in shillings. It doesn't prove anything either way. So we can assume he's not a teenager. Not that I ever thought he was.'

'Okay, let's look at it again: *The art of serial killing.* He thinks of himself as an artist. Perhaps the bastard *is* an artist. Maybe it's even someone you know?'

'I know lots of bastard artists,' I said with conviction. 'He might think of himself as an artist but I don't believe that's what he means here. Usually when people say "the art of this or that is dead" it's a complaint, they're bemoaning the demise of something. As in: "The art of conversation is dead." You wouldn't say "The art of conversation is dead and buried," though. This sentence is too contrived not to be specifically about the next location. And *by George* could very easily be the clue to the location. Another church. Or the George Inn, even. I was there yesterday, meeting Eva. So . . .'

'So I'm stumped.' Tim looked at his empty plate, then at mine. 'Aren't you eating that?'

'Don't even think about it. I'm just slow.' I turned my attention to the grilled sardines on my plate. With Alison getting hungrier by the minute it seemed almost obscene to be enjoying food, but no one would benefit if we starved ourselves. I was almost ashamed when I realized that it wasn't affecting my appetite as long as I managed not to imagine Ali's predicament too closely: Ali, dressed in nothing but a flower-patterned Marks and Spencer's nightie, in a cage, starving. Which she had to be by now.

'Even a crossword specialist wouldn't be any use then,' Tim concluded, eyeing my disappearing sardines with regret.

'No. The first clue was more . . . ecclesiological . . . historical,' I mused. 'We need someone who's shit hot on local history. Someone who'll help with the clues without asking questions.'

'Either that or you'll have to become shit hot on local history yourself, mate,' was Tim's advice.

How fast can you become a historical expert? From the Bathtub Bistro I went straight to an old-fashioned book-shop with creaky floorboards in Orange Grove to stock up on books about Bath. There was an idiotic amount of stuff written about this city. In the end I simply pulled out a huge armful of books, just making sure I didn't have more than one copy of everything, and shoved it at the bemused girl by the till who spent five minutes totting it all up. Then I staggered to the car, poured the books on to the back seat and drove back to the valley.

I spent hours on the sitting-room floor, fuelled by caffeine, surrounded by books about the city I lived in: the history of and guide books to; architectural guides, tourist guides, walking guides; books on famous visitors to the city, photographic records, the history of the World War Two Blitz, learned papers, pamphlets and polemics. Only when my hands started to shake did I realize that I'd probably drunk far too many Turkish coffees and began to calm myself down again with an equal amount of Amarettos. The ashtray was also full again and the packet of Camels I'd opened that afternoon was nearly empty. How many of these did I smoke these days? I had no idea but the fact that I'd developed a richly rumbling cough and bought a carton of two hundred for convenience probably meant: quite a few. By now my head was stuffed with information and historical sketches, images and dates which I'd probably forget just as soon as I walked away from this mess of paper. Some of it might come in handy with a future message from the Doctor, if there was going to be one, or more likely a pub quiz. With this message it didn't help at all. Sure, I knew all about the George Inn by now but none of it had given me even a spark of inspiration.

A thump upstairs, followed by a muffled curse followed by another thump suggested that Annis might be up, though still experiencing some difficulty in keeping her eyes open. I made a cafetière of strong Colombian coffee and when she didn't appear, took a mug up to her room. My knock was answered with something that sounded like 'Ughrlm', which I foolishly mistook for an invitation to enter. Annis was sitting up in bed. She looked even worse than the previous night: her red-rimmed eyes were chased with black shadows and her skin had gone from pale to translucent.

'I brought you some coffee.' I offered her the mug handle first. When she took it I saw her hands shake worse than mine.

'Found anything in Charlcombe?' Her voice was weak, flat and croaky.

'Yes. You were right, Charlcombe was the right St Mary. They have a spring up there, which is what the note referred to.' I pulled the Doctor's message from my pocket and unfolded it. 'In the pool the spring flows into, I found this: the next clue.'

Annis took two seconds to read it, then dropped it on the duvet. 'One ounce of cornflakes? We're just prolonging the agony, Chris.' Tears welled up in her eyes as she stared fixedly ahead, straight into the nightmare of her imagination.

'Stop it, Annis. Stop doing that. Don't . . . go there. I need you here. I need you on board right now. I know solving the clues in the messages won't bring her back but it might keep her alive long enough for us to figure out another way of bringing her back. Until then we need to keep busy, keep engaging the Doctor. So we can get closer and closer.' I didn't tell her how close *he* had come to *me* last night.

Annis blindly emptied the mug and handed it back to me. She read the note again and handed that to me too. 'I'll sleep on it.' Then she fell back on the bed and pulled the duvet over her head.


When the phone chimed in the sitting room I snatched it up. 'Yes?'

'Hi, Chris, it's John from the gallery. Is Ali about?'

'Ehm, no. No, she's not.'

'Well, can you ask her to ring me when she gets in? I'm still at the gallery but she can call me at home if she's back late.'

This was one scenario I hadn't thought about. 'Actually . . . she's gone away for a bit.'

'Gone away? What do you mean?' John asked, incredulous. 'Where to?'

'She's, ehm, gone to see her mother. She's not well. The mother, that is. In . . . Portsmouth.' Even to myself I didn't sound very convincing, but then why should John suspect anything?

'Okay. Have you got a number for her there? It's just that the American couple who bought three of her canvases are going back to the States and want to take them now rather than have them shipped later. So there'll be quite a hole when the show goes to London. I thought she might have a painting or two we could quickly frame to fill that gap.'

'I haven't got her number, I'm afraid. She left in a bit of a hurry. But she's bound to call soon. I'll pass the message on.' Phew. I really should have seen that coming and been ready for it.

Just as soon as I'd hung up the phone rang again. It was Tim. 'Any developments?'

I told him about the tricky phone call from John.

'I wonder how long you can spin that visit to her mother's out. What about the new Doctor's Note? Did Annis see it?'

'I reckon she needs a real doctor's note, there's more than a hangover at work here. I've seen her in her black moods when you wouldn't go within coffee mug-flinging range but this is worse. I'll give her until tomorrow, then we'll have to do something about it. We need Brains of Britain up and running, not hiding under a duvet.'

'Oh mate, you're really not going to like what I've got to tell you then.'

'Wait, don't tell me: you're calling from under a duvet. On a freighter bound for Novosibirsk.'

'Might as well be. Forgot to tell you, I'll be away for a bit. I've got to do a few training days at Southampton Uni. They've got a brand new computer system down there.'

My heart sank. My troops were thinning out drastically. 'Well, that's just great. Didn't know you needed training, I thought you already knew all about computers.'

'Don't be insulting, Honeypot. I'm teaching their staff how to get the best out of their new system. I'm on loan for a few days until they get the hang of it. I'll keep in touch, though, but of course you never check your emails, you lazy sod.'

'I do check my emails,' I said lamely and just a touch mendaciously.

167

'Yeah? I've been sending you outrageous insults on a daily basis for a week now to test that theory and I'm not convinced. Must try harder, Chris.'

'Oh all right. It's such a pain cranking up the computer every day, though,' I complained.

'Then leave it running, you plonker!' Tim advised.


I flipped open a Pilsner Urquell and returned to the avalanche of books on the floor. It would take ages to read them all. I dipped into one, then another, read a passage here and there and soon couldn't remember what I'd read ten minutes ago. It was no help at all. Needham had said that some of the messages they got never made any sense at all, others they solved 'eventually'. What if the Doctor was really quite mad? What if the message didn't mean a bloody thing to any rational being?

A couple of hours later I was well on my way to emulating Annis's vodka performance: the Amaretto bottle was empty and I had slurped through several Urquells without taking much notice until I acquired alcohol-induced dyslexia. I should have gone to bed but my brain was rattling with too much information, too many questions, too much anxiety. I pulled on my jacket and slipped out of the back door into the surprisingly mild and fragrant darkness of the night. I patted my pockets for my packet of Camels, then realized I already had a lit cigarette dangling from the side of my mouth. This was getting ridiculous; I was smoking without noticing it now. Grinding the cigarette into the soft turf with my shoe I vowed to do something about that. Sometime. Then I set off for a distracted midnight tour of my realm in the valley. Adding to the starlight was a sliver of a waxing moon and that was all I needed to find my way around the familiar grounds. I padded across the boardwalk along the millstream, black and slippery and perpetually damp; turned up the hill towards the willows and burgeoning growth that nearly obscured the millpond in summer, another source of nagging guilt; left the pond unvisited but cut across the gently rising meadow towards the single oak, visible in dark outline against the darker strip of woodland behind; avoided the nearby barn full of unpainted paintings and sat down gratefully against the reassuring girth of the tree. Before I'd even thought about it I had taken another cigarette from the pack.

And just as the lighter flared I thought I detected a tiny movement among the moonshadows of the yard. Only now the flame had night-blinded me and it took an agonizing minute or so until I was once more able to make out some of the details of the shacks and sheds and rambling outbuildings by the house. I stubbed out my cigarette and moved sideways into the lee of the studio. From here I could make my way down to the outbuildings while staying in the shadow of the east boundary, which consisted mainly of hazels invaded by thick bramble.

There it was again. A movement in the darkness that had drawn itself up around the shell of a barn where I had hidden Alison's decrepit Beetle. I was still only halfway along the hedgerow when a darkly clad figure walked across the yard. *My yard.* He walked slowly, stopping every so often, turning his head this way or that as if listening, then walked on. By the time I had made my way down there he had vanished into the blackness that sat around Mill House now that the moon had gone in. Still, whoever he was, I ought to have the advantage, knowing the terrain. I slipped out of my leather jacket. It was so full of junk that had disappeared irredeemably into its lining that it could only be a hindrance should it come to a fight. I laid my hand on a foot-long piece of split log: a short fight, if I could help it. Then I moved quietly across the yard and hugged the wall near the kitchen door. The definite sound of footsteps, faint scrabbling noises, like someone trying to prise open the verandah door, then a clang and a half-suppressed oath: my friend had walked into the barbecue. *Good.* But I'd had enough now. My

169

indignation had built up a good head of steam. I inched forward to the last corner of the house, raised the split log shoulder high and charged. He was ready for me. He sidestepped, my log swung into empty space and he got in a painful punch that laid me out by the edge of the verandah. By the time I got up, feeling my mouth for loose teeth, there was no sign of him. A little unsteady on my feet now, I walked into the yard and waited by the front door for a footfall or the crack of a twig under a boot or the grunt of an engine starting up but none came. Not a sound. He'd been reabsorbed by the night.

# Chapter Fourteen

Mid-morning guilt hit me like another punch in the face when I finally woke into grogginess. Standing up in the kitchen I tore a croissant apart and washed it down with an evil brew of French coffee. I couldn't afford to get drunk, or drunk and punched. Who was prowling around Mill House late at night? Did I let the Doctor slip through my hands last night? Had I thought clearly then I might have got my gun and nabbed him. Or followed him to Alison's prison, always presuming it was the Doctor, not some other low-life fancying his chances. Last night I had beat myself up over it. This morning I felt I didn't have the time for that. I had stuff to do, I had to find Alison. I had to solve the clue, too, but the clue, once solved, would guide me to another clue, never to Alison herself. I had found Nikki Reid by looking for Billy. What had Tim said? In that case keep looking for Billy. I grabbed my jacket and keys, fired up the DS and swept out of the yard on a wave of determination. The wave carried me as far as the crack willow at the top of the track and, having spent itself, left me there. I stopped. I sat. I switched off the engine.

Slowly an image of Bath assembled itself in front of my unfocused eyes: not sunlit terraces of Georgian splendour but the unlit, unmapped back- and underside of the city which was my domain as a detective. Finding Alison in that lot was a near impossible task. The police couldn't do it, I couldn't do it. Needham was right, the place was a warren. There was more underground than overground:

171

every house had a basement, each basement had a sub-basement. There were vaults under every pavement and whole streets were laid over cavernous vaulted spaces; there were tunnels and bunkers; underground streams, culverts and channels; there were vaults and cellars that no longer corresponded to the houses that sat above them since they belonged to buildings razed by time, developers or the Luftwaffe. Many of these were unused and forgotten. They said that armed with no more than a crowbar you could make your way across the city from vault to vault without the need to ever come up into the light. People grew mushrooms in the perpetual dark of sub-basements, and cannabis by artificial light. Other cities had crack houses, Bath had crack vaults. Illegal drinking dens, vodka stills and unlicensed nightclubs still flourished down there, more out of long habit now than necessity; unpoliced, undiscovered, undisturbed.

And deep down there somewhere, I was deadly certain, was Alison. Alone. Hungry. In the dark. I would never find her.

A deep, threatening rumble brought me back to the here and now and the sound put a smile on my face. Only one contraption on the planet emitted such awe-inspiring noises and that was Annis's Norton. I waited contentedly until she drew up next to me. In her tatty leather jacket, with all that red hair escaping from under the open-faced helmet and her ancient goggles, she looked quite mad. In a strangely sexy kind of way.

'Now this morning, that's when I really could've done with a pint of coffee, you selfish git,' she shouted happily over the noise that came from between her legs. 'At least you left some in the pot. Didn't get very far though, did you? Come on, we've got a Doctor's Note to pick up.'

'Are you telling me you figured it out? You know where it is?'

'Told you I'd sleep on it. Follow that girl!' She opened

172

the throttle and left me sitting in blue smoke and a world of noise. I checked my ears weren't bleeding and followed at a respectful distance. I had no fear of losing her in the traffic, people everywhere stopped what they were doing and turned to face the World War Two sound effects rolling up their street. We didn't go far on London Road West before Annis gave a hand signal to turn left towards the ancient toll bridge across the Avon. The bloke who collects the tolls simply waved her through: a few pence wasn't worth risking his long-term health for. Annis roared off while I practically threw the money at the boy and set off in pursuit. I didn't have far to go. Annis was already getting off her machine in front of the George Inn. I stuck the DS by the side of the road and jumped out.

'*By George*! Can it be that simple?' I asked into the sudden silence.

Annis pulled off her helmet, took out her earplugs, sensible girl, and shook her hair free. 'It's dead simple. Can't believe you didn't get it straight away. Call yourself a painter?'

'Hey, there's no call for that,' I protested as I followed her across the narrow road and through the lych gate into the cemetery.

'*Dead and buried* means dead and buried.' Annis waved her arms about to indicate the hundreds of graves all around the church. 'And *by George* means by the George Inn.' She set off again, towards the church.

'But who?' I was as mystified as ever.

'You heard of a woman called Patricia Cornwell?'

'I haven't but I have a feeling you'll remedy that.'

'She's a crime writer. American. Quite popular, apparently. Anyway, she got this idea that she knew who Jack the Ripper really was –'

'That's novel. Every few years someone thinks –'

'You wanna hear this? Then shut up. She spent a lot of

money and effort trying to prove that the man who committed those murders in the late nineteenth, early twentieth century was in fact a famous British painter of that period. Got it yet?'

'Wait a minute. *A bit sick . . .*'

'Now he's got it: Sickert. Walter Sickert. And he's buried right here.' She made the appropriate *ta-dah!* gesture.

'Really? I'd no idea. I mean, I know he painted Bath at some point but he's such a London boy in my mind.'

'I know. But he handed his brush back while he was in Bath and so got buried here.'

'So where's his grave?' I looked around eagerly. There were hundreds of graves, some, I had noticed, going back centuries. Headstones were standing at odd angles or had fallen over completely into the soft ground between the river and the canal.

'I don't remember. I found it once. When I was in my first year at art college I was a great fan and came down here and poured turps on his grave, as you're supposed to do with dead painters.'

'You are?' I asked. Now there was something to look forward to.

'Of course. Don't you know anything? Or you can leave a bunch of brushes. But I prefer the libation.' She stopped and surveyed the graveyard, then struck out resolutely towards the centre. I followed. She took a left, then a left again at a tall conifer and along a row of graves.

'Got him?'

'No. I wonder why they don't bury them alphabetically, it would make things so much easier.'

'There's a bloke back there, digging. He might know.' Near the rear entrance through the stone wall that surrounded the cemetery a man in a blue overall, who I sincerely hoped wasn't the ubiquitous Keith Ward, was digging a hole. As you do in graveyards. So, after hundreds of years the place was still in use.

We walked over and asked the pale, soft-fleshed man

standing in his half-finished hole. He looked up from his task and shook his head, uninterested. 'I'm not from around here . . .'

. . . I was just passing and thought I'd dig a hole, I nearly finished for him. Somehow it seemed inappropriate for a century-old graveyard to have guys from 'not around here' dig graves in blue overalls.

'What did you expect?' Annis asked as we walked back towards the church. 'Top-hatted old geezer with crumpled tail coat and a nasty cough?'

'Yes. It's the least I'd expect. With hooting owls as standard.'

'Hooting owls are extra. Always have been. Let's check out the noticeboard in the church, there must be a mention of the famous grave somewhere.'

'Here we are. *Welcome to St Nicholas Church Balhampton,*' I read.

Annis read on: '*A church with historical connections, including the grave of Arthur Philip, First Governor of New South Wales*? Who cares about him? I'm not impressed. No mention of Sickert anywhere.'

'Can I help you?'

An ancient little lady appeared to have grown out of the ground next to me. The frown of concentration she wore nearly disappeared in the extraordinary number of wrinkles that criss-crossed her entire face. She barely reached my shoulder but stood very close to me and appeared to be studying my elbow. At last I noticed her watery irises and the white bands around her substantial walking stick. She was blind.

'We were looking for any mention of Walter Sickert's grave. We don't seem to be able to locate it,' I told her.

'I'm not surprised,' she said with a smile that put wrinkles on her wrinkles. 'He keeps moving around. I'll show you.' She stretched out a hand and put it to the wall. Then walked slowly but steadily to the door, tapped the frame hard with her stick, then set off at a surprising pace into the churchyard. 'They moved him, see? That's why you couldn't find him again, love,' she explained when Annis said she'd visited the grave before. 'His headstone kept falling over. The place is boggy as hell. If hell is boggy, that is.' She tapped the sides of raised graves and headstones with her stick as we passed and sometimes made sudden turns that took us by surprise. But eventually she stopped, sniffed the air, then pointed with her stick at an unassuming headstone a few yards ahead. 'Am I right?'

We walked over and confirmed that she was. *Walter Sickert, 1860–1942.* Even now the headstone seemed to stand at a slant. We walked around the grave. It was adorned with three white lilies in a black tin flowerpot. The flowers were fresh. 'Who looks after the . . .' I began to ask but the old lady was already halfway back to the church. The blue-overalled grave digger was leaning on his spade, studying us – or her – from the comfort of his hole.

We in turn studied the grave, walked around it once more. There was only one place where the note could be and that was under the pot of lilies. The grave digger had gone back to work, yet I was certain we were being watched. I bent down as if to smell the lilies and lifted the pot. Nothing. 'Oh sod it. Hold these.' I plucked the lilies out of the vase, handed them to Annis and plunged my hand into the cool water, feeling around inside. Patently not there. I replaced the flowers and stood. 'I'll get a spade, shall I?'

Annis contemplated the flowers. 'They look very fresh.' She bent down and sniffed the water in the vase. 'You can still smell that plant food they give you in a little sachet with your cut flowers. What if someone changed the flowers today and found the note?'

'Then we're in trouble. We need to find out who looks after the grave, who might have put these here, and hope it's not some admirer who only came once. Where's the blind lady? She might know.'

'She does,' came the answer. She'd done it again. This time she'd grown out of the ground under the pine tree behind us. Did she navigate by memory, sound or smell? 'Are you looking for this?' She held up a piece of paper, folded into a two-inch square.

'We might be,' I admitted.

There was a pause in which she appeared to be considering this, but I realized her thoughts had been elsewhere when she answered: 'I sat for him, you know. I wasn't always blind. Or wrinkled. He was, by then. Wrinkled, not blind, of course. A superb eye, in fact. And not unkind at all. I hate what they're saying now, that he murdered people. It's so unfair. And it's utter rubbish, of course.' I was just about to register my agreement when she held up the note again. 'Now this . . . I haven't read it of course but it doesn't smell right. The note under the pot.' She held it up to her nose and sniffed, then creased her face in disgust. 'Are you sure you want it?'

'Yes, I'm afraid we need the note,' Annis confirmed.

'Well, be careful,' she said, and with a resigned sigh held it out. I took it from her waxy hand.

I sniffed the paper myself. It smelled of nothing much. Of paper, if anything. And it was quite dry. 'What did you smell on this? What's it smell of?' I asked.

She shrugged and turned away towards the church, then stopped, as though reconsidering. 'Unfriendly. Yes. It smells distinctly unfriendly. Perhaps a little bit crazy, too.'

'Come on, what's it say?' Annis prompted. She didn't seem to find anything odd or even remarkable in the old lady's pronouncement, but it struck a chord with me. In Nikki Reid's death cell I had thought I could smell the madness underlying all the other, more obvious smells of human ordure and decay. Did this blind woman smell something similar? Had the note been written in Ali's prison? Or did malevolence and madness leave a physical trace she could detect with her sense of smell, a sense perhaps sharpened by her blindness?

Annis snatched the note from my fingers and unfolded it impatiently. It took only seconds to turn her face pale with pain and anger once more. She threw the note at me and turned a few paces away, looking for the horizon, looking for somewhere far away. I picked it up from where it had fluttered on to Walter Sickert's grave.

FOR MY NEXT TRICK I SHALL – HOW CAN I PUT THIS POLITELY – TALK OUT OF YOUR ARSE, AS YOU'LL DISCOVER WHEN YOU GENUFLECT IN ITS CONTEMPLATION.
REWARD: 1 OZ SEED.

Seeds. Now he was feeding her seeds, like a caged bird. I bit back a scream of anger. Because here it was again, the feeling of being mocked and manipulated for his amusement and, above all, of being watched. 'Annis?'

She turned reluctantly.

'Smile at me. In case he's watching.'

'You think he is?' she asked, giving me a bitter smile. 'I don't give a shit whether he is or not. I just want to kill him. Promise me you'll let me kill him when we catch the bastard,' she said fiercely with narrowed eyes. *When.* When we catch the bastard. The note of faith in our abilities was enough to raise a genuine smile on my own face. I hoped the bastard really was watching us.

'I promise.'

She dug a hand into the inside pocket of her jacket and produced a tiny stoppered glass bottle. 'Sleep well, Walter, thanks for the paintings.' As she poured the libation of viscous fluid on to his grave the air filled joyously with the resinous pine fragrance of Venice turpentine.

We walked back towards the lych gate, the next cryptic message burning a hole in my pocket. She stuck her bright yellow earplugs back in and pulled helmet and goggles on.

'Where to now?' I asked.

She sniffed the air, much like the old lady had done, and scanned the pile-ups of cumulus above.

'Don't know about you but I'm going to arse about on the back lanes of Somerset and terrorize the countryside for a while,' she said joylessly. 'Don't wait up.'

I lit a cigarette and stood well back as she kick-started the monster into life. She roared her anger and frustration through the open pipe of the bike as she thundered past the cemetery. I could hardly hear my mobile chiming over the noise of it.

The air seemed to turn cold when I heard the voice.

'I think you are getting far too much help. This is supposed to be between you and me, Mr Honeysett. So I think I'll even out the odds a bit.'

I didn't even take the time to swear at him, just frantically scrabbled for my car keys, but it was too late. As I looked over my shoulder I could see Annis crashing the Norton into the low wall on the rise of the humpback bridge that spanned the canal. Annis flew forward and cleared the wall, the bike jack-knifed and reared up against it, its engine racing for a few seconds before it stopped in a cloud of dust. I dialled 999, shouting instructions as I ran. A Land Rover had stopped on the bridge, the occupants jumping out, and other people too were running now towards the crashed bike.

I found Annis on the other side of the wall, sideways on the ground in the narrow space between two blue wheelie bins inside a picket fence enclosure. I scrabbled over the wall and into the narrow space where Annis lay groaning quietly.

'Don't move, don't move!' I squeezed behind the bins and unlatched the wooden door of the enclosure to give myself room to move.

'Get me out of here, this place stinks,' she growled at me.

'It's where they keep the wheelie bins, bound to whiff a bit.'

'I *know* that, Honeypot, I had a goddamn *aerial* view of it just a second ago, but I got myself wedged in, so get 'em off me.'

'I think we should wait for the ambulance,' I said soothingly, 'in case you broke something.'

'If you don't get me out of here in two seconds I swear I'll break something when I do!'

'Okay, okay! I'll move one of the bins.' The bins were enormous, full and heavy, but once I discovered you could release the brakes on the wheels I actually managed to move one sideways. Annis plopped on to her front with a loud groan. Several spectators had appeared on the other side of the wall now.

'Has anyone called an ambulance yet?' asked one of the men.

'Don't let her take her helmet off,' advised another one sternly.

'Best not move at all, darling,' said one of the women.

'Would you excuse me?' asked Annis politely and puked decorously on to my shoes.

# Chapter Fifteen

'But she was wearing a helmet,' I protested.

'Wearing a helmet is no protection against concussion and Ms Jordan is definitely concussed. She also has a broken ankle and various cuts and bruises as you can imagine. She needs complete rest. You might be able to see her briefly tomorrow but if I were you I'd call before coming to the hospital.'

I gave up. The woman was right. I remembered concussion from having been clobbered over the head and you don't actually care that much for visitors while you have double vision and fill kidney-shaped objects with puke. I shook hands with the doctor and walked out of the hospital.

Right on cue the weather had turned. Dark, heavy rain clouds had sailed in from the west and threatened to drop their ballast on the city. More depressing still, Superintendent Michael Needham had parked his considerable behind on the bonnet of the DS, talking on his mobile and glowering at me as I approached. He terminated the call and studied the sky for a minute before issuing one of his dreaded invitations: 'Chris. Let's walk.'

I looked around me. 'Why not? It is a lovely car park.'

We walked along the sad rows of visitors' cars. 'Your girl's in hospital and I've just been told even a casual look at her bike says the brakes had been disabled. Now who would do that to a nice girl like Miss Jordan, huh?'

Annis had already told me as much while we waited for

the ambulance. During the time we spent looking for Walter Sickert's grave someone had messed about with the Norton's brakes. She had been very lucky to hit the wall where it was low enough for her to clear it. A few yards further on it was much higher and she'd have flown right into it.

'She's a shoddy mechanic, our Annis.'

'Cut the crap, Honeysett. Someone wanted her in hospital, if not dead. Now if you're not screaming for help from us to find out who did it that means you already know who did it. Right?' He stopped walking and started prodding my chest with a fleshy digit. 'Told you I'd keep an eye on you. You've got yourself involved with nasty people again, Chris. I heard vague rumours about bloody noses and broken legs among our villainous fraternity, all to do with some paintings. And I thought to myself then you might have a grubby oil-stained hand in it somehow, but now I'm sure of it.'

Half of me was relieved that Mike had not connected Annis's crash with the Doctor, the other half was unnerved at his shrewd deductions. So Roy had blamed whoever he got the watercolours from and dished out a painful reminder that he didn't enjoy being robbed. That was something I might think about later.

'Look, let me spell it out for you again,' he went on, turning up the volume. 'I don't mind you guys doing unfaithful spouses or delivering unwelcome mail on behalf of solicitors. I don't even mind you doing missing persons because, frankly, we don't have the manpower to do it properly. But I don't want you to fuck about with criminal cases on my patch!' People were turning around to look at us: big man in a suit telling off leather-jacketed long-haired lout. They liked what they saw.

'Annis's crash had nothing to do with any paintings. In fact we are working on finding a missing person, trying to reunite old friends.' Well, so far I was telling the truth.

Not that lying to Needham would ever cost me a minute's sleep.

'Yeah, right.'

I'd steered us in a neat circle back to the DS and got my car keys out. Needham suddenly stuck his hands into the pockets of my jacket, then half-heartedly patted me down. 'Left your gun in the car, did you?' he said, taking the keys from me and unlocking the door. 'Very careless. What if your car gets nicked, huh? Then you've got a car thief furnished with a gun,' he said while rummaging round in the glove box and under the seats. For a heart-stopping moment I thought he might spot the Webley in its holder under the dash until I remembered I'd left it at home like a responsible gun owner, securely hidden under my pillow. He squeezed out of my car with a grunt. 'I don't know why you bother with the ancient blunderbuss anyway. We'd put you away for just as long for a state-of-the-art Beretta. So you might as well get yourself a decent gun,' he said cheerfully and walked away to where the ghastly Deeks was waiting with his car.

Once I'd got over my astonishment at the Superintendent's rare attack of mirth I started the DS and waited for their grey Ford Mondeo to leave the car park. They turned right so I turned left on to the main road and immediately right again, which eventually brought me on to Weston Road, with the Approach golf course on the left and Victoria Park on the right. Needham turning up at the hospital had given me a touch of paranoia and I checked my mirrors every two seconds. An old Bordeaux-red Volvo some way behind seemed an unlikely candidate for a police tail. I soon relaxed. Needham had probably been at the hospital for another reason altogether and just thought he'd fit in a bit of harassment while he had a spare moment.

I drove into Victoria Park and stuck the DS by the side of the tennis courts, the only ten square yards in the city where they didn't charge you for getting out of the car. The first raindrops were falling by the time I'd walked the few hundred yards to Milsom Street and as I reached the dinky Podium shopping centre that housed the library it began to pour steadily from a charcoal sky.

Upstairs the library had recently been reorganized and the most-used words heard between its rearranged shelves were 'Where the . . .?' Once I'd solved that question myself and found the Local Studies section I absentmindedly – or open-mindedly, I was hoping – browsed the shelves. Most of the books there I had looked at before and dismissed as irrelevant, many I had actually read in my previous study marathon. *For my next trick* . . . Many items here looked self-published, slim volumes dealing with heartbreakingly narrow aspects of life in Bath. *I shall talk out of your arse* . . . Did I really think I was going to find an answer to the riddle here? . . . *when you genuflect in its contemplation* . . . I knelt down to inspect the lowest shelf. I found one quite substantial guidebook I had not seen before. There was nothing else here. I wouldn't save Alison by browsing in the library.

I got my ticket blipped and went across to the awesomely clichéd trattoria, complete with plastic plants, faux fountain and Formula One Ferrari flags, and secured a table by the enormous window. The place was filling up fast with refugees from the downpour outside. From here I could watch shoppers and tourists running for shelter in the streets below but instead I turned my attention to the book. I flicked through it: it was just another guide to Bath. What was I going to do, look up 'arse' in the index? I had to admit it: I hated riddles, had hated them as a child. And for a good reason. I was crap at solving them.

This somewhat dampened my enthusiasm for the plate of pasta primavera the waiter flourished under my nose. I was stumped. Again. With Annis in hospital and Tim at Southampton Uni, Aqua Investigations was down to thirty-three per cent brain power (or less, Annis would say). I should perhaps check my emails, as he'd suggested, and mail him the new clue but what I really needed was a completely fresh perspective. I tried not to enjoy the pasta I shovelled into my mouth when a sudden rattling of rain against the window drew my attention to the drowning streets below. There, on the near empty pavement, just turning into Green Street, was a ratty-haired bloke in a sodden overcoat and the most rancid trainers on the planet. I thought I could smell him from here: Chucky.

I peeled some money on to the table, zipped up my leather jacket and shoved the library book inside. Already standing up I grabbed another mouthful of pasta to fuel the pursuit and ran past the worried waiters. I slalomed round shoppers, hammered down the escalator, skidded along the slippery-when-wet ground floor out into the blinding rain. By the time I had made it into the short but sweet Green Street I was drenched and Chucky was nowhere to be seen. I hiked along to the other end and spied up and down Milsom Street. Nothing. A goat-bearded *Big Issue* seller was sheltering in front of Waterstone's. I squelched across. 'You seen Chucky in the last five minutes?'

'Fuck off.'

I gave him a fiver.

He shoved it in his pocket. 'No.'

'Any idea where I might find him?'

'Fuck off.'

While I retraced my steps to the corner of Green and Broad Street I vaguely wondered whose day this rotten day was, since it so obviously wasn't mine. Or Annis's. Or Alison's. There were pubs on either corner, St Christopher's Inn and the Green Tree, arguably the oldest pub in the city. Both were open but neither so hard up for customers as to allow Chucky inside for longer than it took to register his smell. By now I was ridiculously wet and the rain stung in my eyes and I really wanted to get inside somewhere. So, presumably, would Chucky. But where could he get out of the rain and not be instantly expelled again? One name came reluctantly to mind, though I hadn't heard it mentioned for an awfully long time: the Stone Broke. Could that most desperate and dank of drinking dens still be in existence in the twenty-first century?

The establishment I was looking for was hidden only a few hundred yards and a couple of corners from such respectable locations as the Circus, the Assembly Room and the Museum of Costume. I counted the lamp posts and easily found the house. It hadn't changed. Its black façade, unlike its neighbours', had never been pressure-washed and the well of the basement into which I was staring still sported self-sown trees, giant weeds and a fig that threatened to eat the ground floor. The steps that led down into this dripping rainforest were still urinary green and the first stone step was still broken.

At the bottom of the well I found a pile of cardboard wine boxes turning to mush in the pelter of rain and another pile of bursting binliners. I kicked one: it was full of bottles. So far so good. The naked light bulb directly over the battered wooden door was glimmering. I squinted up at it: fifteen watts; and when did they stop making those? I pressed the doorbell, two short, one long, hoping the signal had remained the same. It took a long minute until the door was opened by a greasy-haired guy in a greasy suede jacket who didn't even look at me as he squeezed past into the rain. I stepped into the short corridor, shut the door behind me and went down the curved stone stairwell to the sub-basement that still housed, by the smell of it at least, the Stone Broke.

Down here a couple of vaulted rooms remained in perpetual dusk and timeless squalor. Voices dropped to a murmur as I entered. To my right, behind a long burnt-out chiller unit with a crack running across its lifeless glass front, stood the equally burnt-out proprietor of the place. He had appeared quite old to me when I'd last seen him, now his skin looked dangerously stretched over his skull and hands. He wore the winning combination of pea-green shirt, strawberry-red bow tie and a suit that even as a painter I could only describe as *beige*. I ignored the other guests – there never were customers at the Stone – and concentrated on the bar and my host so as not to spook anyone, and remembered that his name was Geoffrey. The scratched glass counter was empty and bare, apart from a tin ashtray and a dialler phone the same colour and vintage as the man's suit; in the stone niches behind the bar, lit by strings of coloured fairy lights, a collection of seaside souvenirs made from shells, fluffy with dust, and exotic bottles of duty free liqueurs, all empty.

'Evening, young man.' His greeting appeared to carry a small question mark.

'Evening, Geoffrey, what have we got?' The familiarity of the traditional formula appeared to have a relaxing effect on everyone and conversations picked up again.

'Custard apple liqueur or vinho verde.' His answer had only the faintest hint of regret in it.

'Who's been to Madeira then?'

'The little people.' He nodded in the direction of three male dwarves playing dominoes at a rickety kitchen table. Behind them, stacked floor to ceiling, was a collection of broken valve radios.

'What are they drinking?'

'The custard apple.'

'That's what I'll have.'

'Forty new pennies, then.' Prices were going up everywhere.

Equipped with a glass of the sticky liquid I looked around. The place was covered in dust and cobwebs. A threadbare assortment of carpet oddments and runners covered the stone floor. A few tables, two narrow benches and a couple of faded armchairs completed the furnishings. Apart from the dwarves there was a stupefied-looking woman in her late fifties or seventies, hard to tell, sitting in a legless armchair. Two old blokes, both reading the same paper through thick-lensed spectacles, sat elbow to elbow. In a dark niche all by himself sat a figure I thought I recognized but couldn't immediately place. His severely shorn black hair still glistened wet from the rain. He seemed to stare at a full glass of liqueur with intense concentration. Then I spied the sandwich board leaning against the wall but in the gloom could only decipher the word SIN. Every preacher needed a demon, it seemed. In the furthest corner at another much-repaired table sat Chucky with his back to me. Opposite him, watching me with his lizard eye, sat the man with the burnt face. The dog by his feet was as alert as his master. I lifted my glass in a greeting which he didn't return. Instead he spoke rapidly to Chucky who looked over his shoulder and pulled a painful grimace when he saw me.

The shrill, old-fashioned peal of the telephone cut through the murmur of voices and everyone turned their attention to the bar. Geoffrey stood with one hand resting on the receiver. 'Who's here?'

No one moved or made a sound. He picked up the phone, listened briefly, then said, 'He's not here.' He hung up and turned to one of the old geezers. 'Yours, Barry.'

'Ahh, bullshit.' Barry waved it away.

When I approached Chucky's table only the dog and the burnt man's lidless eye registered me. Chucky looked rigidly in front of him. I circled around and drew up a chair at the narrow end of the table. Both he and his companion had opted for the vinho verde. Both their glasses were nearly empty.

Chucky's face looked a mess. There was old bruising on both cheekbones and across his forehead ran a gaping scar that looked like a cut that should have been stitched but hadn't.

'Hi, Chucky.'

'It's your funeral,' said the burnt man cheerfully, ignoring me. He emptied his glass and returned it with exaggerated care to the table. 'I'm out of here. Come on, dog.' His dog jumped up and followed closely on his master's heels.

Perhaps the rain had managed to wash some of the yuk off Chucky because from where I was sitting I couldn't actually smell him. 'Who's your friend?' I asked.

'Him? Doc Martin.'

'*Doc* Martin?'

'Yeah well, his name's Martin and he nearly was a doctor once and he always wears Doc Martens, so you could say he walked into that one. He's good with illnesses and all that. Gives you pills sometimes if you're feeling shitty, that kinda thing.'

'Where does he get the pills from?'

'Fake prescriptions.'

'How did he get the face?'

'Someone chucked acid at it. At medical school. It was over a girl. It fucking worked, too, she didn't want him once the bandages came off. Whaddayawant from me?'

'I seemed to remember you were going to keep an eye out for Billy for me?'

'So? I never promised nuffink and anyway . . .' He gave me a quick glance, then returned his gaze to the glass.

'And you got beaten up. Badly. Did you get the twenty I sent you?'

'Ah fuck, I got ten.'

'Handling fee, I suppose. Did you find Billy? Did he give you that hiding?'

He snorted. 'I reckon I could take the bastard.' He emptied his glass and returned it noisily to the table. 'Nope. He's got others to do his punching and kicking for him. Especially kicking. I reckon half my ribs are busted. He's got some sort of protection, your Billy. I'm taking a fucking big risk just talking to you.'

I pushed a tenner across the table. He didn't hesitate and made it disappear but not without looking guiltily around the room afterwards. Barry was just leaving, having saved some face by waiting a few minutes before going home to his dinner. He acknowledged Geoffrey with a nod on the way out.

'Who warned you off talking to me?'

'Same people what gave me the beatin', whaddaya-think? Mind you, they gave me forty quid after . . .' He hesitated, swallowed and looked towards the bar. 'I'll just get myself another one.' He made to rise but I laid a persuasively heavy hand on his arm.

That explained how he could afford to drink in such a lofty establishment as this. 'After you told them my name?'

Chucky suddenly looked fragile. 'They're fuckin' psy-chos, man. First they kicked the crap out of me then threw the money at my head. Just threw it at my head. I was bleedin' on the fuckin' pavement.' He twisted from my grasp and got up. 'I'm not going to talk to you any more. Too much shit . . .' He turned and walked away carefully, like an old man, out of the room.

How did a tramp get 'protection' and why? Why had I been looking for him anyway? Perhaps I should get back to Messrs Longbottom, Prangle and Fox, who got me into this thing, and ask some more questions.


It was getting dark early under a sky the colour of burnt porridge but at least the rain had stopped. There was just enough light in fact to hazard a guess at the colour of the Volvo 440 I had spotted in my mirrors. It was a wine colour, claret or burgundy, I didn't care, because just now it was scaring the hell out of me, not a thousand yards from my own front door. It had come slithering out of a gate in the hedge which I knew led nowhere but a tus-socky bit of meadow belonging to a neighbouring farm. It seemed to keep quite a way behind but I knew what the driver was doing since I'd done it myself many times: he kept well back on the straights then accelerated like mad as soon as I turned round a bend out of sight. I couldn't make out the number of occupants, even less who they were, but I felt little curiosity and absolutely no desire to meet them. My advantage ought to be the fact that we were inside my own backyard and that street lighting hadn't yet reached the valley. As I approached the turn-off for Mill House I flicked off the lights, put my foot down and shot past it. I took the next few corners fast and practically from memory, my heart hammered and the DS swayed, then I spied the gap in the hedge and stuffed the car into the entrance of Ridge Farm which I knew was always open. I killed the engine, wound down my window and listened. For a while all I could hear was the bark of the farm dogs further up the hill and the ticking of the cooling engine. Then the sound of a car being hurried along the lane approached and the Volvo shot past. I let the Citroën roll back on to the tarmac of the lane, started up, zoomed off in the opposite direction, flicked the lights back on. Not for the first time was I grateful for the famous suspension on the car as I raced down my potholed and rutted track and shot through my own wide-open gate, throwing up fountains of muddy water from puddles in the yard.

I killed the lights and engine and got out. There was no point closing the five-bar gate, it would only keep out the politest of thugs. Instead I fumbled with the door keys while the faint hum of a car engine grew stronger. Once inside I didn't bother turning on the lights until I'd wrenched open the door to the cupboard under the stairs. Here, by the disappointing glimmer from a battery-powered lamp, I opened up the gun locker. I cracked open the over and under twelve bore, slid two of my special cartridges inside: I had emptied them of lead shot and filled them with short grain rice instead. I had it on good authority that it hurt like hell and might even induce a lifelong aversion to rice pudding but was unlikely to kill anyone. I put two standard cartridges in my jacket pocket in case things got truly hideous and someone decided to answer back. Then I remembered I was a lousy shot and tipped the whole box into my pockets.

Standing in my potholed yard, sniffing at the darkness, I remembered going thug-hunting on my own land once before. It wasn't a pleasant memory so I concentrated on listening. I couldn't hear a thing that wasn't supposed to be there but there seemed to be a hole in the air where a biggish sound had been just a moment ago. I walked quietly and carefully out of the gate and up the track. The darkness wasn't complete. The track showed as a grey band, edged with the dark of the hedgerows on either side and punctuated by the black exclamation marks of the trees. I stood still by the first tree and listened again. There was the rush of the millstream behind me; the rustling of a bird in the hedgerow; the sound of my own breathing; the snorting of a horse several fields away; the splashing of a foot in a pothole and the quiet complaint of its owner: 'Shhhit.'

People always look bigger wearing a mantle of darkness but even when making allowances for the dark and for my angst this guy was no midget. He was walking gingerly on my side of the track, his arms in front, expecting an obstacle or a fall perhaps. Not expecting the cold sensation of a twelve bore in the dark, though. All I had to do was wait. When he drew level with my tree I lifted the weapon and pressed it against his head.

'Shhhit!' he hissed.

'There's a lot of it about,' I concurred. Fear and anger were making my voice shake unconvincingly. I cocked both barrels, a hideous, convincing sound. 'Put your hands on your head and keep walking. Don't piss about or I'll turn you into a regrettable hunting accident.' It occurred to me that doctors picking the rice out of this guy would more likely suspect a bizarre cooking accident. I had no idea what supersonic pudding rice might do to a man's head but suspected that at point blank range the result might be unpleasant. I lowered the gun and prodded his behind with it, urging him forward. And even with his hands over his head and walking carefully through the gate into the yard I seemed to recognize the broad shape, the athletic bearing. I walked him straight into the largest puddle I could make out. 'Wait there.' He groaned as he sank to his shins in muddy water. Then I pressed the weatherproof switch by the door that controls the outside light. Only the one measly bulb hanging from the telephone pole worked but it was enough.

'Hi, Chris,' said John grimly and unapologetically. He was examining the depth to which he had sunk. 'Can I put my hands down and get out of this hole?'

I kept the gun pointed in his general direction. John had been around at Simon Paris Fine Art for a few years now. I'd had the odd drink with him after putting up shows. I didn't really want to be threatening the man with a gun but I was no longer sure of anything. What was John doing here ghosting about in the dark? 'Was that you following me in the Volvo a minute ago?'

He stirred the water with his right foot. 'Yup, that was me.'

'Why, John? What the hell for?'

'Look, can I take my arms down? And can you point that gun somewhere else?'

'The moment you give me a convincing explanation as to what you think you're doing.'

He looked straight at me now. 'Where's Alison?' he demanded. 'And don't give me some bullshit about her having gone away to visit her sick mother in Portsmouth. Ali's mum died when she was nineteen. On holiday in Mexico.'

I sighed. It rang a faint bell. I should really pay more attention. 'So?' Not the cleverest answer but I found the situation distracting.

'What am I to think? I thought perhaps it was something I . . . said and that she didn't want to see me but I was sure she'd tell me herself. I rang a few times, no answer. So I rang Annis on her mobile and there was no answer there either. Then I tried your other mate, Tim Bigwood. Same thing there. I left messages, no one returned any of them. So what's up? What's going on in this place? Where are they all, Chris?'

He had a point. From where he was standing it had to appear a little strange. Not to mention damp. I could think of no explanation that wouldn't sound even less convincing than the sick-mother excuse. 'Oh, all right. Come out of that puddle and get inside.'

He stepped on to dry land and considered me. 'I'm not sure I want to go in there,' he said guardedly. He remained standing by the side of the puddle, his eyes flickering towards the open five-bar gate.

I cracked open the gun and slid out the cartridges. 'Then you'll never find out what happened to Ali,' I said, unkindly perhaps.

'I could go to the police.'

'I wouldn't do that,' I warned. 'Ali's been abducted.'

John followed me quietly into the house.

# Chapter Sixteen

'And you're sure you weren't creeping round Mill House last night? I won't mind, I'd rather it was you, in fact.'

'Not me. Looks like you had another visitor,' John insisted.

I had a pretty good idea who the most likely candidates were.

'Come on, let me help,' he pleaded again.

'Absolutely not. You've not been listening. Annis is in hospital because the Doctor saw us working together. I'm sure he meant to kill her, or at least didn't care if he did. I know how you must feel, especially if you care for Alison. But if he finds out about you, he'll quite happily kill you. You stay out of it. I promise you, we're doing everything we can.' I was sounding more like a police spokesman by the minute, even to myself. At least John hadn't given me any grief about not taking it to the police. But once he had shaken off his shock and disbelief, he was desperate to help. I didn't blame him. Doing nothing was the worst thing about it. And what had I achieved so far? Exactly nothing.

'I can be discreet. He won't find out. How could he?'

I looked around the room. The heavy curtains were drawn across the french windows and I'd lit a fire. The thick stone walls, the heavy ceiling beams, it all seemed so solid, utterly safe. Surely plans could be forged here and secrets would be kept . . . It was all an illusion.

'Where's your car now?'

'At the top of the track.' John waved his hand in the appropriate direction.

'So the Doctor could easily know you're talking to me if he was out there now.'

'I didn't notice anyone out there at all,' he said confidently.

'You didn't notice me out there either,' I reminded him. 'And he might be better at following people than you are.'

He tried to hide his embarrassed smile behind another gulp of Pilsner and emptied his bottle. I took it from him and fetched some more from the kitchen. I realized that the rate at which we were hoovering up the drinks meant that neither of us were capable of driving now.

'This clue.' He picked up the Doctor's note and scrutinized it again. I regretted having shown him the latest one, I should have used one we'd already solved if I really wanted John to stay out of it. *'For my next trick I shall – how can I put this politely – talk out of your arse, as you'll discover when you genuflect in its contemplation . . .* It makes no sense to me but I could show it to someone I know who's quite good at stuff like this.'

'Stuff like what?'

'Well, you know, riddles and things like historical questions. In fact you briefly met him at the show: Keith.'

Keith Ward. Yes, I'd met him just about everywhere since. 'I remember, so what's his story? How'd you get to know him? He doesn't seem your type somehow.'

'Oh, I don't know, we share some interests. Keeping fit is one. That's how we met in the first place, at the half marathon. He introduced me to the re-enactment group. I've been doing that for a couple of years now. But Keith doesn't only know his stuff when it comes to World War Two, he's also a bit of a local historian. He's good at answering tricky questions, too, he's on a pub quiz team. I went once when he had set the questions. He was really good at it. And he's got tons of books about Bath. I could show this to him.'

I weighed up the pros and cons. The cons had it. 'No. Don't show him the riddle. In fact, don't show anyone the riddle. Absolutely no one must know we are engaged in this paper chase.'

John looked hard at me for a moment, then simply nodded. He took a long drag on his bottle of beer. It was empty again but he kept sucking on it to give himself something to do while he wrestled with his emotions. 'Some fucking paper chase,' he managed finally. He got up and walked about, inspecting some of the bookshelves while he wiped his hand across his eyes and breathed deeply. He turned round when he was ready again. 'When you found the other woman. What was it like? The place he kept her in?'

'I don't want to talk about it.' I wasn't just trying to spare John the grief of knowing too much of what Alison might be suffering, I was trying to save myself from having to remember too clearly. 'The Doctor is quite mad. That's what it was like.'

'You think he's mad? But he's managed to outsmart both you and the police so far,' John pointed out.

'I didn't say he was stupid. Just a sick bastard. And when I finally meet him . . .'

We drank ourselves into a stupor. At some stage during the night I woke up. John was snoring loudly on the floor in front of the big armchair. The fire had gone out. I got up, fetched a blanket and threw it over him, then crawled upstairs into my own bed.


It appeared that I'd managed to set my alarm, a good old-fashioned wind-up clock with bells on top which scramble your dreams forever as soon as the thing goes off, ready or not.

Not, was the consensus that morning, mind and body groaning in unison. When I got out of the shower as groggy as I went in I suspected this might not turn out to be the loveliest of days. Just how unlovely it would turn out to be I was still blissfully unaware of.

There was no sign of John. The blanket I had thrown over him last night was neatly folded on the sofa. Apart from that only the nests of empty bottles, the crammed ashtray and the stale fug of alcohol and smoke remained. It smelled as if I had brought the Stone Broke home with me.

The worst thing to do of course is to skip breakfast. Even if you think you can't contemplate it, even if a close friend of yours is on the crash diet from hell – don't skip breakfast. You'll regret it later. I would soon. I couldn't even face coffee and since neither Annis nor I are tea drinkers the alternative seemed to be Alison's concoctions: a choice of nettle or dandelion tea. I settled for a pint of water instead.

It was a warm, bright day with a high, mackerel sky. I furtled in the glove box until I found my sunglasses, rolled down the windows and drove up the track, noticing that I was going to need petrol soon, noticing too late that petrol was the least of my worries: I was going to need painkillers soon.

The BMW that blocked the way disgorged ugliness from its doors and by the time my hungover self had managed to put the DS in reverse one piece of ugliness had stuck a sawn-off shotgun through my window and pressed it in my face. So that's what it felt like. I made a mental note to apologize profusely to John. Perhaps being hungover helped a little. This didn't feel real, surely this was a gangster movie and I'd switch channels to a cookery programme just as soon as I found the remote?

The bit of ugliness kept the gun pointed while another guy, twice his size and just as ugly, opened the door and shouted hysterically 'Out! Out!' in a high voice while pulling me by the jacket. I got dragged and pushed to the BMW and was almost relieved when I recognized Wakey,

Roy's permatanned Surfer Dude, standing by the driver door. His face was set. He made no sign that he knew who I was and looked straight ahead when the two uglies shoved me past him and against the car. I made no attempt to twist out of the big guy's grip so the punch in the kidneys was quite unexpected. The sensation kept me busy trying not to throw up while he ineffectually patted me down for weapons, then punched me in the other kidney. 'In! In!'

The guy with the gun slid into the back seat beside me while the Big Screamer squeezed in from the other side. Three doors slammed shut. 'Drive! Drive!' Apart from tenderizing people's kidneys this guy liked shouting and repeating himself.

Wakey reversed the car expertly up the track, one arm casually over the back of his seat, looking straight past me out the rear window. Once on the road, he drove sedately off. I suddenly remembered what I'd overheard when I sneaked about Roy's place: *I'll get Cannon and Ball over for a bit of extra muscle . . . I know they're a couple of psychos . . .* So Wakey had become driver to the extra muscle and I had become the filling in their sandwich. Cannon had to be the pasty bloke in the white shirt with the ketchup stain, black chinos and smeggy trainers, who absentmindedly stroked his sawn-off shotgun while keeping the muzzle pressed against my waist. The Screamer then was Ball. He snatched the sunglasses off my face, slid open his window and chucked them out.

'Not so sunny where you're going, shithead.' He had the voice of an overconfident five-year-old and a small ugly face floundering in a sea of fat. The tinted window slid up again. He stuck a stubby hand in my jacket pocket and came up with my mobile. He flipped it open. 'No Bluetooth. Complete crap. Still . . .' He pocketed it.

So far I hadn't said a word and was going to keep it that way. I especially had no intention of letting slip that I knew their nicknames. The journey was a short one. Roy's pile soon loomed up behind its high walls but this time I got to go in through the front. The double gate jerked open automatically. Wakey swept the car up the drive and brought it to a crunching halt in front of the cream doors of the coach house.

'Out! Out!' Ball screamed predictably as soon as he had his door open, then dragged me out of the car so energetically my head bounced off the frame twice. He was only a couple of inches taller but had at least five stone on me and was an expert at casual violence. He slapped me around the head, a quick left right left. 'Go on! Walk! Walk!' He pushed me forward with flat, annoying punches between my shoulders until I had stumbled through the left of the two broad double doors into the coach house.

'The Lexus is gone! The Lexus is not here!'

'Looks like Roy had to go out,' said Wakey behind me. I didn't look around, just clocked the inside of the ground floor. There was a motorbike under a silver polythene cover, several slim, wooden cupboards along the right wall and three doors in the wall facing us, all painted white. Everything was clean and tidy, apart from the odd dark stain on the floor. Just oil stains. Relax.

'Shame. I was looking forward to asking shithead here some questions.' Screamer grabbed me by the hair and hauled me along beside him towards the left-hand door, slid back a bolt and opened it. 'Take a seat in the waiting room!' he bellowed in my ear and pushed me in. The door slammed behind me and I heard the bolt being rammed home.


The room was eight by ten with the door on the narrow end opposite a small glazed and barred window. The walls were painted the same cream colour as the rest of the place as far as I had seen it. There was nothing in the room. No chair, no handy bits of metal to fashion into tools, no mattress for shredding into rope. Just me and the throbbing pain in the small of my back. I eased myself on to the floor and stared at the closed door and let out an experimental groan. Then I fumbled a cigarette out of the pack and lit it with shaking fingers.

After a couple of hours the pain eased. By noon I stopped worrying about my kidneys and started worrying about the rest of me. It was cool in the room but the air seemed stuffy and I was thirsty. The high window had once been the opening kind but had lost its handle and long been painted shut. Through its dusty pane I could see the dark foliage of ivy and a bit of sky. I gave the door some closer attention. It was wooden and solid. It had the odd scuff marks where objects had been carried through and scratches made, but nothing else of interest. It opened outwards and had no fittings on the inside, not even a door handle and no hinges to unscrew. I put my shoulder against it; it felt solid. I took a run at it and rammed it with my shoulder but this was no gangster movie; it didn't budge. I sat back down on the cool cement floor and started examining my leather jacket to see if I could find anything that might help, the way you are meant to if your plane crashes in the Andes. Some of the pockets had holes in them and a lot of stuff disappeared into the lining, never to be seen again. The pockets themselves yielded nothing much apart from my house keys, credit cards, my picklocks, which were useless here, and a disintegrating tissue. I wriggled my hand into the lining and dug up a trove of impedimenta: a rubber band (blue), fluff (grey), an antacid tablet (fluffy and grey), three matches, an old five pence piece (had I had the jacket that long?) and a homing device.

I dropped it on the floor like the proverbial hot potato. I was sure it was a homing device, or was it called a *tracking* device? Who cared? How did it get there? Who put it there and what for? How long had it been in my jacket? I had seen similar little things in one of Tim's catalogues, gizmos that worked with GPS, which stood for . . . something, some satellite technology. I stared and stared at it: it was the size of a credit card and less than half an inch thick, hardly weighed a thing and seemed to be made from soft plastic. Nice to touch. Yet just looking at it made me break out in a sweat.

There was one obvious explanation: the Doctor. It explained how he seemed to know exactly where I was at any given time. That still left the other question: when did he get close enough to slip it into the lining of my jacket? The question was academic, considering the ease with which he had entered Mill House to leave his poisonous message in my bedroom. What was I going to do with it? I had to get rid of the thing, naturally, but there was nowhere in this room I could leave it. I scooped it up with the rest of the stuff and dropped it back into my right-hand pocket, the one with the big hole in it, and let it all slither down into the lining again.

By late afternoon I had examined the walls in minute detail, walking round and round in a kind of terrified boredom: I knew that the next thing of interest in my life would probably involve a certain amount of pain. At least I had found no terrified messages scratched into the stone-work by previous prisoners. I had a raging thirst and it was beginning to make me feel weak and panicky. The clever thing would have been to stop smoking but the cigarettes dampened down the hunger and took the edge off my nervousness.

I would come clean, of course, as soon as someone gave me the opportunity, and offer to bring the money round. Hell, there was no one left at Mill House to endanger, so I'd take them round there and hand the case over. I guessed Wakey and the Uglies had just been told to fetch me and we were all waiting for Roy to appear before proceedings could get under way.

By nightfall I had four cigarettes left and felt too grotty to want another one. It was astonishingly quiet up here. I had heard nothing all day but muted birdsong and the worried thumping of my heart. As I crouched in my corner

202

by the door with the darkness closing in around me it became even quieter. I was cold, uncomfortable on the hard and dusty cement floor, and bloody thirsty. I tried stretching out on the floor. It was more comfortable than sitting up. For about ten minutes. I walked around for a while, first clockwise, then anticlockwise in the near complete darkness, then returned to my adopted corner by the door.

The sound of a car engine made me jerk out of convoluted dreams. I stood up quietly, listening. A car door slammed, footsteps on concrete, then gravel, fading. Roy was home. For what seemed an age I sat in the dark, waiting for the return of footsteps that didn't come.

When I woke again it was to a muted dawn chorus, a mouth crackling with dryness and aches and pains all over my body from sleeping on the concrete floor which felt like ice now. I trudged round and round my cell in an effort to warm up and drive some of the aches from my limbs. Perversely, my craving for nicotine matched my thirst. I lit one of the remaining Camels and coughed my way through it with grim determination; it felt like inhaling a desert.

I waited with mounting dread, rolling the conversation I would have with Roy round and round in my head. I told myself not to be pathetic; I thought of the thousands of prisoners all over the world, waiting for interrogation, dreading the arrival of footsteps. I thought of Alison.

I coughed through another cigarette. Being deprived of water had rendered the lack of toilet facilities unimportant but my thirst was becoming a constant preoccupation now. After no more than twenty-four hours I could not stop myself from fantasizing about long cool drinks, beakers of water and chilled bottles of Pilsner. Finally my aquatic musings were interrupted by the noises I'd been waiting for.

Crunch on gravel, footsteps of several people on the concrete, then the bolt was drawn and the door swung open. I stood well back but not far enough. The Big Screamer barrelled through the door and shoved me hard against the wall. 'Back! Back!' He was carrying a cricket bat which he cracked casually against my knee without taking his pinprick eyes off my face. Instinctively I bent towards the pain. He thwacked the bat under my chin. I had the feeling it was one of his favourite tricks. 'Stand straight, you prick! Boss wants a word!' Behind him entered the other half of the duo, minus his shotgun. He stood to one side to let Roy Hotchkiss heft himself through the doorway. The room suddenly felt extremely crowded and painful. Roy was wearing aubergine-coloured trousers and a shirt of palest lemon. He had a napkin stuffed into his collar because he was holding a baguette sandwich in one hand and a green and gold coffee mug in the other.

'Ah, breakf–' was as far as I got before a punch in the solar plexus winded me.

'Shut up! No one's asked you shit yet, shithead!'

'Let the man explain himself, Balls,' said Roy magnanimously. His baguette was bacon and tomato. He took a huge bite and gave me a friendly nod while he chewed.

I'd gone off food for the moment, it was his coffee I coveted. 'It was a stupid idea, I admit it, but I thought it had to be tried, it was just too tempting . . .'

'Too tempting, eh, Mr Honeysett? You can kick the shit out of him now, Balls,' he instructed and stepped back. The Big Screamer lifted the bat shoulder high.

'I can get you the money back here in half an hour, it's all still . . .' The bat connected with my elbow and shut me up.

'Wait a second!' bellowed Roy. Ball looked disappointed. His boss shouldered him out of the way and loomed in front of me. I had no idea a limb could go numb and radiate so much pain at the same time. His bacon and tomato dribbled juice on to my shoes. 'I'm giving you a friendly warning here about staying away from Billy and you're not listening, you're waffling about money. What fucking money?'

'Warn me off about Billy, why?' A suspicion was quickly rising in my mind but had little time to establish itself.

He took a deep breath. 'Why? Listen to yourself. I'd clout you myself if I had a hand free.' He kicked my left shin. 'My brother Billy, you arsehole, I'm going to teach you to leave him alone! Now for the last time, what fucking money?'

'Your money. The . . . you know, the dosh for the John Whites. I've got it.'

'What's he talking about, boss? What's he mean?' whined Ball.

'I can get it to you in half an hour. Quicker if you don't turn me into a complete cripple first,' I assured Roy, whose face had turned the colour of Victoria plum with unexploded anger. He took an absentminded sip of coffee while staring into my eyes, but didn't swallow. He spat it on the floor instead, then poured the rest of the mug after it. 'Bring him.' He turned and walked out.

Once more I was the filling in the Cannon and Ball sandwich; Cannon, who hadn't uttered a word in my presence yet, walked in front while Ball, prodding me with the bat as I hobbled along, trod heavily behind. Through the self-important entrance into the self-loathing interior of Ashton View. The entrance hall was crammed with every type of reproduction antique you could dream of and our footsteps were muffled by a motley collection of Persian rugs from Ikea. I followed Roy's wake into the same drawing room I had once spied on from the outside. Roy let himself fall into the enormous white armchair. I had made it as far as the back of one of the two sofas; a meaty hand belonging to Ball landed on my shoulder, telling me to stop there.

'Where the fuck's Wakey?' Roy reached under the frame of the marble table, and presumably pressed a button there, because Wakey appeared thirty seconds later.

'Yes, boss.'

'Get me another coffee.' He waved an impatient arm at the hired muscle. 'You two wait outside.'

This wasn't really the moment but being a painter I could hardly help noticing that between the fake antiques and china golliwogs and two-for-a-fiver Japanese vases, quite a few prints of English landscape paintings struggled to make themselves seen.

Wakey returned, set the mug with a precise click in front of his master, then withdrew and stood by the closed door behind me.

'Right, start babbling. What are you trying to achieve by snooping round my brother Bill?'

'I had no idea he was your brother,' I croaked, my voice sounding sandpapered.

'Bullshit! D'you think you're the first smartarse trying to get at me through my brother? Never worked so far.' He pointed an angry finger at me.

'I'm a private detective and –'

'I worked that much out for myself, sunshine. Your picture was splashed across the front page of the *Chronic*. Quite the hero. Shame you couldn't have stuck to rescuing damsels in distress. But the important question is: who's paying you?'

'I was instructed by a firm of solicitors to find Billy the . . .' I hesitated.

'Billy the tramp,' he said dismissively. 'I know, that's what everyone calls him, except he never tramps anywhere. He never leaves the city limits. What do your sodding solicitors want with him?' he demanded.

'I wasn't told. All I know is that it might be to his advantage if he contacted them. Longbottom –'

'I tell you what will be to Bill's advantage: when arse-holes like you and your solicitors start leaving him alone!' He took a few deep breaths, then picked up his coffee mug and stared into it. 'You're not going to get anything out of him anyway.' He took a noisy sip, then set the mug down so he could bellow: 'And you fucked me over for the insurance money, is that part of it? Start talking fast, I'm losing patience here!'

He'd gone plum-coloured again so I talked fast and, considering the state I was in, quite coherently. I didn't leave anything out except the names. The more convincing I was the more chance I had of getting out of Ashton View as a walking wounded.

'And I can have it here in half an hour,' I concluded my pitch.

'Can you now? I have a much better idea: I let my boys bulldoze your hovel and then it should be easy to find an aluminium briefcase in the rubble!'

Absurdly I started worrying about Roy's blood pressure as his face went a darker shade of apoplexy and he took a few breaths to calm himself again.

'Your house keys!' He waggled his fingers impatiently. 'Anyone likely to be home?'

I chucked the keys on the sofa, shook my head. 'Cupboard under the stairs.'

'Wakey? Do the honours.'

Surfer Dude grabbed the keys and made to leave. 'Shall I call the guys in?'

'Just go.' He waved him away. And to me: 'I should've known. It was my first thought that somehow you were fucking me over. But insurance companies don't usually go for capers like that, not for a piddling sum like a hundred and twenty anyway and then I couldn't figure out how you could have pulled it off. What gave you the incredibly stupid idea to try and rip me off?'

'Nothing did. I didn't know you were involved until later.' I didn't admit that I'd never heard of him before the watercolour caper. 'I don't like art thieves, that's all. I'm a painter myself when I'm not –'

'Yes, I heard that,' he said. 'My advice is stick to painting.' He pulled himself out of his chair with a grunt and waved me over to the fireplace between the life-sized china

Moors. 'Come here. Look at this.' Over the fireplace, stuffed into a preposterously bright gilt frame, hung a print of a seascape study by Constable. So? What was that going to prove? Then I did a double-take: it wasn't a print, it was the real thing. I looked around. There were several other small paintings imprisoned in gilt frames fighting the good fight against the maroon wallpaper. That explained where the real money went. 'Yeah, that's right. You thought they were cheap repro shit. They're not. They're the genuine article. And these aren't nicked, boy, they're paid for.' He thumped his chest religiously. 'I'm no art thief.'

'I never for one moment thought you were,' I smarmed. 'But then what are you, Mr Hotchkiss?'

His chins jutted. 'I own a chain of discount stores, I thought you knew that. You being a detective and all that. Everybody knows that.'

'The moment they start selling bottles of vodka and packets of fags at the One Pound Store I'll start shopping there. Your warehouse seemed to be full of that kind of merchandise,' I said affably.

'Ah yes, I have other outlets for that kind of stuff. I sell copied designer gear from Russia, cheap booze smuggled in from France, fake cigarettes from Malaysia, and counterfeit CDs and DVDs from Turkey.'

'An honourable trade.'

He stepped closer. 'What would you know?' He grabbed a handful of my shirt and yanked on it. A button popped. 'Armani. Probably real, huh? CDs? DVDs? You probably don't even think about the price of those. Trainers for your kids? The *right* trainers for your kids? Not important to you. But this shit's important to poor people because in their world it matters. It matters because it's . . . self-esteem, it's, it's being able to hold your head up while you walk down the street or not getting bullied in the playground. And it's *your* class who sells them those fucking dreams on telly. "A Place in the Sun", for fuck's sake.

Houses in Spain, all that shit. But you don't pay 'em the wages to ever afford the stuff. I don't know whether you've looked lately but the difference between the haves and have nots used to be an unbridgeable gulf, now it's a fucking continent. It's like being on another planet.' Roy huffed across to the french windows. Outside his huge, black dog was excavating a flower bed. 'They want the football shirts for their kids, the perfume for their wives, the fags and the booze and the latest DVDs to fill their empty nights with. One day I'll kill that stupid mutt. And I sell them to them at a price they can afford.'

In other words, Roy was providing a valuable service to the community. I had no doubt he was providing banking services as well, since no one selling a bit of booze to pissheads needed the persuasive kind of muscle he surrounded himself with. Money lending at extortionate rates, naturally, loans that could never be paid off, debts that simply grew and grew. I also didn't mention that the stitching on his football shirts was shoddy, his DVDs looked grainy and his fags were made from tumbleweed. As far as I was concerned, selling shoddy replicas to the already dispossessed just added to the misery.

In fact I didn't say anything because I wasn't meant to: Roy probably didn't often get a chance to justify his activities. To ordinary people he presented the persona of the self-made businessman while suspecting that they'd loathe him and his new money even more if they knew where most of it came from.

The dog suddenly jumped up and snapped at thin air, probably chasing a wasp. He'd regret it when he caught it. Then he trampled backwards through what looked like freshly planted bedding. In a minute he would crap in it. Roy knew it too and turned away from the window with a look of disgust on his face. It occurred to me that this was as good a chance as I was likely to get to chuck a few of the china horrors at the man and then leg it out through the french windows, though I wasn't at all sure that I could outrun the huge black mutt out there unless I managed to catch him in mid-turd. Then the moment passed, unused.

'You don't look like the type who ever had to worry about that kind of thing,' he said disgustedly.

He was right of course. Though I had seen poverty when I travelled across Turkey, real poverty, without the benefits of social security payments.

'Daddy had a lot of money?' I waggled a so-so with my head.

'Went to a good school?' I nodded.

'University? Art school?' I nodded again.

He walked up to where I was standing, next to a china Moor radiating cold. I thought I could detect a slight wheeze in Roy's breathing. He pointed up at the Constable. 'Can you paint as well as that?' I shook my head emphatically.

'All a bit of a waste then, wasn't it?'

This conversation was beginning to nark me so I changed the subject. 'Is Bill really your brother?'

Roy fixed me with an assessing stare, then mellowed, seemed to sadden. 'He is. Billy is my youngest brother.' Youngest? He looked at least fifteen years Roy's senior; testimony to the power of drink and the street to age a man. 'Might as well tell you since you won't get a chance to do anything with it. Billy is simple. Always was. Learning difficulties, they'd call it today. Billy was backward. Our mum kept him at home because he couldn't cope at school and got into fights a lot. When our mum died I looked after him and my brother Rob. Rob's in Bristol now, doing all right for himself. And before you get ideas, he's a phone engineer. Rob's straight. Don't see much of him these days.' He mused for a moment. 'I kept Billy close, like our mum had done, even after I got married. But he got more difficult as he got older, he drank more and he'd lash out in frustration, shit, we all drank a hell of a lot.' He pulled a grimace and walked over to his aban-

210

doned coffee on the table and picked up the mug. 'One night I had to go out again and left him and my wife at home. Drinking.' He turned round to face me but there was no theatricality in the short pause that followed. 'He was sitting on the stairs when I came back, he'd been crying and he had that look he always had when he knew he'd done something bad. He had blood on his shirt. I knew instantly Lizzie was dead. He'd bashed her head in with a vodka bottle in the front room.' Perhaps this was also a story Roy didn't tell very often. People do like telling me things. Mostly lies. 'They locked Billy up and would have been quite happy to throw away the key. I made sure they didn't and he got out after eight years in various institutions, back into my care. But eight years inside hasn't improved Billy's state of mind. He hates being inside. He lives like an animal, finds himself hiding places to crawl into but never for long, always moves on soon after. Twice I set Billy up with a place of his own. He'd stay for a week then go off and sleep in Vicky Park.' Roy put his mug on the mantelpiece and stood close, speaking quietly into my face. 'And right from the fucking start they tried to make out that it was really me who killed her. That I had somehow persuaded Billy to take the rap for me. And they won't let it lie. Every few years someone gets desperate to take me out of circulation and hang a murder on me, and then they go after Billy. Business rivals, the police, some fucking journalist. But Billy likes Bath. If I bought him a dream home somewhere else he'd come back to kip in a rat hole by the river in Bath. He's got a thing about water,' Roy said without irony. 'And so I'm vulnerable and when I find anyone sniffing round Billy I get twitchy. And you been sniffing.'

He took a deep breath for his next sentence but was interrupted by a knock on the door. It was Wakey, carrying the aluminium briefcase. He dropped it on to the nearest sofa. 'It's all there.'

'I didn't ask you to fucking count it, did I?'

'No, boss.'

'Get the guys.'

Wakey walked out the door and seconds later the uglies appeared. Cannon was once more fondling his shotgun. It occurred to me that in here it was less than useless. The thing was sawn off. If he used it he'd mow down everyone in the room. Unfortunately he looked moronic enough to shoot first and scratch his head later. Wakey seemed to shrink into insignificance behind the bulk and brutal stupidity of Ball who advanced on me.

Roy pronounced sentence. 'There are two things I can't tolerate and that is people going after my brother and people ripping me off. And you did both. Therefore these . . . gentlemen, I nearly said, these guys are going to take you to a quiet place and break your fucking legs.' He gave them the nod. Ball already had a hold of my arm and twisted it up my back.

'Wait a second,' I protested.

Cannon held the door open, Ball propelled me towards it.

'The guy who kidnapped the woman I found, he's got another one. He's got Alison. Who copied the John Whites. You liked her paintings at Simon Paris's.'

On a sign from Roy my arm untwisted.

'Alison.' He rolled the name around his mouth. 'Dark hair, quite . . . round. Like me.'

'That's Alison. He's threatening to kill her if I go to the police. He's sending me riddles, like this one.' I took the Doctor's latest note from my pocket and unfolded it for him. He held it away from him to get it into focus.

'Only when I solve a riddle does she get fed,' I continued. 'You let these guys loose on me and she'll starve to death. He likes to watch them starve.'

It was as though a switch had been thrown inside his head. 'The fucking perv. The fucking pervy bastard.' He stared hard at me for a minute or so. Then he waved his goons away. Regret once more clouded Ball's visage.

'Now this is what you might call a fucking dilemma,' Roy said once the door had closed. 'I fucking hate perverts.' He waved the Doctor's note around. 'He took her to get his revenge on you, is that it?' I nodded. 'He sounds like a right nutter. Pity. She was quite pretty,' he reminisced. 'Even if she did help rip me off. But you see my problem? If I let you off scot-free then it looks like I'm going soft and before you know it every Dick and Harry is having a go. And if I hand out what you deserve then the only riddle you'll be solving is how come you're still alive. So what am I going to do with you?'

'Perhaps we could just say I owe you one . . .'

'Owe me one? You cheeky sod, you more than fucking owe me! No, pal, you'll get what you deserve *after* you've solved your little problem, you understand? The moment I hear you freed that girl I'll be sending some boys round with a little reminder of what happens when you rip off Roy Hotchkiss.' He amiably walked me to the door and opened it. To the goons waiting outside he said: 'See him out. Let him go.'

'You don't want us to break his legs no more, boss?' Ball looked like a boy whose trip to the fair had been cancelled.

# Chapter Seventeen

Why it took all three of them to see me off the premises I don't know. They marched me silently down the drive to the automatic gate and watched me walk through it. Wakey closed the gate. Ball pulled my mobile from his pocket and lobbed it in a lazy arc over the top. 'Catch!' I had to dive on to the tarmac to prevent it from dashing itself to pieces which produced much hilarity on the other side of the gate.

It might have been a short drive from Ashton to our little valley but it was quite a walk, especially if you hadn't had a drink for twenty-four hours and had slept on a concrete floor. I trotted along the road in a stupefied anger at myself, mainly for my ability to complicate my life with irresistible little ideas like the one that landed me in the current mess. I was so thirsty I was quite ready to throw myself into the first puddle of rainwater I found along the road. Fortunately I didn't come across any. After about twenty minutes of walking, however, a thin rain began to fall from a cement-grey sky. For a while I staggered around with my head back and my mouth open, trying to catch raindrops, looking for all the world like the village idiot abroad. Yet no one saw me. I was walking at that time of the morning where country lanes are empty of farmers and ratrunners alike. I'm not one of the world's most natural walkers but I found enough shortcuts and footpaths to get covered in scratches and crud by the time I made it back to my place. I trotted down the track, fantasizing about bottles of beer, when I came across a traffic jam of cars. Of course, I had left the DS where I'd been rudely extracted from it the day before. The other two cars were familiar: one belonged to Eva, the other to Jerry. Still friends, it seemed, but not so they'd sit in the same car. The DS was still unlocked, the driver door open, the keys in the ignition. In the grey light and thin rain it looked eerily like a crime scene, which of course it was. Thirst took control of my brain and made me remember there was still that crate of Pilsner in the back. I levered a bottle open on the rim of the boot and poured the angrily frothing stuff down my throat. Then I let out a burp Chucky would have been proud of and reversed the car all the way into my yard. Eva and Jerry were just emerging from the house as I swung the car into its usual place.

'You had us so worried where've you been bloody hell what happened to you?' said Eva when she took in the state I was in.

The bottle of beer appeared to have evaporated because I was more thirsty than ever. The two of them followed me as I made a bee-line for the kitchen.

'I saw your car in the drive with the keys inside, couldn't find you anywhere and thought something bad had happened. It seemed so spooky I called Jerry to help me look for you.'

'Excuse me while I empty the water pipes. There might be a hosepipe ban very shortly,' I said and started sucking up water straight from the tap. I splashed some over my head too, which probably didn't improve my appearance: unshaven, filthy, just a little weary and damp.

'Did you sleep in a ditch?' Eva could probably smell the beer on me. She felt my muddy jacket with two reluctant fingers. 'We thought you'd been kidnapped or something.'

'I was just about to call the police when you turned up,' said Jerry. 'Blimey, you really are thirsty.'

'I was and I am.' I put the kettle on the stove, shoved

frozen petit pains in the oven and left them shrugging their shoulders in the kitchen while I went upstairs for a shower. Normally, a long hot shower irons out most kinks but today no amount of hot water would straighten me out. I had acquired a painful crick in my neck and a persistent ache in my lower back. My elbow hurt to touch and had gone purple where Ball had practised his swing on it.

I still only felt half human when I got back to Eva and Jerry who sensibly had made coffee and rescued the petit pains from the oven. I plonked smoked salmon, cream cheese, butter and honey on the table. Smiles all round.

'Here's a story you're not going to print,' I began, spreading thick golden butter on to hot bread. 'Roy Hotchkiss sent his goons around to snatch me out of my car yesterday morning.'

Eva's eyes widened. '*The* Hotchkiss bloke, the gangster? He's a complete anus. How did you get mixed up with him?'

How come everyone had heard of the man except me? In consternation I shoved half a salmony bread roll in my mouth so it took me a while to answer. 'I ripped him off to the tune of one hundred and ten big ones.'

Jerry let his mouth fall open theatrically. I noticed his dental work wasn't up to much.

'All in the line of duty,' I assured them.

'And he found out? And wanted it back, I presume? I'm surprised you're alive, Chris,' Eva marvelled. 'The man's bad news. He put a *Chronicle* reporter in hospital a couple of years back just for asking questions.'

'What kind of questions?' I was making a complete mess of myself as honey ran down the back of my hand. I didn't care, this was bliss.

'He never said. He didn't press charges and moved to the Orkney Isles the day he got out of hospital.'

'Good choice.' I had a pretty good idea what questions he might have asked and would've liked to know if he'd

216

got any answers before Roy put him out of action. But if he ran all the way to the Orkneys chances were he wouldn't talk to me, always presuming I found him.

I temporarily forgot about my elbow and set it on the table; it gave a sharp reminder and I winced. I rolled my neck to ease the pain there and it cracked loud enough to startle Eva. 'For crying out loud, will you do something about that, Jerry? He needs a complete overhaul.'

'Be my pleasure. How about it, Honeysett? Free of charge,' he offered.

I don't normally run to doctors and therapists for every piddling thing but my neck was giving me a headache and I felt all out of kilter. 'Can you do it here or do I have to come to your scary clinic?'

'We'll do it right here, just as soon as you're ready.'

'He's not ready until he's told me how he ripped off Roy Hotchkiss for a hundred and ten big 'uns and lived. Come on, Chris, the sooner you tell me the sooner you can give yourself over to the healing hands of Jerry.'

'What for? You can't print it anyway,' I objected.

'I'm just interested. As a friend. And then there's always the possibility you'll get yourself killed, in which case I'll make sure the story gets an airing.'

With friends like these . . . I began telling the whole story, starting more or less at the beginning, which gave me a good opportunity to review the events. It sounded pretty idiotic, a real make-work scheme, even to myself. I left out any reference to the Doctor and Alison's abduction, so Annis's accident must have sounded like pure recklessness.

'You're a marvel, both of you.' She slipped on her shades and picked up her bag. 'While Mr O'Neil here straightens you out I'll drive to the hospital and visit Annis and explain your absence.'

Ten minutes later I was quietly groaning on the floor, having at last found out why people happily handed over small fortunes to Jerry for doing minute things very

217

slowly. He'd found some wishy-washy electronic music I didn't know I had and put that on; it was surprisingly relaxing. Then cupped my head in his hands and started to work his magic. A few minutes into this bliss my mobile chimed.

'I should have made you switch that off. Just try and ignore it,' Jerry advised soothingly.

But I knew I didn't have a choice. I answered it. 'Honeysett.'

'Chris, it's John, John Gatt,' said the excited but strangely warbly voice.

'John, I can hardly hear you, what's up?'

'Sorry, I'm driving. I can hardly hear you either. I've just come from Keith's house. I've got something that might solve our problem of always playing catch-up to the Doctor. But I'm on my way to deliver stuff to London, I'll be back tonight.'

'If it helps us nail the Doctor tell me now.'

'It's not that straightforward. I'll come round to your place tonight, say half nine? Gotta go, there's traffic ahead.'

'All right, see you here at half nine,' I conceded reluctantly. When I gratefully returned to Jerry's ministrations I wondered just how much store to set by John's great discovery. Everyone was an amateur sleuth, given half a chance, and poor John had more motivation than most to come up with ideas. Ideas . . . Alison was slowly starving to death and I was lying on the floor with a belly full of cream cheese and smoked salmon . . .

'You've gone all tense again,' Jerry complained, still moving my head between his hands with hardly detectable movements.

I let myself relax and sink into the carpet. Time I called Tim in Southampton and found out when I could expect him back here, pulling his w– 'Bloody hell!' Jerry had suddenly turned my head to the side, using the edge of one hand as a pivot. An almighty crunch rippled through my neck and upper spine and the sound of it still echoed in my ears. For a couple of seconds I expected a corresponding pain to race up through my head, instead my headache disappeared and my forehead unknotted itself.

'A couple of your top vertebrae were misaligned but that should have sorted it. If not, give us a shout.'

I got up off the floor and stood. It felt as though I was standing straight for the first time in ages. My appreciation for Jerry's skill was at an all-time high and I told him so.

After he'd gone off back into town to get his hands on some paying customers I climbed up the stairs towards my attic office but the open door of my bedroom drew me inexorably towards the cool crisp sheets. Just for half an hour, I promised as I let myself fall across the bed.


When I woke it was early evening and I was shivering in a cool draught from the open window. I closed it and pulled on a thick black sweater. I tried not to feel too guilty about having wasted another afternoon. Part of me had already decided to call Manvers Street and drop the whole thing into the broad lap of Avon and Somerset's finest Superintendent. I had run out of ideas and I couldn't do anything more for Alison. Yet another part of me believed that she was dead. And I had probably killed her with my dithering.

With a black coffee and a stale croissant from the otherwise empty breadbin I eventually climbed to the dizzy heights of my office. Somehow it felt as though I hadn't been here for a very long time. I cranked up the computer and while it percolated into life idly clicked through my phone messages. There really was someone wanting me to find an iguana called Knut. Then I checked my email: there were over twenty messages from Tim, calling me a *lazy technophobe git fossil and what did I have a computer for if I couldn't even drag myself out of the Cro-Magnon era long enough to read my sodding mail* and more in that vein. The last one actually contained some information: he'd be back in a couple of days. Fine. I mailed him the text of the Doctor's latest message and told him to call me, not mail me, if he had any ideas. That reminded me; I stuck my mobile on the charger and went downstairs.

It was getting dark and John would be here any minute. The phone rang. I had no sense of foreboding and for once my instinct didn't let me down: it was Annis.

'They won't let you use your mobile on the ward, then make you rent a phone from them. I want out! Bit groggy still and my ankle's in plaster, a few scrapes, otherwise I'm fine. I just won't be riding any bikes for a bit. Tell me you salvaged the Norton.'

'Not me, but I know a man who did. Jake found it in his heart to take it on, only because it's a British bike and he knows a chap from the Norton Owners Club. He carted it off but said he couldn't find the number plate.'

'Yeah, well, I hadn't got around to registering it yet . . .'

'You're a nutter, you know that? When will they let you out?'

'I was supposed to see a senior doctor this afternoon but he never materialized. Tomorrow, hopefully.'

'Call me, I'll pick you up,' I promised rashly.

I opened the fridge and gave the inside a good hard stare. A couple of rashers of bacon and a lump of Parmesan were the only company for a bottle of white. I opened it, poured myself a generous glass and put a big pan of water on the stove. I chopped the bacon and grated some of the Parmesan, then let a fistful of spaghetti slide into the boiling water and looked up at the big kitchen clock. Half past nine. Glugged some olive oil into a frying pan, an unpeeled clove of garlic and the chopped bacon went in and sizzled away. Fished out the garlic and splashed in some wine from my glass. I beat a few eggs in a bowl with the Parmesan and looked up at the clock: twenty to. Where was John? Drained the spaghetti, quickly dropped it into the beaten eggs and cheese and stirred.

Poured the chopped bacon and oil over it: Spaghetti Carbonara. Another mystery solved. And if John didn't show up soon I'd snarf the lot. I went outside with a mound of it on a soup plate and twirled spaghetti while I stood in the yard, illuminated only by the lights from the house. A few stars were out among the scudding clouds. The damp night-smells of spring and the fragrances of the herb garden around the corner mingled with the strong aroma of Italian food and reminded me of time spent bumming around the heel of Italy . . . A tiny rattling sound made me look up. It came from the direction of the track. Then a lot of nothing. Then it came again. A sort of clunky sound. A bicycle? I closed my eyes and the image of a soldier popped into my mind, overloaded with gear, trying to move quickly and quietly at the same time. I opened my eyes. Surely not. Most unlikely. Now I became less concerned about the rattling than about the lot of nothing. If something was rattling on the track why hadn't it got here by now? And what was it with Italian food and spooky noises? Then the hard, panicked flapping of a wood pigeon halfway down the track decided it. I put the plate down on the bonnet of Annis's Landy, got the big torch from the boot of my car and went looking. This was my place, my home, my land. I couldn't allow myself to get spooked each time I had pasta for supper.

I walked quietly and in darkness nevertheless, treading carefully, avoiding the potholes and deepest ruts. I listened out for more clunking sounds, for the snap of a twig, anything, but couldn't hear a thing. 'It's quiet. *Too* quiet.' The old spooky cliché cheered me up. I flicked on the torch, played the concentric rings of its light along the path as far as I could see it and there was John with his bicycle. He was dead.

I stood paralysed for a moment and the torch beam began to tremble. John's body was lying by the side of the road, his silver-grey mountain bike neatly propped against the dark bole of a tree. The fitness fanatic had cycled across. I knew he was dead before I finally forced myself to walk up to him. There was a dark stain on his sweatshirt, still spreading. His face looked grey, his eyes closed, his mouth wide open. I knelt by his side and went through the motions of looking for a pulse. Nothing. I scrabbled round my pockets for my mobile, then realized it was sitting on the charger in my office. I stood and listened: nothing. I swept the area around me with the torch beam and saw only jumping shadows and moths. I knelt again and lifted his sweatshirt; an ugly puncture mark just below his ribs was the source of the bloodstain. It looked like a stab wound to me but I could leave niceties like that to the pathologist. No doubt I would already get into trouble for having touched the body at all. I turned away reluctantly and trotted towards the house and the phone. I would get a sheet, too, to cover him up until the police got here. Then I stopped in the middle of the track and stood for a while.

John was dead. What could the police do about it? I already knew who killed him: the Doctor did. And by extension, I did. By telling him about Alison, by allowing him to involve himself. I would have some explaining to do when Superintendent Needham skewered and grilled me about how come he got himself knifed on my land. How would I explain what he was doing here? How would I keep Alison's abduction from him? How long would I spend in Manvers Street's poky little interview rooms? How much more time was I going to waste?

I jogged back to the house. In the sitting room I sat by the phone, waited to get my breath back, then dialled Rob and Kat's number. Neighbours of mine at the top of the valley, their smallholding was the source of the black-faced sheep I sometimes borrowed to keep the grass down. They also kept chickens, pigs and a few pretty longhorn cattle and supplied the nearby farm shop with their own meat products. And they had a large cold store. I had hoped Rob would pick up but it was Kat, who was always civil but for some reason not my greatest fan.

'If you want Rob he's in bed. We get up at five, remember? Lifestock and all that . . .?'

'That's all right. I've got a favour to ask . . .'

'Really? You surprise me. Go on then.'

I made her believe that I had come into a sudden 'windfall' of venison I needed to store until I could deal with it properly and she grudgingly admitted they had space for it if I was quick about it.

The thought of what I was about to do made my hair stand up at the back of my neck. I tried not to play through the myriad things that could go wrong and ran upstairs. In the airing cupboard I found a bedsheet and a blanket.

Back outside I looked into the Landy's cab. Keys in the ignition. Annis insisted her heap only moved with the help of certain spells and incantations and no thief would get very far in it. I sent off a short speculative prayer. Eventually the thirty-year-old diesel yawned and woke and I bumped out of the yard. The half-eaten bowl of Carbonara slewed off the bonnet and shattered on to the ground. Didn't like it much anyway. (The bowl. Nothing wrong with my Carbonara.)

Had John really stumbled on something that would help me nail the Doctor? Whatever it was, the Doctor had intended that it would go to John's grave with him. If John's discovery had unnerved him enough to kill . . .

I'm knifing a man in the dark, not a hundred yards from a house I know to be occupied. How sure can I be he is dead? Do I stay and listen to his breath arresting, his pulse slowing, stopping? Or do I make off as fast as I can?

How much would it unnerve the Doctor if he thought John had survived? Could I force him into the open? Could I make him come to me, here, to finish the job and try and finish me? One way to find out.

I stopped as close to the body as I could, let the tailboard down and spread the blanket, then the sheet over the loading area. Standing astride him I grabbed hold of his sweater by the shoulders and pulled. His head flopped back, his sweater came up but very little of John. He'd been tall and muscular when he was alive; he was heavy in death and my elbow sent out protesting stabs of pain. It took a surprising effort to turn, lift, push and drag him on to the back of the Land Rover. I covered his body first with the folds of the bedsheet, then flipped the blanket over. Somehow the edges of the blanket didn't meet in the middle. I was not exactly a stranger to death but this was the first time I'd had to move a dead body and I felt ashamed at my reluctance to touch John's skin which reminded me of cold porridge. In my mind death, decay and disease all seemed to mix into a single revolting entity. I thought I could smell death too, a mixture of faeces and a fungal, rotting sweetness. Unsanctified and undignified by a coffin this felt uncomfortably like picking up road kill. In other words: I wasn't cut out for this.

I drove up the track at a funereal pace for fear of bouncing the body off the back. Once on the tarmac lane that winds its way up the valley I drove a little faster. A dreadful panic was gnawing at me, trying to swamp me. What I was about to do had all the hallmarks of a monu-mental, irredeemable, unforgivable mistake. What if I was stopped on the way there? I put that out of my mind. It was only a two-mile journey, though it felt like the narrow band of road lit by the Land Rover's headlights wound on through the dark forever. At last I bounced into Ron and Kat's yard, a little too hard, perhaps, and apologized silently to John for the rough treatment. A light came on on the side of the squat and functional stone cottage as I walked to the back of the Landy and found with a shock that John's body lay uncovered. I quickly drew sheet and blanket back over him, just in time to prevent Kat seeing what the real cargo was.

'Wrapped in a blanket,' she scoffed as she walked past, wearing the same boots, jeans and grey sweater she had worn on every occasion I had visited. 'Not very professional, Chris. No,' she held up a hand and walked on to the low concrete buildings to our left, 'I don't want to know. I never saw it and neither did Rob.' She unlocked the big metal door in the centre, flicked on the neon light inside and pointed at the walk-in cold store. 'So it's only for a couple of days, right?'

'Right.' I had given myself forty-eight hours. After that I would own up to Needham and admit defeat.

'Okay then. Plenty of room in the back. Since I never saw a thing I naturally can't help you carry it. Lock up and stick the keys through the letter box when you're done. And goodnight.' She dropped the key into my hand and walked back to the house.

There were stainless steel sinks, kitchen cupboards and long work surfaces, all scrupulously clean and depressingly clinical under the hard strip lighting. I rummaged around until I found a big roll of kitchen string. With this I tied the blanket tightly around John's body, all the while fearing that Kat might be watching me from the darkened house. I reversed the car as close to the door as possible, then opened the heavy door of the cold store. It was nearly empty, apart from a steel table and a few cotton-covered cuts of beef hanging from the ceiling and a pile of folded polythene sheeting. I nearly overbalanced when I lifted the tightly wrapped body and staggered to the rear of the room where I laid John down as gently as I could. My elbow throbbed with pain and I felt exhausted. I covered him loosely with the pile of plastic sheeting. If it all went wrong then this was the moment I would remember as the all-time low point in my career and almost certainly the end of it. It was not a good moment. This was not a good place and not a good hour to think what would happen if the Doctor got away; if Alison died of slow starvation.

I locked up, posted the key and fled.

Back at Mill House I emptied the bottle of wine in one long draught and got another from the wine rack in the cupboard under the stairs. The gun locker was open. And empty. I stared at it for a while trying to figure out why my shotgun wasn't there until I realized that I had furnished Roy's goons with my keys so they could retrieve the money. Cannon had added my shotgun to his collection. I would think about that later, I promised myself, much later.

# Chapter Eighteen

I do like to be brought a cup of coffee first thing in the morning, as long as first thing isn't too unearthly an hour, and if it's delivered by a beautiful woman so much the better. Only not one that walks through closed doors, thank you.

'How the hell did you get into the house, Eva?' I growled ungraciously while accepting the mug with one eye open and a minimum of bodily movement.

'Charmed, I'm sure. Well, someone had to pick up Annis from the hospital and you sure weren't going to do it, were you? The coffee was her idea entirely, she's downstairs getting the hang of the crutches. Are you still in a bad state or again in a bad state? It's so hard to tell with you, Honeysett.' She left as abruptly as she had appeared. I opened the other eye and checked the bedside clock. It was half past ten. This didn't fool me into making a sudden move because I knew my brain would slosh about unpleasantly. The coffee eventually helped my nervous system to establish which way was up. Only then was it safe to totter off into the shower.

Some groceries had appeared in the kitchen. Sliced bread. Good Lord, whatever next, soya margarine? Snobbery saved me having to acknowledge that my system was in no fit state to accept solids yet. I made more coffee. The metallic squeak of cheap National Health crutches announced Annis's arrival. She heaved through the door, followed by a breathless Eva. 'I've got the hang of them

now, let me back on the Norton,' she announced, swinging
a foot and ankle in plaster. She was wearing a black vest,
a criminally short skirt and probably not much else. 'Any
news about Alison?' she asked. I gave her a significant
stare. 'It's all right, I told Eva. And swore her to secrecy.
No, don't look at me like that, she's not going to breathe a
word until it's all over.'

'S'right, Gumshoe. This is different.' Eva nodded reas-
suringly. 'You can trust me.'

'And with me on crutches and Tim away you really do
need help. So, are we any further? Did you have any
thoughts about the Doctor's *next trick*? What's with the
mega lie-in? Any developments at all? Are you going to
say something any time soon?'

'Drank too much after I found John's body.' I can be
quite concise when I'm hung over.

As we sat bleakly at the kitchen table I was wrestling with
panic again whilst watching the enormity of the situation
reflected in their shocked, pale faces. Even Annis fumbled
a cigarette from my packet and lit it wordlessly before
demanding all the details. Eva sucked grimly on a fat
hand-rolled cheroot while I told them all I knew. Thought
I knew.

Annis gave Eva's hand a squeeze. 'Looks like I didn't do
you any favours by telling you, Ev. Sorry.'

Next I probed round my jacket lining and produced the
tracking device. 'And then there's this.'

Annis recognized it for what it was immediately. 'One of
Tim's?' she asked hopefully.

'The Doctor's,' I contradicted. 'Found it in the lining of
my jacket. He must know I never go anywhere without it.
Probably been in there for ages. And if he's this high tech
. . .' Instinctively we all looked around the kitchen. 'He
managed to get in here before. He left Alison's clothes on
my bed. The place has to be bugged. Which is how he
knew about John, which is how he'll know about you, Ev.

I think you and Jerry should take a nice holiday somewhere, preferably overseas. New York's fabulous at this
time of year.'

She shook her head slowly. 'I'm used to looking over
my shoulder. Perhaps John wasn't.' She shrugged. 'Should
we be talking here at all if you think he's got the place
bugged?'

Annis's hand tightened around her coffee mug. 'Well if
you're listening then listen to this, you sad wanker: I'm
going to *kill* you! That's a fucking *promise!*' She picked up
her half-full mug and hurled it at the wall where it shattered with a satisfying crack. Her face set hard, she
grabbed her crutches and pushed to her feet but after a
couple of steps one crutch slipped on spilt coffee and she
overbalanced and fell before we could catch her. We both
rushed to her aid but she struggled up by herself. 'Leave
me alone.'

'It's these shitty crutches, I'll find you some decent ones,'
I promised lamely.

She swung out of the door. 'Forget it. Go find Alison,'
she called back. 'And you might do something with John's
bloody bike, you left it by the bloody track!'

We listened to her thump laboriously up the stairs, then
slam the bedroom door behind her. Eva hoisted her bag
over her shoulder.

'You can stay here if you want,' I offered. 'It might be
safer. It might not. I'm fresh out of certainties, I'm
afraid.'

'I wasn't asking for any,' she said firmly. 'No. Let me
copy down that last clue the bastard gave you and I'll see
what the *Chronic*'s archives can come up with. I'm a dab
hand at finding stuff as long as someone bothered to write
it down somewhere.' I copied it for her on a scrap of paper.
She speed-read it: '*FormynexttrickIshall* – *howcanIputhis
politely* – *talkoutofyourarse, asyoulldiscoverwhenyougenuflect
initscontemplation.* Mm. Something there, at the tip of my
tongue . . . no, gone again.' She stuffed it into her bag.

'Right. When the going gets tough and all that. Be in touch. Yuck, it's gonna rain again.'

She bounced her little car up the track, I followed slowly, reluctantly, on foot. As I had hoped, daylight made a lot of difference. Nothing about the spot said murder scene. There was John's bicycle, a state of the art mountain bike, leaning against a willow. Just a bicycle, except to me, the Doctor and anybody into a spot of forensics. I looked around for blood and couldn't see a single drop anywhere. The bike had excellent suspension, I noted as I rode it back to the yard, and didn't make clunky noises. I unfastened the front wheel and chucked it and the rest of the bike in the back of the DS, got in and started the engine. I'd picked up the Webley from my bedroom and was about to clip it into its holder when I had a thought (always a dangerous thing). I walked back into the house and climbed the stairs to Annis's room. The door was open, which I took as a good sign, and Annis was sitting at her desk cum dressing table cum dumping ground with a weighty tome on serial killers. It seemed to have cheered her up. I let the Webley dangle on one finger from the trigger guard. 'Thought you might want this. I'm off out.'

'That's all right, I'll get the shotgun out in a minute.'

'I . . . sent it to be serviced,' I said lightly and let the gun slide off my finger and bounce on her bed.

Then I drove to Jake's under a sky the colour of over-cooked cabbage. It was getting darker by the minute; Eva's weather forecast was set to be spot on.

Jake greeted me with his usual enthusiasm. 'If you've come about the Norton turn straight round, it's not even here. But the prognosis is good, it'll straighten out all right. Now go away before your clapped-out Camembert of a car falls apart in my yard.'

I ignored him, it's the only way. 'D'you remember when you spent six months on crutches after you hit a tree with your mate's hang-glider?'

'I might be bald but I haven't got Alzheimer's. Yet.'

'I was wondering what happened to the crutches.'

'Now there's a good question.' Jake smoothed an invisible beard round his chin. 'Wait here.'

While he disappeared into the house I got out the bike and stuck the front wheel back on. Jake returned on the crutches, powering forward at astonishing speed. 'Handcrafted from finest rosewood. Had them sent over from the States, $875, worth every penny.'

'Cent, surely.'

Jake pulled a long-suffering face. 'For your lady, is it? How's she getting on?'

'Last time I saw her she was sitting in her room with a revolver and a book on serial killings.'

'That probably counts as normal in your household.'

'You'd be surprised. But it's okay, there's just four bullets left in the Webley. Wouldn't be much of a spree. Only I wouldn't go and describe her as "my lady" within earshot or she might actually use the thing.' I pointed to the crutches. 'Want to swap them for a mountain bike?'

Jake hopped around it to survey the offering from all angles. 'You pinched it off a kid or something? You can borrow the crutches, you know.'

'You'd be doing me a favour.'

'I see. If there's any comeback then you'll need these for a long time,' he assured me as we swapped. He bounced the bike on its suspension. 'This come with it?' He detached the small grey bag that dangled from the back of the saddle.

'Repair kit?'

'Says "Kag in a Bag".'

'A cagoule then, I might need one in a minute,' I said, sniffing at the dark skies.

Jake pulled a lime green plastic rainproof out of the bag.

'Mm, perhaps not,' I amended. A battered paperback flipped out from inside it. I picked it up. *Curious Bath: Off the Beaten Track in and around the City.* I stuffed it in my pocket. 'Anything else in there?'

He checked the bag and pockets. 'Nope.'

'All yours, then.' I put the crutches in the back and turned my thoroughly insulted Citroën out of his yard, giving a cheery wave.

Sitting at the kitchen table I reverently smoothed out the slightly bent and crumpled paperback. The front cover had a black and white photograph of the bandstand in Victoria Park, with the title *Curious Bath* above and the legend *Off the Beaten Track in and around the City* below it. By Arthur Bennie. I got up again without opening it, put the kettle on, ground coffee beans and made a big pot of wide-awake Blue Mountain stuff. Then I went back to the little book. I had no doubt that this was what John had got himself killed for and I was afraid of opening it and completely failing to see what he saw.

I opened it. In the upper margin of the flyleaf, written in slightly faded ink, was a familiar name: Keith Ward. There was that name again. It didn't mean anything, did it? So John had gone and borrowed this book off Keith to help with our hunt for the Doctor. Some hunt. Then Ludwig's Fifth started off in my pocket and nearly made me spill coffee everywhere. I grappled with the phone as though I'd never used one before. 'Yes?'

'That was a very stupid thing to do, getting that boy involved. Killing him gave me no pleasure but after the girl survived the bike crash I felt I had to demonstrate my competence.'

The complacent, grating, robotic voice made me want to scream but I fought down the impulse and smoothed out my voice. 'All right, you made your point. Both John and Annis will be out of circulation for a while. It's just you and me. How is Alison? Is she alive?'

There was a pause of a few seconds. Was he digesting what I'd just told him? 'She is hungry, my boy, and losing weight fast. And you can do nothing for her, it seems. I'm getting tired of waiting.'

'I'll be th . . .' I started but the line had gone dead. As usual, try as I might, I could find no trace in the call register of the mobile that this conversation had ever taken place. Hot anger and frustration held me paralysed for a while before I managed to focus my eyes back on the book before me. It was published in 1983 and even then the quality of the paper, print and sparse photographic illustration would have looked cheap, and I didn't recognize the publisher. I skimmed through the ponderous introduction, then started reading the guide. I read slowly, carefully, not wanting to miss a clue, miss the thing that had got John so excited and had convinced him that we could catch our man with the help of this slim volume. Annis appeared on her creaking crutches. I got the rosewood pair out from the car and presented them to her. It earned me an all too brief kiss and a tired smile. I didn't mention the nature of my studies; I was sure the house was bugged and unsure about everything else. Reimmersed in the hidden world of Bath – underground amphitheatres and witches' graveyards – I barely acknowledged the arrival of a bowl of soup and when I'd finished slurping it, couldn't have told you which of the fifty-seven varieties I had sampled.

The guide mentioned St Mary the Virgin in Charlcombe. There was even a picture of the holy spring. I turned the page. The next entry was entitled 'Walter Sickert's Last Resting Place, St Nicholas Church Cemetery'. I sighed. John had been right, this little book might have helped us a lot. I turned to the next entry. 'William Herschel Museum, The Discovery of Uranus'. I stopped in mid page-turning, my hand arrested by an arresting thought. What was that fatuous thing I'd said to Needham? 'Two don't make a series.' I'd been proved wrong. I turned the pages back. The holy spring, Sickert's grave, then the Herschel Museum, then 'Hedgemead Park, The Park

Created by a Landslide'. I stopped reading and started running.

The Wards lived in a small but solid-looking house on St John's Road, not two minutes' walk from the church where I parked the DS, hoping its bonnet might not attract the same attention as the Morris had. Thick, oppressive cloud threatened a downpour but so far had only succeeded in turning mid-afternoon into evening. Street lights were coming on when I opened the gate on the small, immaculately kept front garden and put my finger on the well-polished brass bell button in the centre of the door. I didn't really expect anyone to be there and was quite prepared to make the round of the churches but almost immediately Linda Ward opened the door.

'You!' She shook her head and smiled thinly, adding a chill to the gathering darkness. 'Who've you lost this time?'

'Is your husband at home? I want to speak to him.'

'Do you now? You're in luck, what with the Festival Opening he's taken a few days off. You'll find him out the back. Go round.' She indicated the passage by the side of the house, screened by a white-washed wall from the neighbouring garden. I followed the walkway into the back and entered a war zone.

Two sheds at the bottom of a neat but practically plantless garden had disgorged the impedimenta of World War Two and a man in period British Army uniform was pointing an Enfield rifle at the sky, squinting along its sight. Only his incongruous ponytail spoilt the historically perfect image. Webbing, water bottle, gas mask carrier, all there. What was more startling still was the fact that it all looked so new. As it would have then.

'You've got enough equipment here to fight the war all over again, not just play at it.' I indicated ammunition boxes, radios, tarpaulins, camouflage nets, rucksacks and other equipment I couldn't readily identify.

'That's the whole point of battle re-enactment. And we don't play at it, Mr Honeysett. We see ourselves as a living museum, a historical resource. All our equipment is genuine. These are not toys.' He sat down on a green metal box with black stencilled numbers on the side and leant the rifle against it next to him. 'How can I help this time?'

'I wasn't aware that you helped before. Are you off fighting someone with this genuine stuff or just scaring the neighbours again?' I wandered around, prodding bits of equipment with my shoe, which made Keith frown with irritation.

'The Opening of the Bath Festival, tomorrow night. We're doing a re-enactment in Victoria Park, below the Royal Crescent.'

'And who will you be fighting? Do the Germans send over a detachment of their re-enactors for you to shoot at?'

This appeared to amuse him almost despite himself, judging by his ungenerous smile. 'The Germans don't go in for re-enacting World War Two much.'

'I wonder why.'

'I wonder why are you here, Mr Honeysett?' Keith asked with a sigh. 'I'm really rather busy, as I'm sure you can see.'

'Ah yes, I nearly forgot. Bad news from the front. John can't join you tomorrow.'

'Oh, why is that?'

'He's unwell.'

'Unwell,' Keith echoed.

'Yes. Actually he had an accident on his bicycle. He'll mend but he won't be playing soldiers for a while.'

'Oh dear. He's in hospital then?'

'No, we're looking after him at my house. It happened just outside and the doctor said it would be best not to move him.'

'I'm sorry to hear that, give him my best, won't you? Even though I was quite angry with him this morning.'

I just raised my eyebrows, inviting him to elaborate.

'Oh, he came over yesterday to talk about tomorrow. We talked in there.' He pointed at the larger of the sheds. I ambled over. It was more like a summerhouse, having a desk, chairs, a heater in the corner and shelves and shelves of books, all of them apparently historical. 'This morning I found one of my books was missing. It could only have been John, taking it without asking. It's quite a rare book, too, by a local historian. Long out of print.'

'I'll ask him about it,' I promised.

'No, no, don't bother. If he's unwell . . . It isn't that important.' He rose. The interview was over. 'Thank you for letting me know about John but as you can see I really am busy, Mr Honeysett.'

'Of course.' I made for the passage towards the front of the house. 'Good luck for tomorrow.'

'Luck doesn't come into it.' Keith fingered the muzzle of his rifle. 'Military precision in planning and execution, that's the thing.'

I strode away briskly but tiptoed back and peered around the corner. Keith was standing stiff and still, apart from the hands by his side working themselves into fists.

I called Eva while I walked down St John's Road and asked her to meet me at the Bathtub, which was just down the road. 'Yes, now.'

When I got there myself the place was still closed, though I could see some light at the back. I hammered on the glass. Clive came to the door. 'We're not open yet.'

'I know.' I pushed past him, which isn't easy with a door that narrow. 'But it's going to tip it down in a minute. What are you going to do, let me stand in the rain until you do open? How long has that pot of coffee been stewing on the hotplate?'

'I made it fresh half an hour ago,' he defended himself.

'Fresh and half an hour ago don't go together where coffee is concerned, but I'll have some anyway.'

'Anything for the Great Detective. Hope you don't mind me working while you refresh yourself.' He plonked a mug of coffee on the bar and disappeared into the back. I took a biro and an order pad from behind the counter, sat at the window table and doodled until my new theory had taken shape. The first, ploppy rain pockmarked the pavement when Eva arrived and clicked her car keys against the window. I let her in and furnished her with a coffee.

Clive popped his head around the corner. 'Take the place over, why don't you?' And disappeared again.

'Don't mind him,' I reassured her. 'He works for a living, makes him grumpy.'

'So what's up?'

'We're going to nail the Doctor. Today,' I said, a little dramatically.

'What, with that?' She pointed at my doodles which no longer made much sense even to myself.

'No. With this.' I produced the paperback and opened it at the appropriate place. I was very sure of this. 'Observe. The holy spring. Next item covered in the book, Sickert's grave.'

'So? Coincidence.'

I turned to the next item. 'Coincidence my arse. What's the note say?'

'Ehm, I've got it here.' She fumbled a piece of paper from her pocket. *'For my next trick I shall – how can I put this politely – talk out of your arse . . .'*

'The Herschel Museum. Polite for your arse: Uranus. Old schoolboy joke. *As you'll discover when you genuflect in its contemplation.* Herschel discovered the planet Uranus with a home-made telescope at his house, No. 19 New King Street. In 1781, if you're interested.'

'I am not. God, this coffee is awful. All I want to know is: how's this helping us to catch the Doctor? You've solved another riddle, that's all, Alison gets a handful of seed and we get another riddle.'

'That's not all. He's using the same book, don't you see that?'

'Looks like he might be,' she admitted. 'Oh, I get it. If he does then we'll get the jump on him because we'll already know the answer to the *next* riddle.'

'You're catching on. He leaves me notes. Now it could be that he prepared the whole charade beforehand and all the Doctor's notes are already in place. At the holy spring in Charlcombe the note was floating on the water. It couldn't have been there long. Similar thing at the cemetery.'

'That means we'll be able to wait for him when he delivers the next note because we'll know where he'll put it.' In her excitement Eva took a large gulp of stewed coffee and pulled a face. 'What's the next clue, after the Herschel?'

I turned to the next item in the book. 'Hedgemead Park. According to this it was created after a landslide demolished the houses on that site, Somerset Buildings, in 1875. Lots of people died.'

'Didn't know that.'

'Two pubs were destroyed.'

'Tragic.'

A hairy face, suddenly pressed against the window, made both of us jump. It was Tim.

'You look like you walked down from John o'Groats, not drove up from Southampton,' I admonished when I let him in.

'Thought they might let me go earlier if I stopped shaving. As a last resort I was going to stop showering. Hi, Eva.' He accepted a mug of coffee and sipped it without comment. 'Thought I might find you guys here. What did you do to Annis? The woman's on crutches and came to the door with a revolver in her hand . . .'

I gave him the short version of what had happened and realized it sounded like a catalogue of disasters.

'I turn my back for five minutes . . . Right, what's the plan then?'

238

I suddenly noticed how much I'd missed the kid. I quickly filled him in and waited for his reaction.

'Okay, sounds like it might work. When are we going to do it then?'

'Today. Now.'

'Now? Seriously? I haven't had anything to eat yet,' he complained.

I pointed out that neither had Alison.

When I handed Tim the little plastic homing bug he gave a low whistle. 'GPS, mate. He'll know exactly where this baby is.' To my dismay he picked up the biro and stuck its point into a tiny hole in the casing. 'It's all right, just testing that it's still got power. It has, it's active.'

He nonchalantly let it slip into his own jacket pocket just as Clive appeared and switched on all the lights, inside and out. 'Right, we're open now. Just let me chalk up the specials for tonight and I'll take your order.'

'We're just leaving, Clive, but I might be back later,' I told him.

'There's no rush,' was his advice as we all squeezed out the door into the rain.

# Chapter Nineteen

'So now Tim has the bug in his pocket he'll think it's you at the Herschel Museum,' Eva said. We were trudging through the strengthening rain along Walcot Street. 'But he can't sit in front of a computer all day to keep an eye on where you are at all times, surely.'

'Doesn't need to. Just like you he's probably got a pocket PC that connects wirelessly to the computer he uses to track my movements. But relying on it is where he's making a mistake. Even if I hadn't discovered it that still only meant he'd know where the jacket is. He thinks he's clever but he's given us a weapon.'

'But won't he go there and see Tim instead of you? I've been to the Herschel Museum, it's truly tiny, they're such tiny rooms.'

'That's what I'm relying on. There's no way he could leave the next note there under my nose but it's safe and dry inside so he can put it there as early as he likes. I guarantee it's already there. But unless he changes his habits he'll want to hide the note in the park right under my nose.'

We crossed the road, entered Hedgemead Park at the bottom of Margaret's Hill and puffed up the slope. Below us crawled the rush hour traffic of the London Road but here it was quieter; damp, dark and dripping from every leaf. The park, created on the terraces of washed-away streets, was small but effectively cut in two by a central path in a deep cutting, with gently rusting wrought-iron fencing and gates. There was no single point where both sides could be overlooked. The western part contained the small, circular bandstand and a twelve-foot eagle-crested Victorian drinking fountain in ornate cast iron; the eastern part appeared to have no noteworthy features or structures.

We made for the bandstand to get out of the rain and waited for Tim's call, leaning on the railings and smoking damp cigarettes. I'd switched the mobile to vibrate which I'd never tried before; it made me jump when it went off.

'I've paid my entrance fee and I'm going downstairs.' I could hear Tim's footsteps. 'I've been told the museum shuts in fifteen minutes. The kind people let me in for half price. But this had better be easy to find.'

'It'll be a doddle. Just keep talking, tell me what you see.'

'I'm on the lower ground floor now, level with the garden. It's a kitchen, like a Georgian kitchen, with a coal-fired cooking range and copper pots everywhere, you'd love it. Bit further on ye olde workshoppe-y place with tools and stuff where old Hersch used to grind his lenses. Oh wait, at the other end is a little cinema sort of room with a screen but it's not switched on.'

'Have a good sniff around there. The note says *talk out of your arse, as you'll discover when you genuflect in its contemplation* so there could be something hidden there.'

It seemed like an age before his voice came back. 'Nah, mate, it's immaculately dusted and empty around here, just the projection unit, screen and chairs. I've been on my back on the floor and there's nothing underneath. It's tiny in here, I couldn't miss anything out of the ordinary. I'm going upstairs now.'

I walked around in circles and lit a new cigarette from the last while I waited.

'Okay, here we are, couple of rooms, first one's got glass

241

vitrines and a massive wooden telescope and next door's like a music room with a clapsichord thingy in it.'

'Right. Can you see Uranus?' The question was bound to come up at some stage.

'Not easily, mate. Let me have a look at this telescope. Okay, I'm on my knees now, looking up it and . . . can't see a thing. Ah, this has got to be it.'

'What? What?'

'Well, the telescope is pointing at a ball hanging from the ceiling on a thread, like a paper lantern kind of thing, looks like schoolchildren made it from tissue paper and it has craters and stuff drawn on it and it's painted blue.'

'Is there anyone around apart from you?'

'Not a soul, just the two museum people downstairs. I can hear their till whirring away, they're cashing up.'

'Then get the thing down.'

'I'm not sure they'll like that but I'll get a chair from the music room.'

'I think he's found it,' I told Eva.

'Okay. It's . . . it has a cut on the side, I'll see if I can get my hand inside, whoops, I've torn it. Sorry, kids. Got it! It's not a note, it's one of those keyring digital recorders. Thirty-second memory, to remind you to get milk, that kind of thing.'

'Well done, Tim. Get out of there fast, then play me the message.'

'Just putting the chair back. You know that's the first time you said that?'

'What?'

'Well done. You never said that before.'

'I haven't?' Was that true? 'Bloody well done, Tim. I mean it.'

'Okay, don't overdo it . . . Right, I'm outside. It's one of those black egg-shaped things you can buy for 3.99 every-where. I'll press Play.'

However hard I moulded the mobile against my ear

I couldn't make out any words in the horrible electronic gurgle.

'Did you get that?'

'No, couldn't make it out. What's he saying?'

'It said *Edge closer downing mead with the little man at the North Pole*. That make sense?'

'Kind of. Okay. Walk straight here. I expect he'll call me in a minute.' I rang off.

'Well?' Eva bristled with suspense.

'*Edge closer downing mead with the little man at the North Pole*. Clever bastard. The North Pole was one of the pubs destroyed in the landslide and the park was called Edgemead when it first opened.'

'And who's the little man?'

'I wish I knew. Perhaps he'll be along in a minute. Carrying three pints of mead.'

I switched my phone back to the dreaded Fifth Symphony ring tone and Eva showed me how to switch to loudspeaker so she could hear what was being said. When Beethoven suddenly chimed it made me jump again. 'Yes?'

'It took you longer than it took Herschel to discover Uranus but you got there at last,' came the gleeful verdict.

'Yes, but the clue you left is a bit obvious. You'll have to feed Alison twice in one day. I'm on my way to Hedgemead Park now. Everyone knows about the North Pole Inn and the little m–' The connection was severed. 'He hung up on me.'

'What a hideous-sounding voice, reminds me of the Daleks. You think he's coming here?' Eva squinted into the rain.

'I think he's on his way. We'd better hide somewhere.'

We quit the bandstand. 'But what if he comes and leaves the note somewhere in the other half of the park?' Eva queried. 'There are too many entrances and we can't even see the other side from here. One of us should be over there,' she argued.

I had somehow tried to convince myself that the Doctor

would leave the note near either the bandstand or the drinking fountain but since I had no idea what the 'little man' referred to he could conceivably leave it anywhere. Eva was right but I just didn't like the Hey-let's-split-up B-movie scenario in which the protagonists get picked off one by one. 'Okay. Have you got your mobile?'

She produced it from her bag. 'Never without it.'

'Right. He'll probably leave the note here, around the bandstand somewhere or down by the fountain, but just in case go and hide yourself on the other side of the park. And watch. Just watch. I'll call you on my mobile in a couple of minutes and we'll keep in touch that way.'

Eva jogged away and I walked twenty or so yards to where the path turned down towards the drinking fountain, hardly visible through the rain in the gloom under the dripping trees. There I squeezed behind a couple of rhododendrons and squatted down. It meant I could just peer out and keep an eye on the area while being sure that I wouldn't be seen from the path. Pretty sure, anyway, since I could hardly see out. I dialled Eva's number.

She answered promptly. 'Pizza Express, how can I help?'

'Two Margaritas and a dry change of clothes, please. How's it going?'

'I'm hidden behind a bush right at the northern edge. I reckon I can see most of what's going on. Which is a very wet nothing at the moment.'

'Same here. Don't hang up. Tell me if anyone comes into your area, no matter who they are or what they look like. If they're ninety-year-old Siamese twins on pogo sticks, I still want to know, all right?'

'Allrightallright.'

The greenery soon stopped providing any shelter from the rain, it was coming down too hard for that. While I was huddled there, with rivulets of water finding their way into my clothing, idly wondering how waterproof our mobiles might be, a man appeared at the extreme right of my field of vision on the path. He wore a light grey raincoat and hat, pulled down over his forehead against the rain. He walked at a steady pace until he reached the bandstand, where he stopped and looked back the way he had come. I spotted the leash dangling from his coat pocket before I saw the very wet dog trotting up. Once it had caught up they walked together, both apparently quite happy in the downpour, past my hiding place without once glancing my way. From the little I could see of his face I guessed his age as sixty or thereabouts. They passed out of my vision near the gate to the eastern part of the park.

'One man and his dog coming your way,' I informed Eva.

'I see 'em. They must like the rain. I'm totally drenched.'

After two or three minutes she informed me: 'They left by the bottom exit, I think. Can't see them any more. Anything your end?'

'Nothing.' We settled back into miserable silence. The air had cooled dramatically with the rain, reminding me that it was still only May after all.

'Tim should be here soon,' Eva mused. 'It's not that far from . . . shit . . . hey!'

'What?' I whispered urgently. I got no answer, just a crunching sound followed by lots of static. 'Talk to me, Eva.' I fought my way out of the shrubbery and started jogging, then running. I'd no idea where she had stationed herself and ran wildly into the centre of the place until I spotted a shape on the grass near the upper right exit. I ran to it. It was Eva, sitting on the wet grass, holding her face with one hand and rubbing her back with the other.

'Bastard punched me!' she greeted me.

'Who?'

'Him! I don't know. The Doctor? Could've been anyone. He suddenly appeared in my hideout but I didn't think he expected to find me there.'

I looked around. There was no one in the park apart

from us and a few wet squirrels. I couldn't believe we had messed up so effortlessly. I helped her up. 'What's with your back?' She was still rubbing it.

'I fell over that.' Eva indicated a marble headstone, lying face down by the shrub she had tumbled from. A very small headstone. 'That was what I found in there, completely hidden by the foliage. I fell over it when I got up and he clouted me and it broke off its base.'

'Did you get a good look at him?' I asked, wriggling my fingers under the slick marble and flipping it over.

'Didn't see his face at all. He dived into the shrubbery from behind me. I didn't hear him coming because of the noisy rain and he might not have known I was in there. In fact I'm sure. He made a noise in his throat, like he was surprised. But he could've been anyone, bloke looking for a place to piss, even. What's that thing anyway?'

We were both standing over the dark stone, a foot and a half long, now lying flat in the wet grass. The inscription clearly read:

BACHA
(LITTTLE MAN)
16 YEARS
1925

'Blimey, we found the little man. So it was the Doctor. I'm sure that's where he meant to hide the note, only to find me sitting right on top of it. I didn't mean to get that close to him.' She shuddered. 'Who was the little man, I wonder?'

'Or what. Looks very much like a pet grave to me. Perhaps there used to be a pet cemetery here. Can you remember anything about him at all?' I asked, just as Tim came bounding uphill from the London Road entrance.

'Nothing, only that he was . . . oh, I don't know. No, not really. He wore a raincoat, I think. I heard it swish a split second before he caught me on the chin from the side. And he was gone in an instant.'

'Hi, guys, what's up?' Tim had arrived at our spot, out of breath from the short uphill hike. We explained. 'So it was all for nothing. Our big chance.' He turned to Eva. 'And how's your jaw?'

'Terrible, thanks for asking. But my back hurts nearly as much, I must've caught that stone at a funny angle.'

'You want to go see a doctor?' I was feeling guilty now for not having been more sympathetic before.

'No, but I think I want to lie down for a bit.'

'Why don't you take Eva home and make sure she hasn't done herself some real injury,' I told Tim. 'And thanks for finding the Uranus clue.'

'No sweat.' He fished the little keyring recorder and the GPS bug from his jacket and dropped them into my palm.

As soon as the two had left the park I dived into the sodden foliage behind which Eva had been hiding. There was indeed a concrete base on which the gravestone had sat. It obviously predated the shrubs that by now hid it completely from view. I scrabbled around on the sodden ground but there was no note and no little Dictaphone and no hope. We'd blown it. I'd blown it. I'd mucked it up. Some sodding trap. How stupid. The police would probably have pulled it off. But I didn't.

I fought my way out of the tangle of branches and there he was.

# Chapter Twenty

He was standing quite still by the passage that connected the two halves of the park, forty yards away. In this feeble light and the hammering rain he was little more than a grey silhouette against dark foliage: a raincoat and a hat of some sort. But no face, not from this distance. I could see from his gestures that he was dialling on a mobile. I took mine out and it promptly rang.

His robotic voice made me shudder. He was using his little gadgets even here, looking at me. To me it seemed shameless; provocative beyond endurance.

'You are a very stupid man, Honeysett. I will make you regret this for the rest of your life. And I haven't decided yet how long I'll allow that to go on.'

'It had to be tried, the opportunity was too good to miss,' I said as conversationally as I could and began to stroll slowly along the path in his general direction.

'You think you are clever but really you are a stupid boy playing a game you cannot win. And you have broken the rules. I feel insulted.'

'Rules are there to be broken. Forget the rules. Play a different game. Give Alison up. You can find someone else. You don't need her.'

His voice became barely intelligible as it distorted with anger. 'What the fuck do you know about my needs? My desires? My wants? What the fuck do you know about anything? You think you are an artist and I am a pervert? I am the real artist. I create what hasn't been seen before, what hasn't been dared before. I create perfection. It's people like you who come and fuck everything up. That's close enough. Stop where you are.'

I had managed to close the distance between us by perhaps half, without knowing what I'd do if I got my hands on him. Who said I could overwhelm him in the first place?

I stopped.

'What were you going to do, shoot me? Or haven't you got a gun? Were you going to wrestle me to the ground? Make a citizen's arrest? Huh? You stupid fuck. Either way you'd never find out where she is. I'd never tell you then. You won't touch me. You can't touch me. You can't save her. You can't even save yourself. For you the game is over.'

'No, wait.' But it was too late. The line went dead and he turned away. Three, four steps and he was out of sight. I started walking across the lawn, then ran. It took me no more than five seconds to reach the place where he had stood, another two to make it into the other half of the park. There was nobody. I heard his footsteps, heard him running. He was running down the steps into the street below now. I scrambled over the iron railing and jumped down into the alley, as he must have done, and followed. By the time I skidded on to the slick pavement he had gone. Or had he? There were a few people walking under umbrellas; a car, a Toyota or something, was pulling away from the kerb, another was just disappearing up Margaret's Hill, a Volvo? There was thick traffic at the roundabout. Was he in any of those cars? Had I followed the wrong footsteps? Had he run uphill, was he calmly walking home along Lansdown by now? Was he going home, was he going to Alison, was the game really over? Had I finally killed Alison too? I looked back up the steps, up the alley. It was wet, dark, dripping, empty.

I stuffed my mobile into my pocket and walked blindly on.

The depression at Mill House seemed palpable in the cloying, under-oxygenated, overcharged air begging for the release of a thunderstorm. It was the evening of the Bath Festival Opening, the big event in Victoria Park with music, performances and fireworks. Rain on the opening night was traditional. We were waiting for it with doors and windows wide open to the waiting, silent, unmoving evening. I stepped on to the verandah, my footsteps loud in my ears. The sky seemed close. The headache behind my forehead produced a tingling, metallic smell in my nose. After the amount I had drunk the night before this was a trifling inconvenience, easily remedied by more of the same. I drank warm beer from a frothing bottle. Annis was somewhere in the grounds, swinging away from me and my self-recriminations on her crutches, stone-cold and sober. What sounded like the promised thunder turned out to be a distant train, then silence again. I scanned the granite sky and turned back inside but the sound of an engine quickly brought me out again. I turned right round the house, through the herb garden and into the yard just as Tim's black Audi growled to a stop. Eva was in the passenger seat. Tim got out leaving the car door open and jogged the few yards across to me, fist outstretched. I opened a hand and he dropped a small black keyring Dictaphone into it. 'He might not be talking to you, mate, but he talks to me. Found this taped to the door handle of the TT. Play it.'

I had every intention, I was just stunned. And afraid at the same time. I pressed the fiddly little button.

'One more chance at the Opening of the Bath Festival. A slim chance.'

'Chris, let's go,' Tim urged.

I turned around. Annis stood at the top of the meadow between the oak and the studio, watching us. I held up the tiny Dictaphone, dangling from its chain. She waved a crutch in a wide arc and pointed like a commander directing her troops: go.

I took the Citroën and followed the TT. Tim took us the back way into Bath, barrelling past farms on narrow tracks that eventually spat us out at the top of Lansdown. We dropped down through Winfred's Lane and bullied our black cars through the traffic round St James's Square. We abandoned them, like others had, on the green between Julian Road and Crescent Lane and walked the last few hundred yards. Beyond the green the streets had been blocked off with metal barriers; roads and pavements were full of people coming and going but, like us, mainly coming.

'So what exactly are we looking for?' asked Eva fretfully.

I was thinking the same thing myself. 'Your guess is as good as mine. Let's just get in there and have a good look round.' I tried to keep a positive spin on this but when the three of us reached the entrance my heart sank even further. The park had disappeared under an encrustation of humans. There were so many people the landscape appeared to have changed. The Brock Street entrance had become a claustrophobic bottleneck into which we let ourselves be sucked by the tide of celebrants. There were tents and marquees and ambulances and ice cream vans. There were people standing about, wandering about, people picnicking, playing games, people screaming their delight; people carrying pints of beer, people queuing for pints of beer, queuing for burgers, queuing for ice cream. And from every side came screeching sounds emitting from whistles at the end of sticks of candy and every one of them had an enthusiastic child attached to it. Several types of music were competing with each other and the smells of foods and the exhausts of generators mingled in the oppressive, unmoving air. 'Let's just walk about for a bit,' I suggested feebly, clutching my mobile. We picked our way across the lawn through the narrow gaps left between picnicking

251

groups of people, some with their own flags on poles so their friends might find them in this sea of rugs. Above the ha-ha, in an area roped off from the public, a group of twenty or so World War Two soldiers were unpacking gear from crates and boxes around an impressive-looking artillery piece; it looked as though Keith and his fellow re-enactors were about to start their display; I tried but couldn't spot Keith himself among the men. We took a tortuous route through the mêlée back on to the Royal Avenue. South of the avenue stood the large Victorian bandstand flanked by two stone urns. On it a school orchestra, energetically conducted by a white-haired man, was playing a jolly tune heavy on percussion. The sandwich board preacher was making his laborious rounds too, picking his way amongst the groups of drinking, talking, eating revellers, not finding many takers for his home-made leaflets. Further on people clustered around stalls selling anything from crystals to designer honey. Was the Doctor here, waiting for us? Was he the man sweating past me in a grotesquely large puffa jacket or the one selling balloons by the ice cream van? Or was he miles away, following the signal of the homing device in my jacket pocket?

'Are we just going to keep walking around in circles?' Eva asked. 'And we appear to have lost Tim.'

'How would I know?' I said, irritated by the futility of it. 'The message said there'd be one more chance here at the opening, a slim chance. I can't for the life of me construct that into a more specific location, can you?'

We were on our second circuit, walking away from the bandstand and the infernal percussion piece, making our way up once more towards the Royal Crescent which presided calmly over the celebrations. My mobile chimed faintly over the din. It was Tim.

'Where are you?' I demanded to know, although I could clearly hear the shambolic percussion down the line.

'Just coming up to the bandstand. No use us all walking together, I thought. I'll do the rounds anticlockwise.'

As soon as I cut the connection the phone rang again.

'I'd have thought you might keep your line free for me when a life depends on my every word.'

I looked wildly around me, half expecting to see the dark silhouette of the Doctor again.

'Even the police showed me more courtesy. I have after all decided to terminate our game since you show so little respect.' A loud crackling came over the line. When a second later it repeated itself in my other ear I recognized it as rifle fire from the re-enactment. For the percussion of the shots to come over the phone first he had to be standing very close to them. I grabbed Eva, who was looking at me expectantly, by the strap of her digital camera round her neck and dragged her with me.

'The thing in Hedgemead Park was a stupid idea,' I admitted, trying to keep my voice level while walking fast. 'I apologize.'

'Your apology is not accepted. I do not believe you mean it. You are simply hoping to keep me playing the game until you can catch me.'

I'm trying to keep you talking until I find out what you look like, I thought. I was dragging Eva through thickets of families, through a line of men queuing for beer and laughing at what they thought was a lovers' tiff. The crowd watching the re-enactment stood five-deep. I pushed and shouldered until we made it to the front. The re-enactors were using the area above the ha-ha as their battleground. As we reached them the riflemen that were defending the artillery piece against imaginary attack were firing again from behind sandbagging to our right. The cracks of their .303 ammunition reached both my ears simultaneously. I scanned the spectators while saying: 'No, I really am sincere, you must believe that. And I'm not saying that simply because I fear for Alison's life. I promise you there'll be no more cheap tricks.' I switched on Eva's seven-fold zoom camera and through it scrutinized the crowd as far as I could see, then the people just behind the thick cordon of humanity.

And there he was again. Only this time he was not wearing a hat. I recognized him with an appalled shock. Only how could I make sure? He might just be talking to someone else entirely. Even through the zoom lens of the camera I couldn't see his face clearly enough to match his lip movements to what he was saying. He was talking into the mobile which appeared to have a little gadget fixed to the bottom end and he was walking away slowly as he talked.

'No, I've had enough. It's over. It's over for you and your band of fools and it's over for the girl.'

In front of me a boy wriggled closer to the barrier to watch, his annoying whistle for the moment forgotten. I wrenched it from his hand and blew it hard at my phone. The Doctor yanked his head away from his. 'What the fuck was that?'

Eva had turned white. She had realized not just what I was doing but who I was looking at. 'Oh no. Oh God no.'

'Fuck you, Honeysett. And fuck off.' The line went dead and he disappeared quickly into the crowd.

The boy indignantly snatched his whistle back. I pushed my way free from the claustrophobic press of people, with Eva pulling at my jacket from behind.

'I have to follow him,' I told her. 'I'm sorry. I have to find him again and see if he leads us to Ali's prison. It's my only chance.'

Eva still held me back. 'I know where she'll be. I know the place the bastard would keep her. The fucking bastard,' she added, more surprised than shocked.

'How?' I was desperate to get away.

'He rents a clapped-out building from the MOD up the hill, near Lansdown. As a radio shack to stick his damn aerials on. I'll take you there.' We pushed through the crowd as fast as we could without starting a riot. At the Brock Street entrance I bought a heart-shaped balloon, tied the homing bug to it and let it gently drift up into the clouds. That might give him something to think about. I called Annis at the house but got no answer. I left a quick message, telling her the news and where we were going. I tried to call Tim but his phone was engaged. I left a voicemail message telling him what I knew and to get to Annis in case the Doctor tried to furnish himself with extra insurance.

'You want to drive?' I asked when we got to the car. I thought she might appreciate having something to do.

'No thanks, you drive that thing.'

I hammered on the horn and pushed into the traffic on Julian Road, then shot up towards Sion Hill.

'The bastard,' she said flatly, like a statement of fact. 'The murdering bastard.'

'I know this'll sound stupid but . . . did you never suspect him?'

'No. Although last night, when he hit me, for a split second . . . But of course I dismissed it instantly.'

'Wait a second. You mean you recognized *the way* Jerry hit you? Are you saying he hit you before?'

Eva took a deep breath. 'Yeah, once or twice. That's one of the reasons why we kept splitting up. He's got such a temper. But, you know, he was always *so* contrite the next day. Oh, don't say it, I know, I'm a stupid little woman going *but I love him* and all that. We both know how that kind of story goes but it's not easy when you're in the middle of it, believe me.'

'But the abductions. The murders. What kind of a person . . . You never once suspected anything weird going on? Sorry, no, of course not.'

'Turn right here. You know what they always say after a murderer is caught: "nice man", "family man", or "kept himself to himself", all those clichés that basically say the same thing: you can't tell from looking at the bastards.

255

I know Jerry had a difficult childhood. His father committed suicide when he was ten and his crapulent mother devoted the next four years to eating, drinking and throwing empty gin bottles at Jerry. She weighed twenty-six stone when she died from a heart attack. Jerry was taken into care after that.'

'That might explain the obsession with food or withholding food. But the cranial osteopathy. Caring profession and all that and the violence. I can't put the two together.'

'You go on a course, Chris, simple as that. He was a TV repair man before that.'

'Where now?' I had turned off the main road into a strange, empty little street lined with 1960s-looking buildings behind high security fences. Ministry of Defence country.

'Keep going until the fencing stops and turn down the single track lane.'

As soon as I started down the track the tarmac became potholed and the verges overgrown and uncared for. I could already see what we were heading for. Shielded from the north winds by a row of tattered poplars stood a lone one-storey building. Once a cheerfully ugly piece of functionality, now, staked out by the bare concrete gallows that once supported the security fence and wearing a spiky crown of aerials, it was undeniably menacing. Even up here the air was breathless; the poplars stood still, lifeless.

When I got there I drove into what had been a small car park. Builder's rubble, loose bricks and boards were lying about in it now. The surrounding countryside encroached and reclaimed the edges while thickets of weeds grew from cracks everywhere. I drove up to the desolate building and stopped by the old-fashioned entrance doors. Like the windows they were blind with chipboard.

I ran up the broad and shallow steps. The locks had to be defunct since they were secured with a chain which passed through the solid metal handles on each door. I got the car jack from the boot of the DS, shoved it into the slack of the chain and pumped it hard. It was the handles that gave out first.

Inside, a small vestibule was followed by a short corridor with doors off to each side and a flight of concrete steps halfway along. Like the floors it was covered in decaying wine red lino and over everything lay the dust and detritus of abandonment, except where somebody's feet had recently worn a path through it.

Eva walked ahead into the gloom. 'His radio room is upstairs. He brought me here once when he first moved all his stuff in. He can get good reception from up here apparently.'

Only here and there did needles of grey light enter through chinks in the boards covering the windows. The door to the radio room was unlocked. I could hear the familiar hum of a computer's fan.

'He must have electricity . . .' I found a light switch and flicked it. A triple neon bank, standing upright in a corner of the room, pinged blindingly into life. It illuminated several tables pushed together. On top stood piles of radio and satellite equipment and at least one computer, several blind screens and telephones. Below the tables a snake pit of cables. All over the floor lay pizza cartons, takeaway boxes, crunched-up crisp packets and empty drinks cans.

Out in the corridor I opened all the other doors. None appeared to have lights but even in the gloom I could easily make out that they were empty. I ran downstairs and repeated the process there even though it seemed obvious that no one had walked there for a long time. All the rooms turned out empty.

'Chris! Up here, quick!'

I shot up the stairs. Eva was pointing at a TV screen that had come to life. 'How did you do that?' I asked.

'Just pressed a lot of buttons at random. Usually works for me.'

257

I scrutinized the grainy image. It seemed to be a view of a not quite dark room, and judging from the angles of the faint lights and darks the camera had to be high up. But it was impossible to make out more than that, let alone get any indication of where it might be.

I randomly pressed several buttons on the board in front of us. The image died. 'Never works for me. That was a room somewhere, right?'

'But it needn't be anywhere near here,' she said, indicating the equipment in front of us. 'Perhaps I was wrong.'

'No, it's here. I can feel it. All this feels . . . just right. If you know what I mean.'

She prodded a mould-covered takeaway box with her trainer. 'I know what you mean.'

I dived into the snake pit and followed the cables. The electricity cables went this way and that but a bundle snaked across the room towards the boarded-up window. One corner of the chipboard had been sawn away and the cables disappeared through that, wrapped round with rags. I pulled on the rags, and fresh air and a little light streamed in. A few angry kicks loosened that side of the board enough to show that the cables went through the broken pane. Most went up towards the roof but several thick black cables ran downwards.

The first heavy drops fell as we tumbled outside into the overgrown yard. The radio room's window was at the back of the building. Black cable taped to a down pipe ran to the ground and disappeared into a narrow field of weeds and rubble. 'In there somewhere.' I picked up a splintered piece of timber and began to slash at the weeds. It didn't take me long to find a narrow trampled path that led to the left-hand corner of the field at one end of the line of poplars. It ended at a narrow blackened steel double door in a stone framework in the ground, set at a shallow angle. The little bundle of black cables disappeared into a hole in the stonework.

'Looks like a storm shelter,' Eva said. 'Or is it an MOD bomb shelter?'

I weighed the shiny brass padlock on the doors. 'Might be neither. Could be this is one of the few unlucky farms round here that had bombs dropped on them in the last war and this is what's left. The cellars of the farmhouse might be under here.'

'Can we smash that open?' She looked about her for a suitable implement.

'Don't think we'll have to.' While I took out my picklocks and went to work the clouds let go of their cargo at last and the rain fell, straight and unmolested by any wind. With my wet hands and my eagerness to get in I fumbled, dropped one of my picks and for a couple of minutes got nowhere.

Eva shifted impatiently at my shoulder. 'How long's it going to take?'

I remembered visiting the bowels of the defunct railway station by the light of my lighter. 'Why don't you go and see if my big torch is somewhere in the boot?'

Once Eva had gone I took a deep breath, inserted my picklocks again and the padlock fell open as if by magic.

# Chapter Twenty-One

I heaved on the heavy doors and let the two leaves fall open to either side. Narrow stone steps, worn smooth and round by generations of boots, led steeply away into the dark. Instinctively I went down a few steps for shelter from the rain. That's when the smells came back and I knew I had found the place.

There, just a hint behind the smells of damp earth, of rain, of confined air escaping, was the sweet, cloying odour of cheap air freshener. I took out my lighter and flicked it on. At the bottom the stairs turned to the right and the black cables curved around with them. A whitish, powdery mould covered the wall. I steadied myself against it as I descended the now rain-slickened steps. Five, eight, twelve steps and the narrow stairwell opened out into a larger, vaulted space. Here the other smells were stronger: the ammonia of stale urine, rotted refuse, human despair and human waste. I held my lighter aloft to illuminate more of the space around me. A wooden table, rotten and near collapse, leant against the uneven wall to my left. It was covered with what looked like century-old debris, perhaps to do with farming, perhaps not. I swung slowly around to the right so as not to lose the flame on my lighter. Come on, Ev, how long could it take to get a torch from the car? The lighter was rapidly getting too hot to hold. But I didn't need to wait for Eva. Brushed steel dully reflected my flame: lights on tripods like photographic lamps. I followed the flex down and found a switch, dropped my lighter and blinked a few times in the sudden glare, then looked around. In this low vaulted room rusted relics of what looked like centuries of farming, mouldering wooden things and mounds of unrecognizable substances mixed with twenty-first-century rubbish: more takeaway cartons, cola cans, newsprint and plastic wrappings. Two squat pillars supported the roof. Steps disappearing up into a mound of rubble to my left supported the theory that I was in one of the forgotten underground spaces with no building above ground. A short, gloomy corridor led past the stairs. The black cables snaked along the uneven ground, then curved up and disappeared into a crude hole in the wall next to an ancient door that hung uncertainly in its frame.

'Alison!' I shouted her name at the top of my lungs. Far from echoing the sound of my voice seemed to die on the breathless air. I pulled on the door's thin metal handle. It opened reluctantly, scraped on the ground. Inside it was dark but the smell escaping as the gap widened told me I was there now.

'Ali?' I could see the dull metallic bars of a low cage at the end of the long, low-ceilinged vault but very little else. I felt about on the wall near the door, found the spot where the cables emerged into the chamber and what I guessed was a CCTV camera and light but could find no switch.

One week. It was one week since the Doctor snatched her. Surely Alison had managed to hold out for one week. It was the fear of being frightened, the fear of what I might see, that made me cross the twenty feet or so to the cage slowly, cautiously, as though it might hold a wild beast that could suddenly fling itself at the bars with a snap of its jaws. When I got there I could make out a dark shape, a human shape on the ground, feet towards me, head in the furthest corner of the metal prison. The dull flicker of eyes in the dark.

'Ali?'

'You took your fucking time.' Her voice was slow and

261

hoarse and ancient and beautiful. Her prison was an iron box with a floor space of about eight by six feet, no more than four feet high. She moved with heartbreaking slowness as she dragged herself around so she could huddle by the front of the cage, which was effectively its door. I could make out that she was dressed in a flowery nightdress, stained and filthy.

I grabbed hold of the padlock at the side and got my picklocks out again. 'I'll have you out of here in a couple of minutes. How are you feeling?' It was a stupid question but had to be asked. I angled the lock into the dim light that reached us through the corridor.

'Everything aches. I feel weird. Spaced out. Especially in the dark. I hate the dark. Even more than Jerry O'fucking Neil. You're not going to be ages about that lock, are you?'

'Just a sec . . . You must be bloody starving. Sorry, didn't bring any food.'

'I stopped feeling hungry days ago.'

The lock clicked open. 'There you go.' I pulled back hard on the crudely welded front and it came with a protesting shriek. 'I'll help you out.'

Alison shook her head and didn't move. 'Did you bring your gun?'

'What? No. What kind of a question is that?'

The direction of her gaze answered it for me. He was here.

'Quite a pertinent question actually, Honeysett. Slowly now, no hasty movements, please. I'm glad *she* asked you about the gun. *I* might not have believed you.' Jerry stood just inside the door with the light behind him. It took me a while to make out that the thing he was pointing at me was a crossbow. In the other hand he was holding what looked like my heavy torch.

'Where's Eva? What have you done with her?'

'You're a clown, Honeysett. Don't worry about the stupid cow, worry about yourself for a minute, it might be all the time you have.'

'Why, Jerry? Why?'

'Why am I going to kill you?'

'No. This.' I indicated our surroundings with a sweep of my arm. 'This shit. The abductions, the murders, Jerry!'

'Murders.' He snorted. 'You *would* see it that way. When I first met you I thought you were different, you'd understand the . . . the art, the . . . artistry of what I was about to embark on. But no, not you, I had you all wrong. You probably think I'm mad. Or some sort of sexual deviant and so of course I must be mad. You think you can recognize good and bad and crazy and sane but you can't because you're blinded by what's on the surface, you're superficial, skimming the surface like one of those insects on a pond. You have to go beyond the surface: drain the pond and you'll see what it harbours, its secrets revealed. You have to get down to the bare bones of things – bones, get it? – before you can see what it's all about. Bones, the structure of it. You just don't think. Thinking is where the art begins.' Jerry had flicked on the torch and begun to punctuate his words with stabs of light at me or Alison in the door of her cage or at various points of the room. Slowly he moved towards us. 'You just accept what you've been told. You're just another square, a bourgeois little painter with his bourgeois notions of beauty and acceptability. I heard you scoff at Burns. Snotty tissues in vitrines to you.' He shook his head slowly, pityingly. 'You can't understand him, so you could never understand this. I think deeply, my thoughts penetrate. I reveal the living structure behind the accretions that the wrong kind of living produces. I reduce, I'm a reductionist. I reveal the structure of life just before it departs. I'm a structuralist. I can feel the truth just beneath the skin. I have looked at your truth and your truth is the wrong kind, it's a secondhand truth, handed down to you. But this,' he stabbed a beam of light at the cage, 'is a revelation.'

263

So was Annis's ironic cough from behind him where she had moved into position on her silent rosewood crutches.

Jerry turned slowly, mild annoyance showing on his face, perhaps expecting no more danger than a battered ex-lover. 'Ah, the pretty cripple.' Jerry waved an invitation with his crossbow. 'Come and join the others.'

'Cripple with a .38.' Annis let her left crutch fall away and whipped the Webley from her waistband. 'Drop what you're holding and put your hands up.'

His weapon still trained on Annis, Jerry slowly moved sideways until he could also see Ali and me at the cage. 'You people,' he fumed quietly, almost to himself. 'You people. You are so . . . irritating.'

Ali was pulling herself up by the top of the cage. 'Help me,' she whispered. When I got her standing and leaning against me I realized just how weak her legs had become. Her whole body was shaking with the effort of walking the few steps away from her prison towards Annis. I didn't think it was such a good idea to walk near Jerry's line of fire but she urged me on with a determined grip of her hand on my supporting arm. Jerry lowered the crossbow.

In a near mirror image Tim and Eva came cautiously along the corridor, Tim supporting Eva, who had a blood-stained bandage around her head. He had also armed himself with a length of old lead piping. Eva struggled free from his support as they entered the chamber. Her eyes showed a wild glint. She didn't speak.

Annis hadn't moved or blinked. The heavy revolver remained firmly pointed at Jerry's chest. 'Drop the cross-bow,' she repeated. Jerry threw it aside on to the rubbish-strewn floor with a short-tempered little gesture.

Nobody moved. Tim was leaning against the wall, watching impassively, cradling the length of piping in his arms like a baby. Then I noticed it, too late perhaps. A triangle had formed, a triangle of women regarding none but each other, exchanging quiet glances, holding mute counsel, secret ballot. Alison's body stiffened beside me. I looked at Eva. Her gaze was fixed on Annis's face, which in the twilight betrayed no emotion. I thought I saw the smallest nod. Eva's eyes closed.

Annis fired.

Three times.

# Epilogue

'. . . interference in police business . . . obstruction . . . withholding evidence . . . contaminating a crime scene . . . supplying an illegal firearm . . . being extremely irritating . . .' Needham was near apoplectic with righteous rage. This time he was going to throw the book at me. I soaked up what seemed like hours of his tirade in his office, nodding gravely, showing contrition. He had a point, after all. But success is a strong defence and much of Needham's noise was only there to mask the embarrassment that a private eye had solved the case and his relief that he no longer had a serial killer to find. That the man sported three bullet holes when he found him took some explaining but I had made sure he also found a crossbow bolt in the door frame (the one Annis dodged when she shot Jerry in self-defence). There were just too many witnesses to that for Needham to make much of it, whether he believed the story or not. In the end none of it came to court, though I was invited to attend a couple of uncomfortable hearings where a certain amount of horse trading took place.

I was not invited to attend John's funeral.


I ran straight into one of Roy Hotchkiss's goons one night when leaving the Theatre Royal with Annis on my arm. 'Boss wants a word.' It was Surfer Dude, crammed into a suit. He pointed to the immense Beemer across the street. We walked over and the rear window slid down, just like in the movies. 'I heard you got your friend back,' Roy said meaningfully.

I nodded. 'Is it leg-breaking time?' I asked pleasantly.

He looked away from us, as though he had to think about it. 'I also heard you speak Turkish. That right?'

'Might do.'

'Don't piss about, Honeysett. As you said, you owe me one. I'll be in touch. I have a little Turkish problem you might be able to help me with.'

Which I did, eventually. But that's another story entirely.

It was a few weeks after this encounter when I was able to solve another mystery. Ever since the Albanian café by the bike shop had suddenly closed down Tim had redoubled his efforts to recreate the Special Meatballs, a messy and fruitless endeavour that for some irritating reason always had to happen in the Mill House kitchen. In the photograph below the *Chronicle* headline ALBANIAN CAFÉ OWNER ARRESTED, *Health Officers analyse 'secret ingredients'*, I recognized the thin, middle-aged man in the grotesquely large puffa jacket I had seen at Manvers Street police station after his arrest for bread-soaking offences. Tim turned more than a little green. It was the first time I heard Alison laugh since we got her back.

It was much later in the same year on a Sunday morning, when the leaves were beginning to fall in the strip of woodland behind the studio, that I ran into Billy the tramp on the towpath along the Kennet and Avon canal. It was by pure chance and some time after I had made Longbottom, Prangle and Fox (Solicitors) tell me why exactly I'd been looking for him in the first place. He was carrying a rucksack and several carrier bags of stuff and sweated inside a big, blue overcoat that didn't look too shabby. He refused to stop for me so I walked alongside him. 'I have a little present for you,' I said and pulled out the small velvet pouch I'd been given. 'It's from an American couple who were over here last summer. They wanted you to have it but they didn't know where to send it so I was asked to see if I could find you.' I opened the pouch and let the content slither into my hand: a small, silver crucifix on a chain. I let it dangle from one finger.

'It's a cross,' Billy said. He sounded a little breathless, which was no surprise. It was a fine autumn day with the smell of wood smoke in the air but not overcoat weather yet.

'I know. They must have been Christians. Do you remember meeting an American couple? They said you asked for money but they didn't give you any. They thought you might spend it on intoxicating liquor, don't know who gave them that idea. But you must have told them your name. Do you remember that?'

He seemed to think about it for a while. Then he said emphatically: 'Americans wear checked trousers.'

'They do that sort of thing,' I admitted. 'Why did you say you killed Roy's wife when you didn't?'

'Don't ask me that,' he said. 'You mustn't ask me that.'

'Okay, I won't. Then I'll tell you. Your brother said to you: I did a bad thing, I killed Lizzie. If the police find out they'll take me away and put me in prison and send you to a home and you'll never see me again, so who's gonna look after you? But if you tell them *you* did it then they'll put you in a home and I can come and visit you all the time.'

We walked in silence for a long minute, Billy breathing hard under his labours and the crucifix dangling from my raised finger.

'He said it wouldn't be for long. But it was a long time.'

'Did Roy visit you often?'

'Yes,' he said simply.

We walked alongside each other for a few more minutes until we came to a small stone bridge. Billy stopped and

268

put his bags down. He scrutinized the cross I dangled from my fingers.

'Take the damn thing, will you?' I asked. 'It's been a pain in the arse trying to get this to you.'

'If I take it will you go away?'

'Gladly.'

He took it and I went away.

# Author's Note

Thanks again to Krystyna and Juliet. I'm especially grateful to Clare and Imogen for making my ramblings readable. No thanks at all to Asbo the cat for leaving bits of dead rabbit on my keyboard. What next, horses' heads?